Praise for Ashton Lee and *The Cherry Cola Book Club*

"For anyone who has ever believed in the power of a good book, Ashton Lee's charming novel of a small Southern town with a flavorful plan to save its precious but woefully underfunded library will have you cheering from the start. Clever, sassy and as tasty as an icebox pie, *The Cherry Cola Book Club* is a rare treat. Community activism has never been more delicious—or more fun."

—Erika Marks, author of *Little Gale Gumbo* and *The Mermaid Collector*

"If Fannie Flagg and Jan Karon's Mitford were to come together, the end result might very well be Cherico, Mississippi. Ashton Lee has created a magical town with characters who will inspire readers and bring them back to a simpler time and place. With both humor and moving passages, Lee has captured the quirkiness and warmhearted people of the small town south to a 'T.' Fix yourself a cherry Coke and savor this fun and moving book."

—Michael Morris, author of *Man in the Blue Moon* and *A Place Called Wiregrass*

"Down-home and delicious, *The Cherry Cola Book Club* combines everything we love about Southern cuisine, small town grit and the transformative power of books."

—Beth Harbison, *New York Times* bestselling author

The Cherry Cola Book Club

To Missy from Mississippi —

ASHTON LEE

Ashton Lee

KENSINGTON BOOKS
www.kensingtonbooks.com

KENSINGTON BOOKS are published by

Kensington Publishing Corp.
119 West 40th Street
New York, NY 10018

All Kensington titles, imprints, and distributed lines are available at special quantity discounts for bulk purchases for sales promotion, premiums, fund-raising, and educational or institutional use.

Special book excerpts or customized printings can also be created to fit specific needs. For details, write or phone the office of the Kensington Special Sales Manager: Attn. Special Sales Department. Kensington Publishing Corp., 119 West 40th Street, New York, NY 10018. Phone: 1-800-221-2647.

Kensington and the K logo Reg. U.S. Pat. & TM Off.

ISBN-13: 978-0-7582-7341-3
ISBN-10: 0-7582-7341-X

First Kensington Trade Paperback Printing: April 2013

10 9 8 7 6 5 4 3 2

Printed in the United States of America

For Weesie and Bob, beloved parents

Acknowledgments

My creation of the Cherico, Mississippi, universe would not have been possible without the help and advice of so many friends, professionals, and family members. I must begin with my superb agents, Christina Hogrebe and Meg Ruley, of the Jane Rotrosen Agency, who matched me up with John Scognamiglio of Kensington Books. John makes the editor-author relationship a seamless one.

Next, I owe a great deal to my aunt, Abigail Jenkins Healy, for rounding up and certifying a number of delicious Southern dishes for the recipe section at the back of the book. These dishes appear in the plot, and I thought it would be a homey touch to allow readers to experience these dishes themselves.

Many librarians have contributed to this novel with their encouragement and factual input. Among them: Susan Cassagne, Marianne Raley, Deb Mitchell, Catherine Nathan, Jennifer Smith, Lesa Holstine, Regina Cooper, Susan Delmas, Judy Clark, Jackie Warfield, Derek Schaaf, Alice Shands, the staff of St. Mary Parish Library, in Franklin, Louisiana, Larie Myers, and Angelle Deshoutelles.

Many thanks also to Jerry Seaman for his fishing lure lessons, which I trust I learned well. And to my many Facebook followers at facebook.com/ashtonlee.net, I have appreciated your comments and support more than you know.

1

Books versus Bulldozers

Maura Beth Mayhew shut her sky blue eyes and let the unsettling words that had just been thrown her way sink in for a few tense moments. When she finally opened them, she flipped her whiskey-colored curls defiantly at Councilman Durden Sparks and his two underlings seated at the other end of the meeting room table. Their only distinction was their nicknames—as in "Chunky" Badham, who had not missed many meals along the way, and "Gopher Joe" Martin, the consummate "yes man" if ever there was one. Colorful monikers aside, Maura Beth had no intention of letting any of them roll over her with those bulldozers they kept on romancing as if they were the secret to unlocking the universe.

"You actually think the citizens of Cherico are going to stand for this?" she said, her voice trembling noticeably as the stress crept into her face.

Councilman Sparks flashed his matinee idol eyes and prominent white teeth—the source of his ongoing popularity with many female voters—and leaned toward the town's pretty young librarian of six years standing. "Miz Mayhew," he began, "don't panic. This won't happen tomorrow. We'll give you up until our budget approval at the end of November to rev up that library of yours. Use the next five months to show this Council why we should continue to fund it in lieu of other, more beneficial projects such as our proposed Cherico Industrial Park."

Maura Beth had her response at the ready. "Interesting that you call it *my* library, now that you don't think it has any value. Or maybe you never did."

"Perhaps you're right," he answered, nodding her way. "I remember when I was eight years old and I wanted to participate in summer reading like some of my classmates were doing. They were getting blue ribbons for finishing a certain number of books, and that got my competitive juices flowing. I asked my mother if I could sign up, and I'll never forget how she rambled on about it. She described The Cherico Library as a burden for the taxpayers and told me that the librarian at the time, Miz Annie Scott, did nothing all day but read her favorite novels and try to get in good with all the wealthy families so she could wangle donations. Mom believed it was no coincidence that their children were the ones that always got the ribbons and that I could make much better use of my time playing sports and getting good grades. So that's what I did."

The shock clearly showed on Maura Beth's face. "I had no idea you had such a jaundiced view of the library. But you actually think that grading that tract of glorified cow pasture on the north end of town will pay dividends for Cherico?"

"We're not flying by the seat of our pants here. We've commissioned a study," he answered, brandishing a thin bound volume in the process. "We believe several viable companies would locate here if we prepare the land for them properly. That would bring jobs to our struggling little community. It would mean growth for us in this stagnant economy."

Well, there it was. The broken record of the current crop of local politicians who had gotten re-elected to office in

Cherico, Mississippi, two years ago in the fall of 2010. They had won because they had campaigned with the same stale bumper stickers, but now that they'd gotten in once again, their mantra had suddenly morphed into growth and change. Even if she knew—and Durden Sparks, Chunky Badham, and Gopher Joe Martin also knew damned good and well—that Cherico was not the type of town that wanted to get busier with traffic and attract a lot of those copycat, big-box franchises that advertised on television all the time. It did not even have a daily newspaper anymore—only one of those weekly shopping guides full of coupons, discounts, and special sales gimmicks on certain days of the week.

No, Cherico was small and parochial, even xenophobic at times. It had never taken full advantage of its picturesque location on Lake Cherico, which itself was a finger of the Tennessee River System in the extreme northeast corner of Mississippi. The town was not actually old enough to be called antebellum; indeed, it barely qualified for the Victorian Era with a smattering of homes in the Queen Anne or Swiss Chalet style here and there. Overall, the architecture was muddled and mundane.

Mostly, though, Cherico was full of people who wanted to be left alone, particularly the newer citizens who had built their ritzy vacation retreats and boathouses out on the lake and were therefore not even year-round residents. When they dropped in on the environs during warmer weather for some fishing and skiing, it was only for a few weeks at a time, maybe as long as a month, and they stayed out of local politics as a result.

"What you cannot deny, Miz Mayhew," Councilman Sparks continued after a healthy sip from his water glass, "is that your circulation figures have steadily declined over the past three years, and they weren't going gangbusters before you came here, either. By your own admission, your only regular patrons are Miss Voncille Nettles and the Crumpton sisters, who gather in your meeting room once a month."

"That's an exaggeration," Maura Beth said, her eyes flashing. "We have our regulars who check out books and DVDs. And just for the record, we also have the very respectable Mr. Locke Linwood attending 'Who's Who in Cherico?' His wife, Pamela, was also a regular before her untimely passing, as I'm sure you recall."

"Yes, I do. It was a most unfortunate event. Very well, then. I stand corrected. Three spinsters and a widower attend these utterly fascinating meetings." Councilman Sparks loudly cleared his throat and continued, "At any rate, they gather to run on about their fabled family trees. As if who begat whom is going to change from week to week. Hey, the bottom line is, you're stuck with your genes—good, bad, or something in between—and no amount of flowery window dressing will make any difference, to my way of thinking."

" 'Who's Who in Cherico?' has been the benchmark for genealogical research for many years," Maura Beth proclaimed. "Miss Voncille Nettles spends countless hours researching deeds and such at the courthouse for accuracy. She knows everything about everybody, as well as all sorts of historical nuggets about this town."

Councilman Sparks pursed his lips as if he had just taken a swallow of sour milk. "Tell me about it. I think sometimes we should just set up a cot for the darling lady in the archives and lock her in for the night. Maybe throw in a pitcher of water and a chamber pot for good measure. But Miss Voncille and her followers could just as easily meet in someone's living room as your library. They'd certainly have more space, and I bet she and her little crowd would enjoy a libation or two while they gossip about their dear, dead relatives. Unless you've changed the policy without my knowledge, I don't believe the library allows the consumption of adult beverages, if you will, on its premises. Why, that little bunch could leave you high and dry if they decided they'd had enough of teetotaling all these years. Face it, Miz Mayhew, they're now your only viable claim to fame!"

Chunky and Gopher Joe snickered, winked at each other, and nodded their heads knowingly while Maura Beth did her best to suppress her disgust. She knew those two would never carry on in such a disrespectful manner anywhere other than this special budget session she was being forced to endure without benefit of a single witness. It was clear that as far as they were concerned, she fit the definition of the proverbial redheaded stepchild.

"May I quote you on all that, Councilman Sparks?" Maura Beth said.

"It would be a 'he said, she said' at best, I'm afraid. You'll be gravely disappointed if you try to rally the public, because it's my belief that almost nobody out there really gives a damn about the library. It's my job as a politician to read the tea leaves on all the issues, and I don't think I'm wrong about this one."

Maura Beth shot him a skeptical glance and decided to stay on the attack as long as she could. "I'm curious. Why don't you just close down the library right now? Why wait until you approve the new budget?"

After a particularly patronizing grin and an overly dramatic pause, Councilman Sparks said, "Because we wouldn't want to be accused of not giving you one last chance to turn it all around. Even though we're all supremely confident that you won't be able to, of course."

"Well, I have to admit you've done absolutely nothing to help me up to this point."

"And how's that? I don't profess to know anything about running a library, except the cost efficiency."

Maura Beth allowed herself to roll her eyes as she exhaled. "I'm referring to the fact that this Council has consistently refused my requests to fund a couple of computer terminals so the patrons can come in and access the Internet. That would have bolstered library use considerably over the past several years. It's what knowledgeable patrons all over the country have come to expect. But I guess that didn't suit your long-range agenda."

"There, I have to put my foot down," he said, making a fist of his right hand and pounding it twice on the table like a gavel. "The public can buy their own computers. Everybody I know has one—not to mention all the other electronic gadgets people use now to keep in touch no matter where they are." He cut his eyes first at Chunky, then at Gopher Joe.

"Matter of fact, that reminds me of a joke going around. Stop me if you've heard it. Seems this fella walks into a doctor's office complaining of a peculiar growth on his ear, and now he's constantly hearing bells and loud voices. He's been really worried about it for a while and finally decides to get a medical opinion. 'Do ya think it might be a tumor, or am I going crazy, Doc?' the man says. Whereupon the doc flicks on his flashlight, squints real hard looking around, and finally answers, 'Nope, you're fine. It's just your cell phone.' "

The guffawing from Chunky and Gopher Joe was devastating for Maura Beth. She felt as if they were laughing at her and the joke was their cover. When it had all finally died down, she found herself staring at their wrinkled, solemn faces and wondering if these lackeys had ever in their lives read anything that had not been required for their high-school book reports light-years ago. In fact, she had strong anecdotal evidence to that effect when at a previous meeting, Chunky had rambled on about "all those snooty books in the library like *'Silence' Marner* that nobody likes to read." Even so, she knew she was up against it big-time, and that it would do her no good to continue to aggravate this powerful, privileged trio.

"Very funny joke. But I still have about five months to turn things around," she managed, quickly recovering from her unpleasant mental review. "And if I do so, you'll continue the library's funding?"

Councilman Sparks took his time, casting his eyes toward the whirring ceiling fan as he considered. "I wish I could give you a guarantee, Miz Mayhew. But if you do nothing to change the status quo, The Cherico Library is history. We can't justify the expense any longer. If you should impress us enough, maybe we'll be willing to work something out. Just remember, though—you'll need more than Miss Voncille beating the drum on your behalf. The fact is, there's no millage specifically dedicated to the library, and we think the time has come to stop pretending that we're getting good value for our money in this particular line item of the budget."

Meager as that peace offering was, it was still a vestige of hope from the powers-that-be. Maura Beth caught herself smirking faintly as the session came to an end and she rose from her seat without fanfare. "Please, gentlemen," she told them, nodding in their general direction. "By all means, don't bother to get up. I know you really don't want to."

Alone among the three, Councilman Sparks stood and executed a hurried little bow.

As she made her way down the hall, memories of library science school at LSU suddenly flashed into Maura Beth's head. There had been no course titled "Dealing with Politicians 101," nor even something along the lines of "Elementary Schmoozing." There should have been, though. Some wise professor should have stood before her and the other innocent young library students taking lecture notes and warned them that the political aspects of librarianship were going to be the most difficult to maneuver. That libraries and their scant millages would usually find themselves first to be cut and last to be restored. It always seemed to be easier for politicians to favor the sound of bulldozers in motion over the static silence of the printed word.

Maura Beth walked down the steps of Cherico City Hall and out onto Commerce Street as if she had just been handed a prison sentence. Five months to get cracking. Her shoulders were slumped, and the blazing June sun glinting off the asphalt made them slump even more. It was just past three in the afternoon, and even though she had skipped lunch, she had no appetite at all. What she needed was a big helping of solace, not sustenance. So she made her way deliberately past the familiar lineup of one-story brick and wooden storefronts: Audra Neely's Antiques; Cherico Ace Hardware; Vernon Dotrice Insurance Agency; and Curtis L. Trickett, Attorney at Law, among others. Finally, she reached the shade of the big blue-and-white awning dotted with silver stars belonging to The Twinkle, Twinkle Café. Inside, she knew she would find its owner and the woman who had become her sounding board since her move to Cherico half a dozen years ago—Periwinkle Lattimore.

"Maura Beth, you get your cute little redheaded self in here before you wilt like my famous warm spinach salad!" Periwinkle called out the second she spotted her friend sighing at the delicious blast of air-conditioned relief that greeted her just inside the door. The place was empty, being right in the middle of the no-man's land between the lunch and dinner crowds, but the welcoming fragrance of spices and herbs lingered over the dozen or so tables with their blue-and-white tablecloths and delicate votive candles. Periwinkle quickly pointed to a corner two-seater beneath a mobile sporting an elaborate array of gold and silver metallic stars. "Right over there, honey! I'll wait on ya myself!"

"Oh, I didn't come to eat," Maura Beth said. "Just some much-needed talking and listening."

Periwinkle laughed brightly and headed over to the table with a complimentary glass of sweet tea. "Aha! Deep-fried talking and braised listening—my house specials!"

"And I've come for my fix. Sit with me until someone comes in."

Maura Beth had long ago concluded that the key to the success of The Twinkle, as many locals affectionately now called it, was Periwinkle's willingness to stop at nothing to keep it going. Not just ordering the food and supplies, but doing a major share of the cooking and even helping her waitress serve when the place got overwhelmed. The woman remained lean and indefatigable but somehow never seemed to break a sweat. Her blond hair with its stubborn dark roots was always styled attractively, never disheveled, even if she was seldom without the unsophisticated touch of a wad of Juicy Fruit gum in her mouth.

"So what's on your mind?" Periwinkle said, settling into her chair. "I can tell you're upset about something."

Maura Beth took a sip of her tea, breathed deeply, and then unloaded, covering every detail of the ordeal she had just endured at the hands of Cherico's three heavy-handed councilmen.

"Those . . . so-and-sos!" Periwinkle exclaimed, managing to restrain herself. "You mean you might lose your job? After all this time?"

"It's a distinct possibility."

Periwinkle put her elbows on the table, resting her fists

under her chin as she contemplated. "Tell me true—do you think they would be taking you more seriously if you were a man?"

Maura Beth managed an ironic little chuckle. "Maybe, maybe not. In this case, I just think they're all about shuffling the budget around to suit themselves."

"I don't doubt it. But I wonder if they'd be as willing to bulldoze you—using your words here, honey—if you had a pair. Listen, we women have to fight for everything we get. Do you think I would have gotten the seed money to start this restaurant if I'd pulled my punches in my divorce settlement with Harlan Lattimore? Hell, he wanted to ditch me high and dry, but I bowed up and said, 'No, sir, you won't! Not after thirteen years of marriage, and my salad days are in my rear-view mirror. I helped you make a success of The Marina Bar and Grill, working hard as your secretary day and night, and I'll be damned if you'll leave me out in the middle of the water without a paddle!' "

There was a touch of envy in Maura Beth's quiet little sigh. "You certainly know how to stand up for yourself. Of course I know I can't let these men intimidate me. That's exactly what they want. But I can't force people to come to the library, either. I just don't know if there's a way out of this."

"You gotta have you a gimmick," Periwinkle replied, leaning in while furiously working her gum. "Listen to this. When I was trying to come up with a name for my restaurant, I realized that it wouldn't matter what I called it if my food was no good. I know how to put together a delicious meal, though, so that part didn't worry me. But I thought to myself that a catchy name might just get 'em in the door the first time, and then they'd be hooked. Did I ever tell you that I originally wanted to call this place Twinkle, Twinkle, Periwinkle's?"

They both laughed heartily, and Maura Beth said, "No. So why didn't you? I just love that!"

"Well, I thought it might be a bit too cutesy. So I ran it past my mother over in Corinth, and she said, 'Peri, honey, that sounds like you're running one a' those baby boutiques. You know—where they sell bassinets and cradles and that kinda stuff.' And after I thought about it for a while, I knew she was right on the money. So I put the café part in there so people would know it was definitely a new place to eat. Since then, of course, everyone's shortened it to The Twinkle. It's all worked out, but you need to come up with something that'll get people into your library pronto so you can fend off those fat cats."

Just then, a somewhat plump but still appealing middle-aged woman wearing big brunette hair and a busy floral muumuu flounced through the front door, waving and smiling expectantly all the way. "Periwinkle," she said, slightly out of breath, "I finally found the time to pick up those tomato aspics I ordered this morning. I've been running behind all day with my errands."

Periwinkle stood up and offered her hand as the woman reached their table. "They're in the fridge, cool as a cucumber. I'll run go get 'em for ya." She quickly made a half turn toward the kitchen, but stopped just as suddenly in her tracks. "Now, where are my manners? Let me introduce you two. Maura Beth Mayhew, this is one of my newest customers, Connie McShay. She and her husband just moved here from Nashville about a month ago." Periwinkle paused for a quick breath. "Connie, I'm sure you'll be interested to hear that Maura Beth runs our library. I don't have much time for books myself since The Twinkle takes up every minute of my day, but I'm sure Maura Beth'll welcome a new patron with open arms, won'tcha, honey?"

"I most certainly will!" Maura Beth exclaimed, rising from her seat to shake hands and exchange further pleasantries while Periwinkle hurried off to retrieve the aspics.

"I've been meaning to drop by your library, you know,"

Connie continued with an authentic warmth in her voice. "My husband, Douglas, and I have been so busy settling into our lodge on the lake, though. We've popped in only a week or two every year, but now we're here for good. We still have so many boxes to unpack. I could swear those cardboard creatures somehow managed to reproduce in that moving van on the way down. Anyway, I'm a *huge* reader, and I even belonged to a wonderful book club up in Nashville. We called ourselves The Music City Page Turners."

Maura Beth brightened considerably. "And that's music to my ears. You simply must get your card soon and pick out a couple of the new best sellers we've just gotten in. I use every last cent the library has to keep up with all the popular reads. What's your genre, by the way?"

"I'm the ultimate mystery buff. But I only like the polite kind where they figure out everything over tea and buttered scones. No bloody, gory, true crime forensics for me. When Agatha Christie died, I went into literary mourning for months. No more Miss Marple padding around the village of St. Mary Mead stumbling onto murders committed by the landed gentry, what ho! Or Hercule Poirot waxing his mustache, for that matter."

Maura Beth laughed and was about to reply when Periwinkle reappeared with a small paper bag and handed it over to Connie. "Your aspics are just as snug as oysters in the shell in their little plastic containers in there. Just don't brake for any squirrels on the way home, and they should hold their shape nicely."

"Here's seven bucks, and keep the change as usual," Connie said, chuckling while she proffered a bill she had just retrieved from her purse.

"Much appreciated again, honey," Periwinkle replied, tucking the money into her apron pocket.

Then Connie leaned into Maura Beth as if they had been the best of friends for the longest time. "Don't you just love these tomato aspics? I was hooked the first time I bit into one and got a mouthful of that sinful cream cheese that was hiding in the middle. Douglas makes me get them now practically every other night for our dinner. That's all we seem to eat these days—aspic and whatever fish he catches that day out on the lake. That I end up cleaning, by the way. Some retirement—I've spent most of it so far with stringers and fish scalers. Maybe I need to put my foot down."

"I don't know about that, but you've single-handedly turned tomato aspic into my biggest seller," Periwinkle added. Suddenly, she began giggling and couldn't seem to stop. "I'm sorry," she continued finally, "but I just thought of what a difficult time I had selling my aspic when I first opened up. No one would ever order it, and I couldn't figure out why. I knew there was nothing wrong with my recipe. It was my mother's, and everybody in the family always raved about it. Then one day the mystery was solved when one of my customers, a very polite older man visiting down here from somewhere in Ohio, complimented me on the food on the way out. But he also said, 'Just to satisfy my curiosity, could you tell me what *icepick* salad is? Your waitress recommended it as an appetizer, but it sounded pretty dangerous to me, so I passed on it. I've just spent a fortune having most of my teeth capped.' "

Both Maura Beth and Connie looked halfway between amused and bewildered as Periwinkle caught her breath once again.

"I know, ladies. I had that same expression on my face when that dear little man asked me that question. The deal is, there's a certain type of Southern accent where people pronounce words like nasty as 'nicety,' glass becomes 'glice,' cancer turns into 'kindsuh,' and, of course, aspic winds up as 'icepick.'

Maybe you've run into somebody who does that. Anyway, my waitress at the time, Bonnie Lee Fentress, was the sweetest little thing, but that's the way she spoke, and she had no idea she was scaring people to death when she mentioned that item on the menu and left it at that. So I sat down with her and straightened out her diction, and lo and behold, my aspic was reborn. The rest is delicious history."

"I most certainly agree with that," Connie said while glancing at her watch. "Oh, I still have a million things to do, ladies. Let me run now. So nice visiting with you both."

"Don't forget about your library card!" Maura Beth called out as Connie exited as quickly as she had entered, hurling a muffled, "Will do!" from out on the sidewalk.

"I really like her," Periwinkle said as she and Maura Beth resumed their seats. "She may be living high on the hog out on the lake, but she's the salt of the earth—just my type."

Maura Beth was gazing at her tea in silence and let a few awkward moments go by. "Oh, yes, I know she'll be a welcome addition to Cherico, particularly since she's a reader," she finally offered, coming to. "I must track her down if she doesn't keep her word and come by for that card. She's given me an idea that might help the library out. It came to me just this second."

"Shoot!"

"That book club she said she belonged to," Maura Beth explained. "I need to pick her brain about that. Maybe we could get something like that going here in Cherico. You know, get people into the library to review books and socialize with each other. Maybe that's the type of gimmick you were talking about earlier that I could use to put the library back on the map."

Periwinkle looked particularly thoughtful and then nodded. "Couldn't hurt. I think you need to get on it right away, though."

"I knew I did the right thing coming in here to talk things over with you," Maura Beth added. "That shoulder of yours has come in handy quite a few times over the past several years."

Periwinkle reached across and patted her hand affectionately. "Hey, what are girlfriends for?"

2

Turn That Page

The Cherico Library wasn't much to look at, and it was even harder to find. Tucked away on a little-used side street at the sinister-sounding address of 12 Shadow Alley, it had originally been a corrugated iron, farm implement warehouse seventy-something years ago. A decade later, a few wealthy matrons who decided it was time to improve the town had come up with the idea of starting a library and had even donated some of their inherited money to get one going. The City Council back then had been as indifferent as the current one was, however, and had done as little as possible in converting the warehouse into a suitable facility. The unproven rumor was that the lion's share of the funds had been cleverly pocketed by a couple of the politicians, including Durden Sparks's father. It seemed that Cherico had never suffered from an excess of integrity.

A few unimpressive improvements had followed over the years, consisting chiefly of tacking a couple of flimsy white columns onto a pedestrian portico and creating a cramped meeting room inside. There was no loading dock—just a back door—no off-street parking, and the building contained only a stingy 3,500 square feet of space for the librarian's office and shelving the entire collection. Although the fiction was more current, the nonfiction needed weeding for the more topical issues—but Maura Beth barely had enough of a budget to keep the patrons in best sellers, newspapers, and periodicals. It even made her feel guilty to endorse her own paycheck, which was far from what anyone would have called generous.

Oh, sure, it was enough for her to shop for groceries at The Cherico Market, pay the apartment rental, manage the note on her little Prius, and get her hair curled the way she liked at Cherico Tresses. But putting anything aside for the future—such as for a wedding, provided she could ever meet the right guy—was completely out of the question; and she was genuinely embarrassed by what was left in the coffers to pay the two circulation desk clerks that alternated workdays.

"I feel like a missionary in a foreign land sometimes," Maura Beth had confessed to Periwinkle shortly after they had first met. "I'm bound and determined to make everyone here in Cherico understand what a library is for and that they need to take advantage of it. Of course, I'm the first to admit that I got this job straight out of library school—right after my big booster shot of idealism that came with my diploma."

"Don't ever lose that kind of dedication, honey," Periwinkle had advised her back then. "No matter what happens. Because things'll bear down on ya both sooner and later. I speak from experience."

One week after the latest disheartening session with the City Council—another bona-fide example of "things bearing down"—Maura Beth was leaning back in her office chair and reflecting upon that memorable conversation with Periwinkle nearly six years earlier. Momentarily, Renette Posey, her Monday, Wednesday, and Friday front desk clerk, knocked on her door and popped her head in.

"There's a Mrs. Connie McShay here to see you. I just finished fixing her up with a library card," she said in the disarmingly sweet and girlish voice that had become her trademark. It was the main reason Maura Beth had hired the inexperienced eighteen-year-old permanently. She was, in fact, surprisingly good with the public—diplomatic beyond her years, even—and the library needed all the help it could get.

Maura Beth was hardly able to restrain herself, snapping to attention. "Yes! Show her in!" She'd been anticipating this meeting for the last five days, hoping that it would turn out to be the kickoff for holding on to her job and keeping the library open.

"Thanks so much for chatting with me over the phone and working this into your schedule," Maura Beth continued, as the two women shook hands and took their seats across from each other.

"Oh, it's my pleasure," Connie replied, quickly surveying Maura Beth's tiny, windowless office cluttered with book carts, uncrated boxes from wholesalers, and stacks of review journals. "Well, you weren't kidding about the lack of space here and the library being an afterthought with your politicians."

"Yes, I have to do practically everything around here. Order the books, process them, pay the invoices, even check things out when my clerks take their lunch break. I have no children's librarian, and no one in reference or technical services. It's a wonder that I even have this computer." Then she leaned in and lowered her voice. "Not to mention the lengths I go to in order to keep the collection safe. For instance, there's a supply of peanut butter crackers behind the front desk for Mr. Barnes Putzel. He's getting on up there, and his younger sister takes care of him. When he first started coming in, he'd spend all his time in reference and would eventually end up banging volumes of the encyclopedia together like a pair of cymbals. We had no choice but to ask him to put them down and leave. Then, his sister came in one day and suggested we offer him a couple of peanut butter crackers on the sly before he headed over to reference. She said they always calmed him down at home. So, I followed her advice, and we've had no trouble with him ever since. He's in heaven poring over the encyclopedias in blessed silence with no wear and tear on the bindings. The worst we have to deal with now is his peanut butter breath when he comes over to say good-bye."

"I have a thing for peanut butter crackers myself," Connie remarked, nodding with an appreciative grin.

"Yes, well, keeping the reference material safe with crackers is only a part of the reality of the small-town library with practically no funding. You have the patrons who don't understand why we don't have every best seller on the shelves yesterday, but don't bother to bring their books back because 'they've already paid for them with their taxes, so why not keep them?' Would they take a jackhammer and remove a piece of Shadow Alley out in front of the library because they'd paid for the streets and sidewalks? Not to mention the ones that show up with several boxes of moldy books from the turn of the century—not the millennium, but 1900, or even earlier—that they've just found in the attic and want to donate to us. 'If you'll pay for the fumigation,' is what I want to say to them, but instead we just end up having to smile politely and dispose of them as soon as they've left. You wouldn't believe how many people there are who think libraries don't take money to run and that everything gets on the shelves with the wave of a magic wand."

Connie was frowning and shaking her head now. "Is it really that bad here?"

"I wish I could say I was exaggerating."

"I can tell you're not," Connie continued, "because I'm

still shocked by that ultimatum those councilmen gave you. I nearly dropped the receiver on the floor when you told me that. Nobody could get away with that sort of thing in Nashville."

Maura Beth pounded her fist on the desk for emphasis. "But Nashville, this isn't! That's why we've got to put our heads together and see if we can get a book club going. We've got to get more warm bodies in here and boost our circulation figures. I need your input as to how The Music City Page Turners worked, and we'll go from there."

Connie patted her well-sprayed and therefore inert bouffant hairdo and then settled back in her chair. "We had nearly thirty people in our club, mostly women, but there were a few men who showed up eventually. And you wouldn't believe what a fuss some of the divorced and widowed women made over them. They acted like high-school coeds. But that's another story for another day." She chuckled richly and cleared her throat. "We didn't start out with thirty, of course. Originally, we were just a group of seven and built from there. We concentrated on popular Southern writers, either classic or newcomers that had hit the big time. We'd meet quarterly, allowing six or seven weeks for all the members to read the selection for that particular quarter. So we ended up reviewing four books a year."

Maura Beth nodded approvingly. "Southern writers—I like that. I think that would work here. Faulkner, Richard Wright, Winston Groom, Willie Morris, Larry Brown—"

"Oh, we eventually got around to most of those men you mentioned and many more, of course," Connie interrupted. "But, oddly enough, we started out with Southern female writers like Margaret Mitchell, Eudora Welty, and Harper Lee—icons like that. I know our core of women really appreciated it, from the way they dug deep into the discussions. I like to say that it was probably all about heeding voices with estrogen in those early days."

"I've never heard it put quite like that," Maura Beth said, her laughter reflecting her surprise. "But there's no reason why we shouldn't go with that approach here. We could even call ourselves The Cherico Page Turners."

"Sounds good. It's not like we had a copyright on the page-turning concept."

"So, anything else I need to know about your club?"

Connie thought for a while, then perked up. "Well, I kept the books when we got big enough. I was always good with figures. Oh, and I almost forgot. We eventually brought our favorite dishes to these affairs—casseroles, layered salads, lemon and chocolate cake squares, just to name a few—and we learned to do our reviews fully sated after a few mishaps. When there were only seven of us starting out, we sat together in fairly close quarters. That's when we discovered that it's pretty distracting having someone's stomach growling loudly just when you're trying to make a serious literary point. You feel like you're being criticized right that instant."

"That's too funny!" Maura Beth exclaimed. "But it sounds like you ladies got past all that and literally made a delicious time of it."

"Not only that, but hardly anyone ever missed a meeting. Why, you practically had to be hospitalized with the swine flu or recovering from an auto accident not to show up."

A look of determination gripped Maura Beth's face as she set her jaw firmly. "And that sort of loyalty is exactly what we need to jump-start this library again. Only I was thinking that since we have just about five months to work with, we ought to shorten the reading time for our selections. We need to try to squeeze at least two meetings into our agenda before the deadline. I don't think one would be enough to gather any momentum and impress anybody, much less that bunch running City Hall. But once we're good and established, we can try a more leisurely pace the way you did in Nashville." She brought herself up short, flashing a grin. "Listen to me, going on as if we've got this thing in the bag."

"There's nothing wrong with that. You should definitely act like it's a done deal."

Maura Beth nodded enthusiastically and busied herself making notes, leaving Connie to mull things over during the ensuing silence. "Have you thought about how you're going to advertise the club, Maura Beth?" she finally said. "We printed up tons of flyers for our meetings and distributed them to all the branches in Davidson County, plus we found lots of restaurants downtown that let us tack them up for their lunch crowds."

"Flyers would absolutely work," Maura Beth answered, looking up and momentarily putting down her pen. "I know how to do that, and I could get Periwinkle to hand them out to all her customers at The Twinkle. I could also put a sign-up sheet on our bulletin board here for people who might be interested. Maybe we should have an organizational meeting first to see if we can even get this thing off the ground. I wish there were some way I could get the rest of those Music City Page Turners to follow you down here."

Connie smiled warmly. "I'd love the familiar company, but I'm afraid I have no following to speak of. Actually, Douglas and I weren't planning to move into our lake house for five more years, when we'll both turn sixty-five. We still feel like newcomers to Cherico. So even I shouldn't be here. But we sat down one night by the fire over a good bottle of Chianti, and Douglas told me he'd finally had his fill of trial lawyering for one lifetime. All the legal loopholes and angles were just wearing him down. He said all he really wanted at this stage of his life was to indulge his better nature and drift in the middle of Lake Cherico, sip beer, and catch a few fish. Then he asked me if I'd be willing to give up my job at the hospital so we could just move. You see, I'd been an ICU nurse since I graduated from college, and we'd both been socking away a good bit for our retirement."

"I've always admired you folks in the medical profession," Maura Beth offered. "I'm afraid I faint at the sight of blood, but I'm glad there are people who don't or the rest of us would be in big trouble."

"Frankly, I wondered if I would miss it," Connie added. "Especially the reality that I was always taking care of people on the brink. There was nothing more distressing to me than seeing somebody flatline. Oh, the finality of that monotonous sound, and the sorrow and trauma that it represented—I never did get used to it! On the other hand, I got such a kick out of seeing my patients recover and get on with their lives. That made it all worthwhile. I guess that's why I don't have trouble gutting all those fish Douglas catches. I'm not the least bit squeamish—I've seen it all." Then she suddenly leaned forward. "Do I have on too much perfume?"

Maura Beth cocked an ear and blinked twice. "What?"

"Sorry," Connie said, retreating slightly. "I just finished an entire stringer of perch before coming here. I was afraid my hands might smell too fishy no matter how many times I washed them. So I spritzed on some of my Estée Lauder for good measure. Too strong?"

Now that she was being asked to focus on it, Maura Beth actually thought that Connie had overdone it a tad. But she had no intention of saying so, as her best public servant instincts rose to the occasion. "I hardly even noticed it."

"Good," Connie replied, allowing herself to relax. "So, what's our next step?"

Maura Beth handed over the notes she had been making, and Connie scanned them quickly, suggesting a few changes. The two of them went back and forth a couple of times and finally came up with a suitable plan: Maura Beth would design and produce the flyer, but Connie would pay for everything out of her "mad money," as the library simply lacked the funds to pull it off; they would allow a period of two weeks for people to sign up for the club; then Maura Beth would call an organizational meeting at the library and officially get things under way.

"I only hope somebody else will show up," Maura Beth observed, arching her eyebrows dramatically.

Exactly when Maura Beth had come up with the idea of hand-delivering one of her flyers to Councilman Sparks, she could not recall. But she had run it past both Periwinkle and Connie before acting on it, and the three of them had decided that an aggressive approach was the best one to take. She needed to let the councilmen know she meant business about proving the library's worth and would be pursuing that goal immediately.

At the moment, she was standing in front of City Hall with its massive, three-story Corinthian columns—indeed, the ornate building dominated the otherwise low skyline of the town—while she summoned the courage to mount the steps and walk in to have her say. At all costs she must shrug off the lingering traces of intimidation that innumerable sessions with these politicians had produced.

Five minutes later, she found herself sitting in the councilman's outer office, staring uncomfortably at his personality-free secretary, Nora Duddney. In all the visits she had paid over the years, Maura Beth was quite certain that she had never seen the woman come close to registering an emotion of any kind.

"Miz Mayhew! You're looking lovely as ever!" Councilman Sparks exclaimed, bursting through the door unannounced after a tedious ten minutes had passed. "So sorry to keep you waiting, but I have the City of Cherico to run, you know. So many departments, so little time. But do come in and tell me what's on your mind!" He gestured gracefully toward his inner office, turning on his bankable charm full-bore, but Maura Beth couldn't help but notice that Nora Duddney was as charmless as ever, blankly typing things onto her computer screen.

"So, what brings you in this morning?" he began just after they had settled comfortably into their sumptuous leather chairs. Whatever financial problems the City of Cherico might be having, they were clearly not reflected in the opulent décor of the head honcho's office. It had the aura of one of those upscale designer showrooms with Persian rugs covering the floor, as distinguished-looking as the touch of gray at Councilman Sparks's temples.

Maura Beth drew a deep breath as she leaned forward and handed over the flyer. "I'd appreciate it very much if you would read this, please. It will explain everything to you."

He quickly accepted the paper and commented immediately. "My, my! Is this color supposed to be some shade of gold?"

"The printer called it goldenrod, I believe."

"Cutesy name. But a little loud, I think."

"The other choice was bubble gum pink. I don't know what happened to everyday white."

"Aha! You were caught between a rock and a hard place! In that case, you chose wisely. Color is such an intriguing part of life. Myself, I'm partial to bright, flaming red."

After making quite a production of holding up the flyer and thumping it noisily a couple of times, Councilman Sparks chose to read out loud, his tone deliberate but managing to impart a hint of mockery at the same time:

> *Announcing the organizational meeting of The Cherico Page Turners Book Club! Be one of the first in town to review classic Southern literature and sample delicious potluck dishes with your friends and neighbors. Circle the date. Friday, July 17, 2012, at 7 p.m. in The Cherico Library Meeting Room. Let us know you're coming by signing up today at the library or at The Twinkle, Twinkle Café on Commerce Street. We hope to see many of you there.*
> *Sincerely,*
> *Maura Beth Mayhew, Librarian, and the*
> *Rest of Your Friendly Cherico Library Staff*

"I'd like for you to attend," Maura Beth said the instant he stopped reading. "And the other councilmen, too, if they'd like. You don't actually have to sign up and participate. Just drop by and see what we're trying to accomplish."

He patiently began folding the flyer several times until it had been reduced to a small square of paper, which he then pressed between his thumb and index finger for an awkward length of time. "Well, first, I'd like to say that the way you capitalized the line about the staff there at the end really made an impression on me," he began at last. "Just imagine how much more forceful it would have been to have used all caps. I do question whether three people is a staff, however."

Maura Beth managed to force a smile, refusing to let him get to her. "I'd like to have more personnel, of course. I'd even like to have a whole new library, for that matter. But it all takes money, as you well know."

"Yes, that appears to be the crux of the matter between us,

doesn't it?" Then he abruptly switched subjects. "As for your invitation to the other councilmen, I think Chunky would definitely show up for the free food. He'd be the first one in line. But I know he wouldn't sit still for the rest of it. There are times I could swear he can't even read his utility bill. But he comes in handy with bringing certain voters into the fold. As for Gopher Joe, he'd come if I told him he had to, but you wouldn't get a peep out of him all evening. No, I think maybe I'd better make this a solo appearance on behalf of the Council. Just call it an executive decision."

"Then you'll come?"

"I enjoy keeping an eye on you, though I have to admit, I didn't expect something like this to pop up. You've been a busy little honeybee since we last got together, haven't you? Doing your frantic little dance to show the way to the pollen, it appears to me."

Maura Beth was feeling emboldened now and pressed on. "According to what you've told me, I have nothing to lose except my job."

"You have spirit, Miz Mayhew. I like the way you stand up for yourself. It's a very attractive quality among so many."

"Thank you for saying so. Oh, and you don't have to bring a dish with you, by the way."

"I assure you, I hadn't planned to. I can't boil water, and my wife's not much better. Evie and I eat out as often as we can. But I do appreciate you giving me a heads-up about this club of yours. The truth is, I detest surprises of any kind, especially successful ones." Then he rose quickly and said, "If there's nothing else, then, I'll be seeing you on July 17th at the library. I know you really don't believe it, but this office is and always has been open to you."

After she'd left and was heading down the hall, Maura Beth began to get an uneasy feeling about the exchange she'd just had with the man who had hired her. It would be beyond foolish to trust his slick, wolfish demeanor when she imagined him viewing her as Little Redheaded Riding Hood just ripe for the waylaying. He had been far too compliant about everything, and she ended up wondering if she really wanted him there as an observer after all.

3

Missing in Action

The July session of "Who's Who in Cherico?" was well under way in the library's drab little meeting room with Miss Voncille Nettles holding forth in her inimitable fashion.

". . . and this is a photo of the Doak Leonard Winchester Family showing off the brand-new First Farmers' Bank of Cherico building," she was saying. "I'll now pass it around for your perusal. Note especially the big white bows in the ladies' hair. That was all the rage around the turn of the twentieth century. I know that from my research, of course, not because I was actually there."

Everyone laughed and began eagerly inspecting the picture, while Miss Voncille looked on approvingly. Though approaching seventy, she projected the vigor of someone ten to fifteen years younger. Especially impressive was the resonance of her voice, even though she was not a large person. Whenever she made genealogical and historical pronouncements as she was now to her handful of followers, they always lapped them up as the gospel truth. Criticisms or disagreements quickly brought out the sharpness of her tongue, enabling her to live up to her prickly surname. Despite the short fuse, however, there were still traces in her face and in the way she carefully arranged her salt-and-pepper hair of the great beauty she had once been, making people all the more curious about her perennial spinster status. If nothing else, she remained the town's most impeccably dressed woman with no place to go.

On this particular evening, Maura Beth had decided to join Miss Voncille and her loyal members—the Crumpton sisters and widower Locke Linwood—with the deliberate intention of recruiting for her book club. It would be easy enough, she reasoned, to chat with each of them over the fruit punch out of a can and store-bought sugar cookies they routinely trotted out for refreshments. In fact, she had already put a self-serving word in edgewise while ladling a plastic cup for Miss Voncille and was fully counting on closing the deal immediately after the adjournment.

All of a sudden, Mamie Crumpton was shouting about something, and Maura Beth was yanked out of the thoughtful review of her evening agenda.

"Why, Voncille Nettles, you take that back this instant. You simply must retract that outrageous statement. It is most certainly the lie of all time!"

As the older and decidedly overbearing maiden sister of one of Cherico's wealthiest families, Mamie had already begun hyperventilating, heaving her ample bosom. Her detractors around town—and there were more than a few—had often conjectured that one of these days she was going to puff herself up so big during one of her tantrums that pricking her with a pin might just send her flying all over Cherico like a deflated Goodyear blimp.

The unassuming and far daintier Marydell Crumpton uncharacteristically joined the attack. "You made that up out of a whole lace tablecloth, Voncille Nettles, and everybody in this room with any knowledge of this town knows it!"

"See?" Mamie added, wagging a bejeweled finger. "You've

upset my little sister, and you should know by now how hard that is to do!"

"Neither of you has to get so worked up and take everything so seriously!" Miss Voncille exclaimed, deliberately averting her eyes from her accusers. "This is just par for the course for you, Mamie. You haven't changed in all the years I've known you!"

Maura Beth blinked in disbelief at the heated exchange, realizing she had not been paying close attention to Miss Voncille's latest pronouncement. "Now, everyone, please calm down."

"I have a right to be upset. Armadillos, indeed!" Mamie repeated, practically spitting out the words. "I've never heard such a ridiculous thing in my life. The Crumpton Family has been solvent and respectable from the instant we set foot on these shores. We would never have stooped to the activities you describe. So, once and for all, are you going to retract this incredible fabrication of yours or not? Really, I have no earthly idea what could have gotten into you!"

Miss Voncille folded her arms and turned up her nose at the challenge, just sitting there saying nothing.

"Very well, then. I'll take that as a 'no,' " Mamie declared, rising from the table with all the authority she could muster. "Come along, sister dear, we don't need to be dignifying this with our presence any longer." Whereupon the two of them huffed out of the meeting room, slamming the door behind them and leaving Maura Beth and Locke Linwood sitting in place virtually stupefied.

Miss Voncille finally broke the awkward silence. "Mamie Crumpton always has to have her way. She's so pompous, and there's this morbid side she's had since we were girls in school together. That's an incredible story in itself. Would you like to hear it?"

Maura Beth leaned in with all the poise she could muster. "Another time, perhaps. But I'm afraid I was daydreaming a bit when you revealed whatever it was in your lecture that got the Crumpton sisters so upset. So sorry. Would you mind repeating it?"

Miss Voncille shrugged. "I meant no harm. I just thought we could inject a little fun into one of these outings."

"Well, then, please tell me all about the fun."

"Oh, very well. After I was through talking about the Winchester Family, I said that I'd found an old newspaper article about Hyram Crumpton, their grandfather, opening up a business downtown that specialized in stuffed animals and other novelties like flower baskets made out of armadillo shells. I also said he had to do it because he'd previously gone bankrupt." Miss Voncille was unable to suppress a giggle or two. "And, yes—I made it all up."

"For heaven's sake, why?"

"Maybe I've gotten a little bored with 'Who's Who?' after all these years. The words *deadly dull* come to mind," Miss Voncille confessed with a sigh. But her tone was not particularly contrite, and she even managed to look a trifle smug there at the end.

Locke Linwood straightened his shiny silver tie and noisily cleared his throat to gain the floor. "Miss Voncille, I'd like to tell you something very important and of a personal nature, if you don't mind."

"Go right ahead, Mr. Linwood," Miss Voncille replied, looking intrigued.

"Would you like some privacy?" Maura Beth put in, thinking on her feet.

Locke shook his head of thick gray hair emphatically. "Please stay right where you are, Miz Mayhew. I don't mind you hearing this. It seems to be a night for speaking with abandon."

He appeared to be gathering his thoughts and did not say anything immediately. Maura Beth could not wait to hear what was on his mind, noting the profound lines of displeasure creasing his face. She had never associated frowns with this lanky, distinguished man, as it was well-known to everyone that he and his late wife, Pamela, had been the happiest of married couples for nearly forty years. After her passing, he had surprised everyone by continuing to attend "Who's Who?" by himself, but even then had never exhibited a hint of sorrow in his expressions.

"Miss Voncille," he began at last, "my dear wife and I always enjoyed your diligent efforts to shed light on our family histories here in Cherico. No one could possibly be better researched than you are. We considered you the ultimate authority, and you know we didn't miss many meetings. But I think this so-called joke of yours at the expense of the Crumpton family was in questionable taste, no matter what kind of boredom you say you're going through. It was a complete disappointment to me."

He paused for a moment and swallowed hard. "Not only that, but, well, things have been mighty lonely for me since my wife passed, and I was actually thinking of asking you out, believe it or not. I hope you don't think that's too forward, but there it is. Except that after your behavior tonight and the way you've just shrugged it off as if it was nothing, I realize I don't really know you at all. You're not who I thought you were. There now, I've gotten that off my chest."

Miss Voncille's face dropped noticeably, and she seemed at a loss for words for the longest time. Finally, though, she regained her composure. "Mr. Linwood, I'm not an easy person to surprise, but I have to admit you've just accomplished that." She paused briefly to throw up her hands. "At any rate, it seems that you and Miz Mayhew are in agreement about my behavior. So perhaps I should just go ahead and apologize."

Maura Beth reacted first, but not before finding the polite, formal exchange from the older generation a bit on the endearing side. Was she possibly witnessing the budding of a future romance? "Miss Voncille, I think it's the Crumpton sisters who need your apology. If you lose them as members, you've gotten rid of two thirds of your following."

"Yes, I realize that."

"If you ladies will excuse me, then," Locke said, rising from his chair and squaring his shoulders. "I think I'll call it an evening." He made his way slowly to the door, turning back at the last second with a gentlemanly bow. "But, Miss Voncille, I want you to know that I don't discourage easily. Despite what happened tonight, I fully intend to be here for the next meeting."

"Another surprise! What am I supposed to make of all that?" Miss Voncille exclaimed after Locke had left the room. But Maura Beth could sense the false bravado in her tone.

"We could talk about it, if you like. Would you care to have a heart-to-heart over more punch and cookies?"

Miss Voncille's reply came only after a great deal of fidgeting with the notes she had prepared for the meeting, as if they would somehow acquire some sort of magical powers and tell her what to do. "Oh, why not? Getting things off your chest seems to have worked nicely for Mr. Linwood."

Maura Beth waited as patiently as she could, seeing that Miss Voncille was having some difficulty getting started, but finally broke the ice herself. "I hope you regard me as more than just a librarian by now. I know six years isn't that much history between us in the grand scheme of things, but I've always prided myself on being a good listener. But first, let's keep our energy levels up." So she headed for the refreshment table and poured them each another cup of red punch with maraschino cherries on the bottom, brought back a couple of cookies wrapped in paper napkins, and the exchange began in earnest.

"Locke Linwood was right when he said he didn't really know who I was. He's in good company because very few people know what I'm about to tell you. I can sum it all up in two words, though," Miss Voncille explained after nibbling a cookie and sipping her punch. "Frank Gibbons."

"Frank Gibbons? Who is he?"

"Only the love of my life," Miss Voncille explained. "Today's been rough on me. It's been forty-five years since Frank literally dematerialized. I should have known better than to schedule a meeting of 'Who's Who?' with that so heavy on my mind lately. It comes and goes, of course, but what's worse is that I took it all out on the Crumpton sisters and their money and haughty ways. But I still shouldn't have lashed out at them. I'm bigger than that."

Maura Beth put on her most sympathetic face and lowered her voice accordingly. "So tell me more about this man disappearing into thin air."

"Well, no. You misunderstand. You see, he was a soldier who lived over in Corinth. My parents didn't approve because they said he was from the wrong side of the tracks. It was true that his family didn't have a lot of money or social position, but that didn't mean a thing to me. I was madly in love. Still, very few people here in Cherico even knew this little affair was going on because my parents wanted it like that. From the very beginning, they said they knew it would never last. That would turn out to be the cruelest thing they would ever say to me, and I never forgave them for it." Miss Voncille broke off for a few moments for another swallow of her punch.

"Frank had just introduced me to his family over the Christmas holidays back in 1967. They were as sweet as they could be to me, even though I knew there would be serious in-law problems down the line. Nevertheless, we fully intended to get engaged, no matter what. But in January, Frank was deployed to Vietnam, and we had to put everything on hold. I don't know how well you remember your history, but that was January of 1968. Shortly after he arrived over there, the North Vietnamese launched the Tet Offensive, and Frank's company ended up right in the middle of it."

"As I matter of fact, I do know about the Tet Offensive, even if I wasn't around," Maura Beth explained. "We librarians are always getting refresher courses in everything under the sun when we help students research their school reports. The teachers never stop assigning papers on the Vietnam War, and we're open much later than the school libraries are. Anyway, I know there were a lot of casualties among our troops during that terrible period. So are you telling me Frank was one of those?"

Miss Voncille absent-mindedly snapped her cookie in two, briefly staring down at what she'd done in astonishment. When she looked up, she picked a spot on the wall above Maura Beth's head and spoke to it. "It was the worst thing that can happen. He was officially declared MIA, which doesn't allow for closure. Of course, I never got it. He's still MIA all these many decades later. He was just gone, and no one knew where to find him. I kept in touch with his mother until she died, but there was no further word.

"Of course, there was a memorial service for him over in Corinth, which I sneaked off to when the time came. But it just wasn't the same as putting his actual remains to rest. You might not think that's such a big deal, but, believe me, I'm sure it would have helped me heal. Meanwhile, I busied myself with my school teaching until I retired and then took on all this genealogy research after that and . . . well, here we are sitting side by side, sipping punch and discussing it all as ancient history."

"I'm so sorry about Frank," Maura Beth said, shaking her head slowly.

Miss Voncille brushed away a few cookie crumbs from the

palm of her hand with her napkin. "Sometimes, just when I think I'm really over him, something like this bubbles up to remind me I'm not. I mean, like making up a lie about someone skinning armadillos for a living. Of course, those Crumpton sisters have truly annoyed me beyond belief over the years. Mamie, in particular, has managed to make it very clear that my having to earn a living as a schoolteacher practically made me a peasant in her eyes. For that reason alone, I think she had my rude nonsense coming to her. Maybe that will help you understand what I did this evening a little better."

"Just between the two of us," Maura Beth confided, leaning in, "there have been times when Mamie Crumpton has walked into the library and treated me like a servant—ordering me to get a book off the shelf for her without so much as a 'thank you' later."

Miss Voncille started nodding compulsively. "That's Mamie in a nutshell—emphasis on the 'nut.' As far as I can tell, all that money of hers has insulated her from the hard knocks most of us receive in life—such as what happened to me and Frank."

"Well, I haven't experienced your level of pain," Maura Beth said, her voice wavering a bit. "But these lost loves are tough. I got jilted at LSU by a South Louisiana boy named Elphage Alphonse Broussard, Jr. We dated for three years, and I was convinced Al was going to ask me to marry him. Once, he even joked about having a gigantic wedding ceremony on the fifty-yard line of Tiger Stadium with Mike the Tiger in his cage roaring his approval right next to us. Instead, he suddenly made a big deal out of whether or not I'd convert to Catholicism before the ceremony. When I said no, he broke things off very abruptly. It made me suspect there was someone else waiting in the wings, and he was just using that as an excuse. He'd been so indifferent on the subject of religion before. Why, he didn't even like putting on a costume and going to Mardi Gras parades to catch beads and doubloons, which is a complete betrayal of the culture down there. Believe me, college kids live for it. And . . . I've been a little skittish ever since."

"But you haven't remained missing in action like I have, I hope?"

"Oh, my girlfriend, Periwinkle Lattimore, keeps an eye out for me when someone she thinks I might be interested in wanders into The Twinkle. She even takes pictures with her cell phone on the sly and sends them to me. The problem is, we don't exactly have the same taste in men. After all, she's almost forty, and I'll be thirty in two years."

Miss Voncille arched her eyebrows and managed a wry smile. "You say that as if you don't have most of your life ahead of you—although I will admit the pickings are slim here in Cherico."

Maura Beth felt the tension that had filled the room earlier quickly draining away now, and she decided to resume pursuit of her original mission. "Unfortunately, you're right. By the way, I'd like to know what you thought of my Cherico Page Turners. Maybe you could join us? You've probably spotted the sign-up sheet by the front desk. I was thinking that with all these tempers flaring in 'Who's Who?' maybe you could give genealogy a rest for a while and try something a little different while everyone cools off."

Miss Voncille closed her eyes for a brief second trying to remember. "Books and potluck? Was that the gist of it?"

"Essentially. But we thought we would concentrate on Southern female writers in the beginning and maybe bond with each other in the process."

"I don't know if that sort of gaggle would work out for me. I'm used to running the entire show."

"Then what about this?" Maura Beth continued, not willing to let her wiggle off the hook so easily. "Weren't you intrigued by what Mr. Linwood said to you? I mean, the part about asking you out. I'm sure it took us both by surprise."

"At last . . . we get around to that." Miss Voncille let the statement just sit there for a while before moving on. "The truth is, I'm flattered. I had no idea he was thinking along those lines. He was always a man of few words, holding his wife's hand the way he did and letting her do all the talking. As for myself, I've blocked out contemplating male companionship over the years. That's what lack of closure will do for you."

"It's very fortuitous that you've brought up the concept of closure," Maura Beth explained, deciding not to beat around the bush any longer. "Even if I mean closure in an entirely different context." Then she told Miss Voncille everything she had also shared with Connie McShay about the disquieting ultimatum from the City Council. "I realize you have other options besides holding your meetings here, but I wanted you to know what could possibly happen in just a few short months. Does Cherico really want to be without a library?"

Miss Voncille looked and sounded distressed. "I've never cared for the current crop over there at City Hall. Actually, the only one that matters is our very own banana republic hotshot, Durden Sparks. You're originally from Louisiana, aren't you?"

Maura Beth said she was.

"Well, Durden fits the Huey Long model of governance from down your way. Or maybe he's more like Edwin Edwards was with those flashy good looks. I taught Durden in junior high, and he was so conceited and full of himself the way he'd stand up in front of his fellow history students and give an oral report that sounded like he was being nominated for President of the United States at a political convention. It was all I could do to keep from giving him an 'A' in Demagoguery. These days, of course, I can name you scores of silly women who vote for him time after time just because he makes them fantasize and swoon. Not me. My Frank wasn't all that handsome, but he was brave and he stood for something. That's my definition of a man."

"Well, then, there's your incentive. Why don't you sign up and show Councilman Sparks and his cronies that they just can't do whatever they please?" Maura Beth continued, proceeding full speed ahead now. "And not only that, since you're a woman who likes to take charge, why don't you consider inviting Locke Linwood to accompany you to the first meeting? He's already surprised you. Maybe you could surprise him."

Maura Beth saw she had struck a responsive chord when Miss Voncille actually seemed to be blushing. "Very well, then. You've convinced me. I'll become an official Cherico Page Turner." Then she suddenly turned thoughtful. "As for Mr. Linwood . . . I don't want to rush into that one. I think he's looking for a different version of me. I'll have to sleep on it." The next second she was glancing at her watch and rolling her eyes. "It feels like it ought to be later than it is, but then, I ran everybody off tonight, didn't I? It was definitely not my most successful lecture, I can assure you."

Maura Beth reached over and patted her hand warmly. "Oh, I don't know. First, I have to thank you for joining my little club. And then, I think you and I got to know each other a lot better after all this time. Locke Linwood hasn't really gone anywhere, and I'm willing to bet the Crumpton sisters will come back into the fold with a little diplomacy on your part."

"Got a delicious recipe for crow?" Miss Voncille quipped, gathering up her notes and photos and tucking them into the folder she'd brought along.

"Come on," Maura Beth replied, chuckling as she dangled her impressive collection of keys before them. "We'll sign you up and then close down together."

★ ★ ★

It was just past nine when Maura Beth walked through the door of her cozy one-bedroom apartment on Clover Street and collapsed on the rust-colored living room sofa her parents had shipped to her three Christmases ago from their hometown of Covington, Louisiana. *It'll go with your hair when you sit on it,* her mother had written on the card that had accompanied it.

Actually, it *was* a pretty close match. Auburn, whiskey, or rust—those were the adjectives that had been used most often by the admirers of Maura Beth's hair. But she herself had thought, rather playfully at times, that her mother's sentiments weren't particularly grammatical. Which was she supposed to sit on—the sofa or her hair?

Whatever the case, she sometimes enjoyed entertaining herself with the question for lack of anything better to do after coming home from work. Tonight, she was happily remembering the last thing Miss Voncille had said to her as they were walking under the portico of the library into the steamy July evening air. "Your Cherico Page Turners are no longer missing in action! Miss Voncille Nettles, reporting for duty!"

They had both laughed, waved good-bye, and headed toward their cars down the street.

Back on the sofa where her hair had blended nicely into the fabric of one of the big cushions behind her, Maura Beth suddenly realized that all those cups of fruit punch had coated her throat with sugar. She needed a nice glass of ice water, so she jumped up and headed toward the fridge and the big pitcher she always kept inside on the middle shelf.

The phone rang on the way over, startling her, but she reached the crowded kitchenette counter soon enough. Whoever was on the other end of the line opened the conversation with an enthusiastic, "Guess what?"

Maura Beth immediately played along, easily recognizing

Periwinkle's down-home voice. "And hello to you, too. Don't tell me. You have another picture of a person in pants for me. Or is it another set of twin cowboys passing through from Dallas on the way to become country singers in Nashville? One for you, and one for me."

Periwinkle produced her usual hearty laugh. "Even better. Someone signed up for your book club tonight over here. She just left—in fact, we closed the place down together we had so much fun chatting. You won't believe who it is!"

"Enough guessing games," Maura Beth said. "Just tell me."

"Okay, here goes. It's Becca Broccoli!"

Maura Beth frowned immediately. "Who?"

"Surely you've heard of her. Becca Broccoli of radio fame? Haven't you ever listened to her show on WHYY?"

"Periwinkle, I don't listen to the radio or even watch much television," Maura Beth said, growing slightly impatient. "I'm always curled up on my sofa reading the free galleys all the publishers send us librarians. How do you think they get the buzz going for their new writers? We're their foot soldiers in spreading the word."

"Never mind that. This is exciting news. Becca Broccoli has a cooking and recipe show on local radio—how do you think I get some of my best ideas for The Twinkle menu? I listen to her faithfully every morning."

Maura Beth mulled things over, still somewhat puzzled. "Cooking on the radio? Not exactly a visual medium. And what's with the name Broccoli? That can't be real, can it? Is she one of those vegans or vegetarians?"

There was the faint sound of paper rustling, and then Periwinkle explained. "I'm holding the sign-up sheet in my hand right now. I didn't know this before, but Becca's real name is Mrs. Justin B-R-A-C-H-L-E. She told me tonight over her bread pudding that since her name was pronounced like broccoli, she decided to go ahead and capitalize on it. Thus was born *The Becca Broccoli Show,* weekday mornings at seven-thirty. Don't you realize what this means for your club?"

"She can review cookbooks for us?" Maura Beth ventured, unable to resist.

"Seriously, now. Think about the publicity angle, girl. She can mention the club over the radio whenever she has a mind to. She has a huge audience. You're a bit slow on the uptake tonight!"

Maura Beth briefly debated whether to mention all the hoopla at the "Who's Who?" meeting but thought better of it. "Sorry, it's been a long day. But I've got a sign-up myself at this end. Miss Voncille Nettles of 'Who's Who in Cherico?' is on board. So now we'll have at least four people for our organizational meeting next week. And if you could find a way to join us—"

"Like I said before," Periwinkle interrupted, "I just don't have the time, honey. Not to read books and run the restaurant six days a week, too. Just let me hand out flyers here at The Twinkle and talk you up that way. Reading recipes is more my speed. Anyway, you got you a good one in Becca Broccoli, and who knows how many more'll eat at The Twinkle and end up in your club?"

"Thanks, Periwinkle," Maura Beth said. "You really are my eyes and ears, even without your cell phone camera."

An hour later, Maura Beth was propped up in bed against her purple pillows, smiling down at her wiggling, freshly painted, pink toenails. "You are such a girlie girl sometimes, Maura Beth," she said out loud, pouting her lips playfully.

Anyone surveying her bedroom would have thought so. She had changed the nondescript wallpaper she had inherited to a lavender floral design, and her solid lavender bedspread picked up the theme. What little money she had managed to put aside—with significant help from her parents, of course—

had been spent on the brass bed, which was the centerpiece of the room. Altogether, it was an environment that had yet to welcome its first male visitor, and Maura Beth wasn't particularly happy about that.

Before turning out the lights, she decided to open the top drawer of her night stand and retrieve her journal. She had been keeping it off and on since her freshman year at LSU, and whenever she needed a boost of any kind, she would trot it out and turn to page twenty-five. Tonight was one of those nights.

It read:

THREE THINGS TO ACCOMPLISH
BEFORE I'M THIRTY, PLUS A P.S.

1—Become the director of a decent-sized library (city of at least 20,000 people).
2—Get married (but not out of desperation).
3—Have two children, one of each (natural childbirth—ouch!).
P.S.—Hope one of the bambinos has red hair. (We're such a minority!)

Maura Beth gingerly rubbed the tips of her fingers on the page and slowly closed the journal. Then she put it away, sighing resolutely. Would any of those things ever happen, even past thirty?

4

Out of the Mouths of Babes

It was nearly ten after seven on the evening of July 17, but the organizational meeting of The Cherico Page Turners had not yet begun. Maura Beth had decided to disdain the meeting room because of the claustrophobia it never failed to produce. Instead, she was standing behind a podium she had placed in front of the circulation desk in the main lobby, gazing out at the half-circle of folding chairs arranged before her. Connie McShay, Miss Voncille, along with her guest, Locke Linwood, and Councilman Sparks had arrived early and were talking among themselves in their seats. But Mrs. Justin Brachle (aka Becca Broccoli) had not yet made an appearance, and Maura Beth was beginning to worry. Their numbers were paltry enough as it was.

"If Mrs. Brachle doesn't show up within the next five minutes, we'll begin without her," Maura Beth announced.

But no sooner had those words escaped her than the celebrated Becca Broccoli breezed through the front door wearing a summery yellow frock and apologizing profusely as she approached the group. "I know I've kept everyone waiting," she began, "but I had to feed my Stout Fella. That's my husband, Justin, you know. He was trying to wind up one of his real-estate deals over the phone, and he just wouldn't come to the table—" She broke off and flashed a smile. "I guess none of you are really interested in all this. Except, I owe you an introduction, at the very least. I generally go by the name of Becca Broccoli these days, and, again, I'm so sorry I'm late." Finally, she sat down in the open chair next to Connie, who offered her a gracious nod.

Maura Beth couldn't have been more surprised. Not at the tardiness, nor the rambling, breathless monologue, but at Becca's actual appearance. This petite, perfectly accessorized, very attractive blonde did not match the voice on the radio that Maura Beth had taken the time to tune in to the day after Periwinkle had informed her of the sign-up. That next morning, she had envisioned the woman loudly enumerating the ingredients for spicy beef stew as matronly, perhaps even as tall and ungainly as Julia Child had been. Instead, Becca was more like a bouncier, much younger version of Miss Voncille.

"Don't worry," Maura Beth replied, briefly waving her off. "You haven't missed a thing. We've all just been getting better acquainted. So, shall we begin?"

But before she had a chance to mention the first item on her scripted agenda, Councilman Sparks stood up and stole the floor from her. "We're a pretty sparse crowd, aren't we? Is this going to be enough to have a viable book club? I'm just a kibitzer, you know, so don't mind me."

It was Connie, however, who answered his question, turning toward him with a deferential smile. "We started out with seven people for The Music City Page Turners in Nashville, Councilman. It only takes a few dedicated readers to make a book club work."

"Yes, we'll worry about numbers later," Maura Beth added, eager to take back control. "And there's no need for anyone to stand while speaking. We're going to be very casual in our approach."

Councilman Sparks resumed his seat with what amounted to a mock salute. "As you wish."

Maura Beth offered a perfunctory but still civil, "Thank you!" and then moved on immediately. There were a few parliamentary issues to resolve first—such as confirming the head of the club and the necessity of a treasurer. It was decided that Maura Beth would continue to lead and see to it that there were multiple library copies of the books they would reviewing, while Connie would handle the bookkeeping, since she had performed that function so admirably for The Music City Page Turners.

Next came the matter of coordinating the menus for each meeting—something that perhaps only Maura Beth had considered. "After all," she continued, "I think we'd prefer an appetizer, entrée, and dessert for our get-togethers. Someone needs to make sure we have a balance of dishes with a few timely phone calls to the others. Volunteers?"

Becca glanced first one way and then the other, checking for competition. As no one else budged, she said, "I'll be happy to do that since I'm planning menus all the time for my shows."

It was exactly what Maura Beth had hoped to hear. She had even thought about phoning Becca the day before to ask if she would willing to assume the food planning duties. Since the two women had never met, however, she had concluded that it might be too forward and chose to wait until the meeting got under way when they were face-to-face.

"I, for one, would be delighted to have you do that for us," Maura Beth replied, "and I assume that the rest of you feel the same way? Show of hands?"

Councilman Sparks rightfully abstained from voting, but everyone else was on board.

"I'm honored, ladies and gentlemen," Becca stated, while scanning the group with a smile. "But I did have one question.

Will we be reviewing cookbooks from time to time? I feel I have special insight into their effectiveness."

Maura Beth was trying her best to conceal her surprise. The flyer had made it quite clear that Southern literature would be the focus of the club. "To be honest with you, I thought we would sample each other's dishes and exchange recipes as we saw fit," Maura Beth explained. "But our discussions would be strictly literary."

"Didn't you know that I'm publishing a cookbook next year? I'm calling it *The Best of Becca Broccoli,* and I'll be transcribing some of my most popular radio shows. Of course, I was hoping it would be the subject of one of our future meetings."

Maura Beth felt her body tensing up at the wrench that had just been thrown into the works. It was imperative that she think on her feet and strike the right note. "I see no reason why we can't consider that down the line. You say your cookbook is forthcoming anyway," she pointed out, proceeding carefully. "For now, though, I believe we need to concentrate on our famous Southern female writers and get firmly established. We can make the rest up as we go along."

Becca settled back in her chair, offering up a pleasant little nod. "I'll just keep everyone posted on the progress of my cookbook, then. And I'll be more than happy to autograph copies when it comes out."

"Very good. We'll look forward to that," Maura Beth continued, returning to her notes with a decided sense of relief. "Now, the next item I have down here is our club name. Are we all in agreement on The Cherico Page Turners? May I have a show of hands?"

Everyone except Councilman Sparks raised their hand briefly, but Connie continued to wave in the studied manner of Queen Elizabeth on the balcony at Buckingham Palace or a newly crowned Miss America walking the runway.

"Yes, Connie? Do you have something to add?"

"Well, I was just thinking, Maura Beth . . . maybe we should consider going with something original instead of copying somebody else."

"But you were the one that told me all about The Music City Page Turners."

"Yes, I know. But if you'll bear with me. Something happened recently that I just have to share with y'all." She took a moment to gather her thoughts, obviously amused by what she was about to reveal.

"Our daughter, Lindy, has been visiting us from Memphis with our little granddaughter, Melissa. We told Lindy we weren't quite ready for visitors yet, but she wanted to come anyway. She said, 'Melissa misses her Gigi and Paw.' That's what the little angel calls my husband, Douglas, and me. Anyway, she's just eight, and she still has trouble with certain words—like Cherico, for instance. So after a few days, she said, 'Gigi and Paw, I just love visitin' with y'all here in Cherry Cola, Mis-'sippi!' We just thought it was the cutest thing ever. So I was wondering if we might consider calling ourselves The Cherry Cola Book Club instead of The Cherico Page Turners? What do you think?"

Subdued *oohing, ahhing,* and nodding rippled through the half-circle, and it was Miss Voncille who spoke up first. "I like it. It gets my vote. Locke, you'll go along with it, won't you?"

"Whatever you ladies prefer is fine with me," he said, patting her hand. "I'm only here because of Sadie Hawkins sitting next to me."

"But you didn't say no to me, Locke Linwood!" Miss Voncille exclaimed, looking smug.

Becca then offered her approval, and finally Maura Beth chimed in. "It's highly original, if nothing else. And since I haven't had any logos printed up yet, I don't see why we can't change our minds. Ladies' prerogative, as they say."

All the women were chuckling or rolling their eyes, but it was Maura Beth who truly offered up the exclamation point. "As they also say—out of the mouths of babes. So, many thanks to your precious granddaughter, Connie. Looks like we're now officially The Cherry Cola Book Club. Maybe the name alone will intrigue people enough to join."

"And we could add the cherry cola part to the menus," Becca suggested. "I mean, nothing spruces up a soft drink like dropping a few ice cubes and cherries into a tumbler and then giving it a shake or a stir with a swizzle stick. Add a twist of lime, and you've got a cola to remember—especially in the summer heat."

Connie gave Becca a gentle nudge and chuckled softly. "That sounds marvelously refreshing, of course, but did anyone ever tell you that you talk like a recipe?"

"I'd be in trouble if I didn't, considering the thousands of shows I've produced!" Becca exclaimed. "Oh, yes, my Stout Fella says all the time that I'm very fluent in listing ingredients!"

"What I want to know is how you keep that cute little figure of yours while hanging around the kitchen so much?" Connie continued. "Mine blew up on me years ago. My figure, not my kitchen, of course."

Everyone present enjoyed a good laugh, and Becca said, "No big secret. I do all the cooking, but Stout Fella does all the eating around our house. He's gained about forty-five pounds since we got married ten years ago. I really should put him on a diet for his own good. Last time he went to the doctor, his cholesterol was up in the stratosphere. If I could just stop him from 'islanding' his ice cream, for starters."

Connie's brow furrowed dramatically. "Islanding? You mean scooping?"

"No, I only wish he would scoop. It's when Stout Fella hovers over a half gallon of ice cream with his big spoon. He starts digging around the edges where it's softer, and then he keeps going around and around and deeper and deeper until he's eaten enough to make an island out of the middle."

"What does he do with the middle?" Connie continued, still looking puzzled.

"Oh, he eventually gets around to that, too. Another time, he chips away from the edges until the island has completely disappeared. The point is, he consumes thousands of extra calories at one standing. I've informed him of the existence of bowls, but he won't use them because he knows they would make him commit to a finite amount."

Sensing that she was losing control of the meeting again, Maura Beth stepped in and abruptly switched subjects. "Ladies, this is all very fascinating, but I wanted to get your opinions on when to schedule the next meeting. We need to decide how long it will take us to read our first selection."

"Exactly what is our first selection, by the way?" Miss Voncille wanted to know.

"I planned to go into that, too," Maura Beth explained. "I had one particular classic in mind but thought we'd discuss it first. We might as well do that right now and then worry about the scheduling later. So, to cut to the chase, what does everybody think about getting our feet wet with the very dependable *Gone with the Wind*?"

"I've waded in that pool before with The Music City Page Turners," Connie explained. "It's been a few years, though."

"So you're less than enthusiastic?" Maura Beth said, sounding slightly disappointed.

Connie shrugged while patting her hair. "I'll go along with the majority, of course, but it's just such familiar territory to me."

"We'll branch out, I assure you," Maura Beth explained. "Harper Lee, Eudora Welty, Ellen Douglas, and Ellen Gilchrist won't be far behind."

"Getting back to *Gone with the Wind,* though," Miss Voncille began. "I'd like to know what could possibly be said about Margaret Mitchell's only contribution to literature after all these decades? Hasn't it been done to death and then some? Because the truth is, I don't know if I can get through all those dialects again. I read the book way back in high school and never deciphered a word Mammy said. Did slaves really talk like that? Lord knows, I don't want to get into that can of worms called political correctness, but I *am* a student of history, and it seemed so exaggerated."

Instead of being discouraged by the negative comments, however, Maura Beth was actually pleased. "But that's exactly the sort of observation I'd like for us to be discussing in the club. We don't have to stick to the same tired angles, as if all criticism has been chiseled in stone. We can explore new and original concepts."

Miss Voncille looked pensive but sounded placated. "We can bring up anything we want? No matter how outside the box?"

"Absolutely. You can be as revisionist as you like. All writers should be open to interpretation forever, even if we tend to bronze and retire them."

"On the other hand, you can always rehash the movie," Councilman Sparks quipped unexpectedly. He was sitting back in his chair with his arms folded and a supreme smirk on his face. "Which would seem to lead to the obvious next question: Will your members fall back on watching Clark Gable and Vivien Leigh instead of taking the time to actually read the book? And how can you prove they didn't take that DVD shortcut?"

Maura Beth quickly realized that her fears about Councilman Sparks attending the meeting were not groundless. Clearly, he was there to make trouble with his subtle digs, but she was not going to give him the satisfaction of showing her irritation. "If members would like to view the film in addition to reading the book, I would certainly have no objections. That would make an excellent point of comparison for our discussions."

"Clever girl. You should run for office with that answer," Councilman Sparks added. "I couldn't have put it better myself."

"So, if there's no further input, shall we vote on my suggestion?" Maura Beth continued, ignoring his comment.

After a few more stray remarks that produced no fireworks, the vote was unanimous in favor of *Gone with the Wind,* even though Becca reminded everyone not to forget about her forthcoming cookbook as an aside. Then it was decided that the group would take a month to read the novel and reconvene on August 17 to discuss it—a straightforward enough proposition.

Councilman Sparks, however, continued to play devil's advocate. "What if someone else enrolls in a few weeks and doesn't have enough time to read the book? Will you allow use of *CliffsNotes*?"

Maura Beth waited for the awkward titters to subside before answering. "This isn't a course, and we're not here to be graded, Councilman. We're here to think, have a good time, and enjoy some good food." Then she decided it would be best to pull the plug. "So, if there are no other questions . . . I think this organizational meeting will come to an end."

"And don't forget, I'll be giving y'all a call to work out who's going to bring what to eat," Becca put in at the last second. "We'll try to make sure everyone whips up one of their best dishes."

Maura Beth did not much care for Councilman Sparks lingering behind after everyone else had left. She did not want to hear what he had to say, knowing quite well that it could not possibly be of a constructive nature. Nevertheless, she resumed her position behind the podium, subconsciously viewing it as a means of protection as much as anything else. Then she plastered a grin on her face and looked directly into his eyes as he spoke.

"I admire your organizational skills, Miz Mayhew," he began. "You run a tight ship just the way I do. But perhaps it's time you faced up to the possibility that your tight ship is also sinking fast. I'm just wondering if all this furious activity of yours isn't much ado about nothing. I hope you realize that a handful of people picnicking in the library is not going to alter the equation here. It may end up amusing a few intellectual types in the community, but I can't see it becoming popular with the masses. I just don't think that dog will hunt in Cherico."

Maura Beth frowned. "We're just getting off the ground. Don't you think you should cut us a little slack?"

"I know you're intelligent enough to understand that even if you doubled the number of people you had in here tonight, it wouldn't be enough to keep the library open when we bear down on the budget," he said, arching his eyebrows.

But she matched his glibness with sturdy body language of her own, leaning toward him with her chin up. "You've made that quite clear. Maybe I have more faith in the public than you do. But never mind that. I still think it's odd that you just don't close me down right now, particularly if you're so sure that nobody will care."

"Are you daring me to do that, Miz Mayhew?"

She cleared her throat and swallowed hard. "Yes."

"Impressive," he answered, turning off his dazzling smile in an instant. "You called my bluff. Chunky and Gopher Joe are way too intimidated to even try something like that. The truth is, if I don't know anything else, I know my politics. And if by some miracle, you should pack every resident of Cherico into your little library five and a half months from now, I don't want to be on the outside looking in. I'll pretend that I knew you'd succeed all the time, and no one will be the wiser. I'll have my attendance at every one of your meetings as my proof, too. So, thank you very much for the invitation to shutter you sooner rather than later, but I think I'll keep all my options open. For the time being, that will be my official position."

Maura Beth took a deep breath, having weathered the latest go-round. "So you'll be dropping in on our review of *Gone with the Wind* next month, I take it?"

"I wouldn't miss it. I've always wanted to observe a literary hen fest."

"We'll do our best to amuse you," Maura Beth replied, matching his sarcastic smile. "And maybe Becca Broccoli can even get someone to cook up an omelet just for you. Perhaps a little cheese added to make you feel right at home."

He leaned over the podium and winked. "Yum, yum!"

As she watched him walk away from her after their perfunctory farewells, Maura Beth steadied herself by grabbing the podium and whispering the phrase she had used earlier in the evening when they'd changed the name of the club. Over and over it came out of her like a soothing mantra: "Out of the mouths of babes . . . out of the mouths of babes . . . out of the mouths of babes . . ."

But when Councilman Sparks reached the front door, turned, and gave her a neat little bow, she couldn't help herself, knowing full well he couldn't hear her at that great distance: ". . . as well as charming rascals up to God-knows-what."

5

I'm Scarlett, You're Melanie!

It was beyond annoying to Maura Beth that Councilman Sparks's snide prediction that the group would end up rehashing the movie version of *Gone with the Wind* stuck in her craw over the next couple of weeks. That, and the lingering feeling that she might have been a bit too heavy-handed with the others at the organizational meeting of what was now to be called The Cherry Cola Book Club. It seemed that no one really wanted to read and review *Gone with the Wind* again except herself, but she had prevailed with authority. Yes, she had promised them that they could explore new angles and ideas regarding the time-honored classic, but she herself had failed to come up with anything viable, despite constant brainstorming. Was anyone else having any better luck?

In fact, she was about to dial Connie McShay's number from her office one slack afternoon when Renette Posey appeared in the doorframe, holding the library's DVD copy of *Gone with the Wind* and looking decidedly puzzled.

"I'd like to ask you a quick question. Don't worry—there's no one waiting at the front desk to check out. Even worse, there's nobody in the library at all. Hasn't been all morning," she explained on the way to Maura Beth's cluttered desk. "It's about this movie I'm returning. I got curious when I read your *Gone with the Wind* flyer."

"Yes?"

"Well, I watched it last night for the first time with a few girlfriends of mine, and we did the slumber party thing in pajamas at my apartment. I know, it sounds lame, like something out of high school. We fooled with each other's hair, talked about boyfriends, popped popcorn, and ate all sorts of junk food. But after the movie was finally over—it went on forever, and thank God for that intermission so we could all take a bathroom break—we sat cross-legged on the floor in a circle and came to the same conclusion."

Maura Beth straightened up in her chair. "And what was that?"

"Well, we decided that every one of us acted in real life like either Scarlett or Melanie, for the most part. We even wondered if every woman might fall into one category or the other. Do you think there's anything to that, or is it just a silly, slumber party idea from a bunch of single girls on a sugar high?"

Maura Beth couldn't help but snap her fingers and smile. "Renette, I'd give you a raise if I had the money!"

"Really, Miz Mayhew?"

"I wish I could, of course. But that's a great idea you and your friends had. By the way, which character were you? Or should I say, are you?"

"Oh, everyone thought I was a Melanie," Renette answered, growing quieter and hanging her head slightly. "I've been called a goody-goody too many times to be anything else. But that's who I am—I like helping people."

"You certainly do!" Maura Beth exclaimed. "You're a star with our scanner, and you tell the patrons about their overdues with honey dripping in your voice. They never get mad—I've gotten so many compliments about you."

Someone calling out, "Hello?" from somewhere in the library broke up their exchange, and Renette turned, dashing toward the front desk to attend to her duties. But Maura Beth made a note to herself to find a way to give her pleasant young clerk a little more in her paycheck, even if she had to juggle a line item or two in the books to get the job done. Landing in her lap from an innocuous slumber party was the perfect angle for the upcoming *Gone with the Wind* outing.

"Declare your allegiance!" would be the challenge she would issue to Miss Voncille, Connie, and Becca over the phone with supreme confidence. "How do you see yourself in today's world—as a Scarlett or a Melanie?"

Suddenly, she could sweep aside the insecurities that had been plaguing her about her leadership style and choice of material. She could even tempt Periwinkle with the ploy, especially since her best girlfriend had already generously agreed to send some sherry custard along from The Twinkle as an extra dessert.

"If things start to go wrong," she had told Maura Beth over the phone just a few days before, "you can at least get you a little buzz off the sherry. Sometimes, when I go home alone, that's all I have to look forward to."

"Now, come on, Periwinkle. Enough of the lonely, sherry custard-eating, sob stories," Maura Beth had returned before signing off with a friendly promise. "I'm going to find a way to get you to take a break from that kitchen and into our book club if it's the last thing I do!"

For the moment, however, she had to run Renette's slumber party angle past her existing membership, and she decided that Connie would be the first she would dial up.

"Are you busy?" Maura Beth said after Connie answered. "You sound out of breath."

"Well, you caught me. I'm out here on the pier grunting in a very unladylike manner with the fish scaler and hoping somebody will rescue me with a cell phone call like you just did."

Maura Beth made a sympathetic noise under her breath. "Douglas isn't pitching in?"

"Nope, he's off to The Marina Bar and Grill for a round or two with his fellow fishermen. He did invite me to join him, but they're all about watching sports on TV and telling off-color jokes out there. Not my style."

Maura Beth changed the subject quickly, launching into the exchange she'd had with Renette. "So what do you think of the Scarlett and Melanie debate?" she concluded.

There was silence at the other end for a while. "Your idea reminds me of something," Connie said finally. "I know. Getting a Girl Scout badge for something that's really a stretch. Only this one would be for adults. You know, who gets the Scarlett badge and who gets the Melanie badge to sew on her blouse."

"I wish I could see your face now," Maura Beth added. "I can't tell whether you like the idea or not from what you just said."

Connie broke the modest tension with a generous laugh. "Of course I like it. Maybe I didn't express myself so well. It's probably these fish fumes poisoning my brain cells."

"You're too much. But thanks for the vote of confidence on my idea."

Next up was Miss Voncille, who seemed to be in an unusually prickly mood. "Do we have to dress up in costume?" she inquired after Maura Beth had explained everything. "What I mean is, if I decide I'm a Scarlett, do I have to rent one of those antebellum dresses complete with hoopskirts? Actually, I suppose I'd have to do the same if I were a Melanie. And my hair isn't long enough to be done up in ringlets the way they did back then. So that would mean I'd have to buy a wig. I can tell a woman wearing a wig a mile away. And men in bad toupees no matter what the distance."

"This isn't a costume ball, Miss Voncille."

"Thank goodness!"

"So what's your verdict?" Maura Beth continued.

"Fine with me," came the reply, though with little enthusiasm. But a sudden infusion of warmth soon followed. "What I'm more excited about is my friendship with Locke Linwood. We're starting to go out on dinner dates and such. Of course, it's all very innocent at the moment, you understand, and I'm trying very hard to soften my image on these occasions."

"That's lovely to hear, Miss Voncille. You keep at it. We'll expect both you and Mr. Linwood at the meeting in your regular clothes and hair."

Then it was time to speak with Becca. Seemingly not to be outdone by her unpredictable friends, she offered an off-the-wall proposal once Maura Beth had given her all the facts.

"I think it's a really cute idea," she began, "but why don't we make it even more of a theme than that? Everyone could make up a recipe that they think Scarlett or Melanie might have preferred to make or eat, and we could all compare notes."

Maura Beth took a deep breath and tried her best to smile through the phone.

"I'm pretty sure neither Scarlett nor Melanie did much cooking in flush times. And after the Yankees came through and burned up all the crops, recipes were a fond memory for a while. Getting anything at all to eat was the goal. I appreciate your creativity, Becca, but let's just stick with the personality angle this time around."

After they'd hung up, Maura Beth sat frowning at her desk for a few moments. Tricky stuff, this book club business. It was a delicate balancing act once people were in the fold, but it had to be worth the trouble. A kaput library was simply unacceptable.

The next day, Maura Beth decided she would keep Councilman Sparks in the loop, too. Of course, he hardly qualified as either a Scarlett or a Melanie. However, she could easily picture him wandering into the library smelling great, looking spiffy, and smiling from ear to ear to perform his irritating kibitzing act with aplomb to throw her off her game. Well, even though there had been no course at LSU in Dealing with Politicians 101, the truth was that she was living it now, like it or not, and there was no better way to learn her lessons than to face the politician in question without fear. Perhaps she could even throw him off his game.

"We'll be reading and commenting on *Gone with the Wind* from a particular perspective," she began, sitting across from him in his inner office one afternoon. "All our members are women so far, as you know very well from the organizational meeting." Then she explained the Scarlett versus Melanie theme to him and waited for his response.

Councilman Sparks took an awkward amount of time before answering while staring her down, but Maura Beth made a concerted effort not to fidget in her seat or otherwise indulge nervous body language. "Are you going to go feminist with this club, Miz Mayhew?"

"I wouldn't put it that way, no."

"Because I was going to say that you might just be ruling out fifty percent of the population of Cherico with a girlie-girl approach," he continued, flashing one of his dazzling, but completely insincere smiles. "Some men like to read, too."

"Are you a reader, Councilman?"

He produced a peculiar laugh that came off more like an intrusive sound effect. "When it suits my purposes."

"No doubt."

He calculated a moment longer, tightening the muscles of his face further. "You're so full of unexpected visits these days. So, was this one to prepare me to do well at the upcoming book review and 'all you can eat' buffet? Or was it to suggest that I stay away because I couldn't possibly fit in?"

"Oh, I don't think wild horses could keep you away. But I did think it was worth mentioning that I intend to give this project my all. When I first came here, I promised myself that I would make a success of the Cherico Library, and by that I meant to turn it into the type of facility that people just couldn't do without. I admit that it's been hard, slow going these past six years, but you may have ended up doing me a favor by challenging me the way you have. I trust you'll bring out my best professional instincts."

Councilman Sparks shrugged his shoulders and seemed to relax his posture. "You have a penchant for soapboxing, Miz Mayhew. Maybe you could moonlight in my next election and write speeches for me. That is, in case this library thing of yours doesn't work out."

At that point Maura Beth knew it was time to leave. She had summoned her courage to face her adversary once again and dealt with him aboveboard. Yet, he always had an answer or a clever quip for everything—a master of one-upmanship. She knew his intention was to wear her down, but she just couldn't let that happen.

"Well, if you'll excuse me, Councilman," she said, rising from her chair. "I have a library to run."

He rose across from her without smiling. "But for how long, Miz Mayhew? For how long?"

* * *

After what seemed like two months instead of two more weeks, the August 17th inaugural meeting of The Cherry Cola Book Club finally arrived. Once again, Maura Beth had chosen to stage the festivities in the library lobby instead of the meeting room; but she had gone online and ordered some decorative touches to offset the drabness of the premises. As before with the flyers, Connie had been delighted to step up and fund them. Surrounding the refreshments table laden with the various dishes all the women had brought were blow-up movie posters of the stars of *Gone with the Wind*—Vivien Leigh, Clark Gable, Leslie Howard, Olivia de Havilland, and Hattie McDaniel. Maura Beth, Renette, and the Tuesday, Thursday, and Saturday front desk clerk—the amiable, hardworking Mrs. Emma Frost—had reinforced the Technicolor stills with cardboard backing and had spent the previous afternoon standing them up against some of the folding chairs. There in the background, the five Hollywood legends would bear silent witness to the drama that would be unfolding.

At one point Maura Beth had thought about blowing up balloons and tying them to the shelving here and there to add a more festive party accent. She had even gone out and bought a big bag of them with every color of the rainbow showing through the plastic. But she had backed off at the last minute, opting for the gravitas of the library instead. So much better, she had reasoned, that her literary trial balloon not be interpreted so literally.

As for the food, it was a smorgasbord of tempting aromas, colors, and appealing presentation. Becca had done an admirable job of coordinating the menu, keeping egos in check seamlessly. She herself had offered to cook up her chicken spaghetti casserole for the evening's entrée, and everyone was fine with it. Connie had been quite adamant about her contribution: "Assign me anything but fish—nothing with gills and scales, please. If I never cook another fish in my life, it will be too soon!" So the two women readily agreed that a frozen fruit salad would be in order from the McShay household. Miss Voncille thought her jalapeno cornbread would complement Becca's spaghetti and revealed that she would be bringing Locke Linwood as a guest once again; and Maura Beth's chocolate, cherry cola sheet cake in conjunction with Periwinkle's sherry custard would satisfy everyone's sweet tooth there at the end.

"I see you've taken my comment to heart, Miz Mayhew," Councilman Sparks offered after briefly schmoozing the others and surveying the posters and buffet just past seven. He was, in fact, ridiculously overdressed for the occasion, falling just short of black tie apparel, and his cologne announced itself the second he entered the room.

Maura Beth took a sip from her plastic cup, filled to the brim with Becca's summer cola drink recipe swimming with cherries and a tart twist of lime. "And what comment would that be? I don't exactly memorize all your pronouncements."

They walked together past the photo capture of bug-eyed Hattie McDaniel, distancing themselves a bit from the others. "I'm referring to Mammy here," he pointed out. "Looks to me like you're just rehashing the Selznick production with this bigger than life approach. As in 'the movie was so much better than the book.' I believe I mentioned you might end up doing that."

Maura Beth refused to bristle, giving him the most serene of her smiles. "Ah, but I assure you, we'll be exploring uncharted territory tonight with our Scarlett versus Melanie debate—right after we've all enjoyed this delicious repast. So, shall we make our way back to the table and help ourselves? I'm about to tell everyone to dig in. We eat first, then discuss."

At which point she did just that, and a line began to form by the stack of serving trays, paper plates, plastic silverware, and napkins next to Connie's saucers of frozen fruit salad. "I hope you don't mind the informality." Maura Beth continued to the gathering. "I thought we could balance our trays on our laps. The Cherry Cola Book Club won't be about putting on airs."

In fact, no one seemed to mind the balancing act once they had helped themselves and claimed their chairs, and the chatter that bubbled up between bites and sips was natural and friendly. Even Councilman Sparks was on his best behavior, concentrating on Connie with his banter; then it came to Maura Beth in a flash that the McShays were potential voters now that they had moved to Cherico permanently.

"I was thinking that the City Council ought to consider a Welcome Wagon concept," Councilman Sparks was telling Connie at one point. "Perhaps we could convince a few civic-minded ladies to visit new residents with brochures and flowers—that sort of thing."

Connie nodded in noncommittal fashion as she broke off a piece of jalapeno cornbread. "I'd be more interested in a chapter of Fisherman's Anonymous. You don't have one, do you?" She chuckled and then began explaining her husband's recent addiction to spending most of his time casting his line out on the lake. "I expected my Douglas would be out there now and then, but it's turned into an obsession with him. That, and tossing back a few at The Marina Bar and Grill."

Then Becca joined the conversation with vigor. "Husbands and obsessions—no greater truth exists in the world today. Take my Stout Fella. I don't know if anyone's told you this, Connie, but my Justin single-handedly developed all those home sites out by the lake. I'm sure you bought your lot from him."

"Don't get jealous, but I do remember a big, good-looking man," Connie revealed.

Becca waved her off. "Believe me, anyone who built out on the lake dealt with my husband. His real-estate projects are his oxygen. All he does is eat and talk on his cell phone. Eat and e-mail people. Eat and text, eat and Tweet."

There was polite laughter at the last comment, but Becca's demeanor remained serious. "I wish I could find the humor in it, I really do. I'm sure you all know by now that I do my cooking show weekday mornings, so I'm always in the kitchen trying out new recipes. I suppose you could make a case that I'm obsessed with food. But not the way Justin is. He eats everything I fix him and even wants to lick the spoon. He's insatiable. When we were first married, he was tall and trim—quite the athlete." She hesitated as she blushed. "I know I shouldn't have started calling him Stout Fella, but, well, he's gained so much weight that I couldn't help it. Maybe I thought I could shame him into eating less, but he got to the point where he admitted he actually liked being referred to as Stout Fella. He said it made him feel like he was a big comic book superhero."

Miss Voncille put down her fork and gave Becca an engaging smile. "I haven't had the chance to say this to you yet, but I would have gotten around to it eventually tonight. I've been a huge fan of your *Becca Broccoli Show* since you first came on the radio. I've copied down all your comfort food recipes, and they've turned into staples for me." She paused for a second and put her hand on Locke Linwood's shoulder. "Why, I fixed your macaroni and cheese with bacon bits just the other evening for myself and my gentleman friend here on one of our dinner dates, didn't I?"

Locke acknowledged her remark by patting his stomach with a contented little smirk on his face. "It was so irresistible I had an extra helping, and I don't normally do that. I like to stay in shape."

Becca rolled her eyes in exasperation. "Oh, I wish I had never invented all those rich, comfort food recipes as my main focus. It's what's really gotten Stout Fella in trouble. That, and the recent explosion of ice-cream flavors!"

"There's so much emphasis on eating smart these days," Miss Voncille added, pausing for a thoughtful frown. "I don't want to tell you how to run your show, but maybe you could put the broccoli back in *The Becca Broccoli Show*. After all, you're in charge of the recipes."

"You're absolutely right," Becca replied, nodding enthusiastically. "I can change the equation if I want. I could put together some episodes that would definitely put the broccoli back and then follow through by fixing the same recipes at home for Justin and myself. Now, let me see, what should I call them? Anyone got any ideas?"

"Calorie-Conscious Comfort Food?" Miss Voncille suggested.

Becca screwed up her face and then smiled diplomatically. "Thanks, but maybe too much of a tongue twister."

"Comfort Food without Calories?" Connie offered.

Becca laughed. "That would be outright fraud. There's no such thing."

"Don't I know it!" Connie exclaimed.

Then Miss Voncille tried again. "Downsizing with Comfort Food?"

Becca perked up immediately. "Oh, I like that. I think it just might work. A clever play on the state of the world today. I'm indebted, Miss Voncille."

"Oh, happy to help out. Perhaps you could keep us informed about these new episodes and let us know when the first one will be broadcast so we can all be sure and tune in. In fact, I'll be upset if I don't hear from you."

The mutual admiration society continued throughout the rest of the meal, and not even Councilman Sparks could disturb the camaraderie that was developing among the group.

Then, after everyone had raved about the sheet cake and custard and stacked their trays, it was time for the serious business of The Cherry Cola Book Club to get under way.

"By now, I'm sure all of you have had plenty of time to think about our theme tonight," Maura Beth began, standing behind the podium. "So, who wants to be the first to tackle 'I'm Scarlett, You're Melanie!'?"

Councilman Sparks quickly raised his hand and did not wait to be acknowledged. "I just wanted to assure everyone here that I'm definitely not in the closet, so I'm neither."

"Your contribution to our meeting is very amusing, Councilman," Maura Beth said, as brief, muted laughter broke out. "But now it's time for some real thought."

"I'd like to go first, if you don't mind," Connie said. And as there were no objections, she took the floor but remained seated. "I just wound up a long career as an ICU nurse at a hospital in Nashville. I know I went into that occupation in the first place because I felt I could do all the vital, detailed things that nursing requires. But despite all this moaning I've been doing tonight about my husband and his devotion to fishing, I really do have an empathetic personality. One of the things I did best when our daughter, Lindy, was growing up was to stroke her forehead patiently when she felt bad or had a temperature. It takes that kind of touch and tendency to be a good nurse, I believe. And that's why I think I'm a Melanie. Maybe a somewhat firmer Melanie at times. But still a Melanie."

There was a ripple of polite applause, but Connie held up her hand like a school crossing guard shepherding children. "I had something else to add, though. There's a sequence in *Gone with the Wind* where Scarlett tries to tend to the maimed and dying soldiers at the field hospital. But she just can't stomach it, apologizes to Dr. Mead, turns on her heels, and runs away.

She just doesn't have the temperament for it. Reading that passage this time around, I had a frightening vision of a high-tech Scarlett working as a nurse in a modern hospital. I envisioned her going around to all the patients that annoyed her and pulling the plug on them in one of her ongoing hissy fits. I love that expression, by the way—even though I couldn't find it in my dictionary." She waited for the subdued chuckling to subside.

"Maybe you think I'm being too extreme in my observations about Scarlett. But remember, she told Mammy she didn't want to have any more children because of what giving birth to Bonnie Blue had done to her figure. That's not a life-affirming instinct. It's completely self-absorbed. Melanie would never be capable of that kind of behavior—at least not as written by Margaret Mitchell. So, I think you can definitely count me in Melanie's soft, sweep camp, and I'm proud to be there pulling people back from the edge."

More polite applause followed. Then Maura Beth said, "I think we'd all agree with your analysis, Connie. Very thoughtful. So, let's score one for Melanie. Now, who wants to be next?"

It was Becca who volunteered from her seat. "I don't know about going around pulling the plug on people," she began, "but I have to say that I'm a Scarlett. I suppose I have the sense of entitlement that she always had because she was born at Tara, but mine comes from a different source. I think I've earned mine through hard work. I don't think our culture recognizes merit enough these days. This radio personality of mine, this Becca Broccoli I've become, materialized out of nowhere. I went to bed one night, knowing I had this fifteen-minute radio show to produce after a chance meeting with the program director of WHYY at The Twinkle. We were sitting at adjacent tables, raving about the food to our waitress, and he happened to lean over and say to me, 'I wish there was somebody in Cherico who could teach my wife how to cook like this!' And something inside just egged me on, and I flat out told him I probably could since I loved cooking. One thing led to another, and somehow we came up with the idea of my doing a radio show. Finally—something to do with my degree in communications. Anyway, the very next morning I woke up with a doable gimmick." Becca paused for a coy giggle.

"I liked the possibilities of this character immediately, plus my married name has always been impossible for people to spell. I discovered that Becca Broccoli was a different side of me—she was the take-charge person I'd always wanted to be. Scarlett was like that from the beginning. When she wanted something or someone, such as the incredibly dull Ashley Wilkes, she went all out. What Scarlett wanted to be was mistress of Tara, but she never really achieved it. On the other hand, I wanted to be mistress of the airwaves, and now I have the most popular show on radio station WHYY, The Vibrant Voice of Greater Cherico. That last part always makes me laugh. What are we—maybe five thousand people counting any pregnant women waddling around? Oh, believe me, I know I'll never get a Grammy for being Becca Broccoli. People in the Beltway or out in Hollywood will never hear of me. I live in flyover country. But I'm still proud of what I've done. So perhaps I'm Scarlett, but with a well-adjusted, saner attitude."

After a brief round of applause, Maura Beth put an exclamation point on Becca's testimony. "Now that's the sort of Scarlett I wouldn't be afraid of meeting up with at the top of a dark landing!"

It was Miss Voncille's monologue a few minutes later, however, that had the group riveted to their seats. "I know I started out with Scarlett's fire and headstrong personality," she was explaining. "It was my intention to have it all—a loyal husband from a good family, however many children we decided to have, a fine house with all the trappings. You name it, I didn't see why I couldn't have it if I applied myself. That, of course, was very much the essence of Scarlett. But like Scarlett, I made a crucial error"—she broke off suddenly, putting her hand up—"give me a second, please."

Sensing what Miss Voncille might be about to reveal, Maura Beth spoke up in code. "We value your privacy above everything, Miss Voncille."

"I appreciate that," she resumed, taking time to catch her breath. "But I'm fine. I don't intend to go into a lot of detail here. What I was about to say was that Scarlett made the crucial error of falling in love with the wrong man. Or at least thinking she was in love with him. In my case, I fell in love with a soldier who went missing in action in Vietnam. We were engaged to be married, and when he didn't come back, I found myself embracing Scarlett's rougher edges. It's hard to forget that Margaret Mitchell's first description of Scarlett on the opening page is that she *was not beautiful*. But she ultimately fell back on her strength and the more cunning aspects of her personality. What I fell back on was being a tough, no-nonsense schoolteacher, and lately I've been running 'Who's Who in Cherico?' like a Third World dictator. I know I'd like to try and be more like Melanie, but for the time being, I have to say I'm camped deep behind the front lines in Scarlett Territory."

This time there was no applause. For some in the room it was the first time learning of Miss Voncille's long-held secret about her lost love. Suddenly, they understood why she was the way she was, and that seemed to have inspired respectful silence with gentle smiles.

"Thank you for sharing that with us," Maura Beth said at last. "That can't have been easy for you."

But Miss Voncille immediately put everyone at ease by

chucking Locke Linwood on the shoulder. "Life goes on, people. In fact, he's sitting right next to me in a coat and tie and a twinkle in his eye."

Locke actually seemed to be blushing even as he smiled. "I reserve the right to remain silent."

The laughter that followed cleared the way for Maura Beth's finale, which began with unexpected praise as she remained at the podium. "Before I give my take on this premise of mine, I'd like to thank you, ladies, for being so candid about your lives. You've held nothing of importance back in letting the rest of us know who you are. It occurs to me that maybe we've got something more than a book club going here. I hope this is just the start of our meaningful friendships."

Aside from a skeptical expression from Councilman Sparks, Maura Beth saw nothing but approval reflected in everyone's face as she proceeded. "As for myself, I know that Melanie has always been part of my library personality. In *Gone with the Wind,* she would have been the first to help any lost soul find their way. I grew up thinking it would just be terrific to help people find the right book to read on a stormy evening or locate the perfect source for a report they were doing. As a child, I loved scouring the shelves for something fun to check out, and I can still amuse myself that way as a grown-up and the director of this library." But her easy smile began to fade as she continued.

"There's another side to Melanie that I must mention, however. She was often naïve and a bit too trusting, and I do believe I've been guilty of that here in Cherico. I haven't always stood up for myself the way I should have. A good dose of Scarlett's determination is what I really need. Unfortunately, there are those in this community who feel that a library is a luxury for bored housewives who are too cheap to buy their own copies of best sellers at the nearest bookstore. And that's one of the milder sentiments I could conjure up for public consumption. Those people don't see the library as the educational and job-hunting resource it's always been. But at this juncture of my life, I feel that this little library—corrugated iron siding and all—is my Tara, and I intend to fight for it with every ounce of my strength. So the truth is: I'm in the midst of transforming myself from a Melanie into a Scarlett while trying to retain the best qualities of each. To my way of thinking, both characters ultimately represent what all women should strive to be. The right blend of kindness and ambition never goes out of style."

Amidst muted but genuine applause, Councilman Sparks spoke up loudly. "My goodness, Miz Mayhew—that reminded me of the scene where Scarlett gets down on her knees in the dirt, berates a carrot, and declares that she'll 'never go hungry again!' Why, you left not a dry eye in the house with the intensity of your monologue!"

Maura Beth, however, rose to the occasion. "Maybe it was a bit on the hammy side, but then, I was trained to be a librarian, not an actress. My milieu is shelving, not the stage. Or biographies, not Broadway."

"Touché!" he exclaimed, actually appearing to enjoy the repartee and even blowing her a kiss.

"This was the most fun I've had in ages!" Connie added. "And that includes all those years with The Music City Page Turners up in Nashville. We never mixed our reads with our lives quite like this. It's a different approach, but I like it."

"I have a point to make, though," Locke Linwood put in suddenly. "The food was mighty delicious, but I think the discussion was apparently for ladies only. I mean, nobody asked me if I thought I was a Rhett or an Ashley."

Miss Voncille gave a little gasp as she looked him in the eye. "Now, Locke, you told me you weren't even going to bother to read the book. You said I could do all the yapping, and you were just coming with me for the big spread."

He hung his head, sounding a bit sheepish. "I lied. I'd never read it before. Never saw the movie, either. I guess I wanted to find out what all the hoopla was about."

"Imagine that," Miss Voncille replied, sounding pleased and surprised at the same time. "I thought everyone had seen the movie at least once. It's like admitting you've never seen *The Wizard of Oz* or heard of Judy Garland."

"Well, Miz Mayhew?" Locke asked.

Maura Beth was puzzled. "Well, what, Mr. Linwood?"

"Aren't you going to ask me if I'm a Rhett or an Ashley, or do you have to be a woman to make these important literary connections?"

The request met with laughter throughout the room, after which Maura Beth popped the question. "Okay, by all means. Which are you, then?"

"Of course, I think of myself as a Rhett. My late wife, Pamela, always told me I was her hero."

"You were certainly that," Miss Voncille offered. "Anyone who ever saw the two of you together could confirm it. I saw it at every meeting of 'Who's Who?' that you attended."

"Does this mean that you consider yourself a bona-fide member of The Cherry Cola Book Club, Mr. Linwood?" Maura Beth said, seizing the opportunity.

"Why not?" he answered quickly. "I agree with Miz McShay over there. This is the most fun I've had in a while."

"Wonderful, and welcome aboard officially!" Maura Beth then glanced over at the front desk clock and decided to test the waters. "I see we've been at this business of dining and discussing for an hour and fifteen minutes now. Does anyone have any other thoughts about the novel? They don't necessarily have to be related to Scarlett and Melanie."

"I'm just curious," Becca said. "What was the final total on that? I mean, how many Melanies and how many Scarletts did we end up with?"

Maura Beth scanned the notes she had scribbled throughout the proceedings and emerged chuckling under her breath. "It's not all that clear, actually. I have Connie down as a Melanie, Becca and Miss Voncille as Scarletts—although with reservations in my estimation—and myself as a work in progress."

"That's hedging," Becca insisted. "Here in the South we always take a stand. It's in the lyrics of 'Dixie,' you know." She began humming the tune until she got to the proper spot in the chorus and then began singing. " '. . . *in Dixie Land I'll take my stand, to live and die in Dixie* . . .' "

"Point well-taken," Maura Beth replied. "Very *Gone with the Wind,* as a matter of fact. Okay, then, I'll err on the side of Melanie for myself. Just for the time being, though. I have lots of things to accomplish before I'm thirty."

"Tell me everything, girl!" Periwinkle exclaimed after her last customer had left a little past nine. She had just flipped the blue-sequined sign hanging on the front door of The Twinkle from OPEN to CLOSED. "Did anybody get tipsy on my sherry custard? It's actually happened before. Some precious little ole lady had two of 'em one night, and it took a coupla grown men to escort her out the door. Maybe I should put a customer warning on the dessert menu."

Maura Beth laughed as they claimed a table in the middle of the room. "No, I think your custard went down smoothly. No hiccups, just raves. My ooey, gooey, chocolate, cherry cola sheet cake was a winner, too."

Periwinkle settled in, leaning forward with her gum going a mile a minute. "Okay, enough about the food. How did the meeting go? Was Councilman Supremo there throwing off his usual sparks?"

"Oh, yes. Dressed to the nines, too. He looked like he was going to a wedding. Or maybe he was supposed to be the groom. But he behaved, for the most part. Or let's just say, I handled every curve ball he threw me. He even blew me a kiss, believe it or not. He's an odd duck, that one. Anyway, I'm here to tell you that The Cherry Cola Book Club took flight without a hitch this evening. Everyone contributed in a meaningful way, and we ended up with two Scarletts and two Melanies. Oh, and a Rhett!"

"As in Butler?"

"As in Mr. Locke Linwood demanding that I ask him if he was a Rhett or an Ashley. It was so cute, and he's now officially a member."

Periwinkle eyed her intently. "Well, I guess you know I'm in the bunch with Scarlett branded across their foreheads. I'm too feisty to be anything else."

"Scarlett on steroids, perhaps?"

Periwinkle drew back playfully. "Now, sweetie, I'm one of the good guys, remember?"

"Just kidding, of course. I definitely need more of your spine. Anyway, we got a lot accomplished tonight, including all the important decisions for the next meeting. Before we adjourned, we put it to a vote and decided that we'd be reading *To Kill a Mockingbird* this coming month. We'll be getting together on the evening of September 19th, as a matter of fact." Maura Beth gave her friend a hopeful look for emphasis.

"I still don't see how I can swing it, honey," Periwinkle insisted, reacting instantly to the unspoken appeal. "Let's put it this way. If my restaurant bid'ness is going great guns and I've got standing room only all the time, then I simply won't have the time to participate in the club. And if I have so much slack that I can loll around reading and choosing which fictional characters I most resemble, then I'm in deep . . . well, let's just be ladylike about it and settle for the term . . . financial trouble. Does that make sense?"

"Of course. But I was thinking just the other day about your restaurant and my library—particularly about how busy you are. Not to mention that long drive you make round-trip every day to and from The Twinkle. I mean, your house is halfway between Cherico and Corinth. Don't you get bored at times?"

Periwinkle shrugged. "Just part of making a living, honey."

"What if I could spice things up a bit for you?"

"What do you suggest? Cumin, paprika, or something stronger like cayenne pepper? I've got 'em all on the shelf."

They both laughed. Then Maura Beth said, "I was thinking that you could use our audio books to liven up your travel. Our selection is modest due to our budget, but the patrons that use them swear by them. So, what do you say? How about joining the club officially by being a good listener?"

Periwinkle was all smiles. "I think you should recruit for the Army, girl. I'm all ready to sign up under those circumstances."

"Wonderful!" Maura Beth exclaimed, clasping her hands together. "We'll finally get you a card, and we can take it from there."

"And how about if I send over something extra to the buffet this time? Like my aspic."

Maura Beth cut her eyes to the side with a saucy smile. "Can't argue with that."

"Of course, I'll keep handing out your flyers to my customers. I assume you'll be printing up a new one for the *Mockingbird* book?"

"That's the plan."

Then Periwinkle grew serious, briefly stopping her gum and leaning in. “So do you think all this’ll be enough to keep those weasels at the City Council from shutting you down?”

Maura Beth sighed plaintively. “Too early to tell. It’s very hard to predict Councilman Sparks. All I can do is plug away.”

6

Back in the Saddle Again

Miss Voncille's tidy cottage on Painter Street was one of two dozen or so homes in Cherico built around the turn of the twentieth century in the Queen Anne style and had been the only thing of value she had inherited from her parents, Walker and Annis Nettles. It was graced by a small but immaculately manicured front yard featuring a mature fig tree on one side of its brick walkway and a fanciful, green ceramic birdbath on the other.

"Isn't this quaint!" Maura Beth exclaimed, as she and Connie stood in front of it early one humid August morning.

"Exactly the sort of place I would expect Miss Voncille to live," Connie added. "Very spinster schoolteacher-ish."

Just then Miss Voncille spotted them and flung open the front door. "You're right on time, ladies!" she called out. "Come on in. I've got coffee, hot biscuits, and green-pepper jelly waiting for you. We have about fifteen minutes to eat before Becca's show starts!"

Once inside, Maura Beth was surprised to discover a veritable jungle of potted palms set in sturdy ceramic containers. Some were enormous and obviously quite mature, their fronds spreading out like great, spraying fountains. Others were much smaller and newer, but there was hardly a nook or cranny in the front part of the house without them. Nor were they absent in Miss Voncille's bright yellow kitchen, where the three ladies eventually sat down to breakfast in a cozy little nook.

"I've got the station tuned in and everything. All I have to do is turn it on," Miss Voncille explained, as she poured steaming coffee all around. "Please, help yourselves to biscuits. Everything's homemade, including the jelly. I grow the peppers myself in the backyard."

After everyone had sufficiently fussed enough to fix their plates, Maura Beth began making small talk. "I just think it was so generous of you to invite us over here for Becca's first 'Downsizing with Comfort Food' show. She called me up yesterday to tell me how pleased she was that we were all getting together to hear it. She's a bit nervous about it."

"Oh, I know, but it's the least I could do since I put the idea in her head," Miss Voncille said, after swallowing a bite of biscuit. "Besides, she's given me so many great cooking ideas over the years, I want to support her any way I can."

"We all do," Connie added. "From what she's told us, she needs every bit of help she can muster in getting her Stout Fella into shape."

Miss Voncille took a sip of her coffee and drew herself up with great authority. "Ladies, I just love the way we're getting to know each other. I don't have to tell you that I haven't been terribly social over the years. And I don't consider pontificating about genealogy to qualify, either. That's why participating in the club is doing me so much good. It's just what I need, and I thank you again for prodding me to join, Maura Beth. So, I wanted to take the bull by the horns and explain all these potted palms in the house."

The comment took both Maura Beth and Connie by surprise. Neither would have dreamed of bringing up the subject, but it was Maura Beth who found something to say that didn't sound insincere. "Well, if you feel it's necessary."

"Yes, I really do. The house didn't look like this when my parents were still alive. They hated houseplants. But this is my tribute to Frank, my MIA sweetheart. He disappeared in the jungles of Vietnam, as I've explained." She paused, smiling at all the greenery she had strategically placed around the room.

"But the last letter I got from Frank before he went missing was so full of life and his special spirit. You would never have known he was in the middle of a war. He went on and on about how beautiful and exotic all the palm trees were. The line that especially sticks with me after all these years is where he said the entire place would be a wonderful spot for tourists if everybody wasn't shooting at each other. Perhaps he was imagining what it would all look like in peacetime someday. And then he said that before he finally came back to me, he wanted me to go out and buy a bunch of potted palms to welcome him home. How could I not honor his request?"

"They're beautiful," Maura Beth managed, not really knowing what else to say.

"They're also a form of closure for me," Miss Voncille continued. "Since Frank was officially MIA, I wanted to be sure they were always here if he did ever return to me by some miracle. I take care of them year after year and replace them if they die, and all of that gives me great comfort. It may seem nutty, but that's the truth."

"I understand. Whatever works for you," Maura Beth said, while Connie just nodded with a smile.

"Most people who've visited me probably think I'm just a crazy old maid who went gaga for palms. Of course, I gave up worrying what other people thought about me a long time ago."

"Well, this green-pepper jelly of yours is beyond delicious, and so are your biscuits. It all just melts in my mouth," Connie said, trying to lighten the mood a bit.

"How gracious of you!" Miss Voncille exclaimed, her face a study in delight. "I grow the peppers, along with my basil, mint, and rosemary in my backyard plot. And you know, I may have even gotten the jelly recipe from one of Becca's shows." She checked her watch and perked up even further. "Oh, we're just a few seconds away from the debut of the new regime. Now, ladies, you leave everything right where it is. I'll clear the table later. Let's just sit back and give Becca our undivided attention, shall we?"

Then she rose from her chair, headed over to the clunky old radio sitting on the counter, and turned it on just in time for the pre-recorded station ID: *"You're listening to WHYY, The Vibrant Voice of Greater Cherico, Mississippi!"* The theme music that Becca had chosen several years ago—a meandering, nondescript instrumental full of acoustic guitar chords—announced the beginning of yet another episode of *The Becca Broccoli Show.* After another twenty seconds or so of music, Becca's distinctive voice came through loud and clear.

"Good morning, Chericoans! I'm Becca Broccoli, and welcome once again to my little treasure trove of recipes and cooking tips, coming to you every weekday morning at seven-thirty right here on WHYY. As always, the best fifteen minutes you can spend to get you in and out of the kitchen fast to the applause of your family and friends. Today and over the next few days, however, I'm going to be doing something I've never done before, and that is, put an emphasis on more healthful recipes. We're calling it 'Downsizing with Comfort Food.' As in 'let's go down a size or two and still enjoy our food.' " Becca paused for a little chuckle. *"Yes, listeners, we're going to be putting the broccoli back in* The Becca Broccoli Show. *Not literally, of course. I don't want you to panic and throw Brussels sprouts at*

me. More healthful doesn't mean horrendous. Good for you doesn't mean god-awful. Believe me, we're not going to be throwing out the baby back ribs with the bathwater here. . . ."

The three ladies sitting around Miss Voncille's table laughed out loud, and Connie exclaimed, "Great start! Way to go, Becca!"

"Oh!" Maura Beth added suddenly. "What if we want to write any of this down?"

Miss Voncille shook her head emphatically and made a shushing sound. "Not to worry. Becca told me she'd bring copies of all her new recipes to our *Mockingbird* session next week."

". . . and you may be asking yourself what the reason for all this is. It's simply that I want my family to get good checkups when they go to the doctor. We all need to be more proactive about our health while we still enjoy our comfort food. So this morning I have for you my new version of tomatoes and okra," Becca was saying as the ladies concentrated on the radio broadcast once again. *"Yes, I know some of you think okra is too slimy, and you don't like its texture. But I've got a few good tips for you that'll make it easy to avoid most of that slime. My goodness, this sounds like something out of* Ghostbusters, *doesn't it? Who ya gonna call—Becca Broccoli?!"*

There was more laughter from the ladies. "She's nailing this so far," Maura Beth observed. "Although this is only the second time I've listened to her."

"I want to see what happens when she gets to the actual recipe, though," Connie added. "De-sliming okra is a mighty big promise. I haven't seen it done in my cooking lifetime."

But Becca delivered within a minute or two. *". . . and the key to cutting down on the slime is to sauté your okra quickly on very high heat. Don't let it lie around in the pan because it will end up oozing all those juices some people just don't like. Another tip: Cut your okra on the bias so that you end up with diagonal slices. That way more of the surface has contact with that high heat. Isn't it interesting how the simplest tips can make your life so much easier in the kitchen? Now, we'll be right back to talk about the versatility of tomatoes and okra for your more healthful lifestyle after this message from our sponsor."*

As the latest deals from Harv Eucher's Pre-Owned Vehicles held no interest for the ladies, they began their chatter once again.

"I know Becca has to be telling the truth about the high heat," Miss Voncille commented. "I practically stew my okra on simmer in the pan. But then, I don't mind the slime. I guess it's an acquired taste."

Connie was shaking her head and wagging a finger at the same time. "I never could get my Lindy to eat it. She always claimed it made her feel like she needed to clear her throat. But my little granddaughter, Melissa, just loves to eat it in gumbo. Of course, she doesn't even know it's in there mixed up with the rice and the onions and the chicken. She's too distracted pushing her spoon around, and she says, 'Gigi, I cain't find the gum in here!' So, I made up a cute little ditty for her, complete with cheerleader-type hand gestures—I forget the tune now—but the lyrics went: 'Who took the gum outta the gumbo, hey? Who took the gum outta the gumbo, hey?' Oh, she danced around and went wild!"

The ladies' laughter erupted just as Harv Eucher's revved-up blather about taking advantage of once-in-a-lifetime trade-ins finally came to an end, and Becca's voice returned for some blessed relief.

"Welcome back to 'Downsizing with Comfort Food' on The Becca Broccoli Show. *Next, we want to talk about using tomatoes and okra as a side dish or—as I most often prefer it—as a staple ingredient in my chicken or shrimp gumbo . . ."*

"There you go!" Connie exclaimed.

". . . and it's my suggestion that your pantry should never be

without several jars of what I call my all-purpose gumbo base. Here in the middle of the summer with everything fresh and in season is when you should be putting up that gumbo mix for those cold weather evening suppers looming ahead . . ." Becca continued.

"I'm not a canner," Connie admitted with a smirk. "I'm from the crowd that thinks Mason jars should be used to serve up humongous cocktails. Why, it's all the rage at certain restaurants up in Nashville."

The others nodded agreeably even as Becca rolled through her script. "*. . . and another tip for lightening up that gumbo base would be to go with about half as much butter when you sauté. Keep your garlic and your salt and pepper for that all-important seasoning. Just take the plunge and use olive oil instead. It's part of the Mediterranean diet that's becoming increasingly popular everywhere. They say a little olive oil and an occasional glass of red wine does wonders for longevity . . . and maybe even your love life. Of course, for those of you out there who are teetotalers, just go with the olive oil and skip the wine . . .*"

Miss Voncille leaned in and raised an eyebrow smartly. "I wonder how these instructions about substituting olive oil will go over with the devout butter believers. I know people from church potluck suppers who think 'Thou Shalt Use Only Butter in Everything' is the eleventh commandment."

"My mother was one of them," Connie added with a wink. "If she had a headache—she'd spread butter on a few aspirin and go about her business."

The ladies couldn't seem to help themselves from that point forward. Whatever Becca said, they had an aside or witticism ready, and they were somehow able to coordinate the two seamlessly in the manner of an old-fashioned television variety show act. It wasn't criticism as much as it was a form of "dishing with the girls," and it made the show's precious minutes fly by with plenty of laughter in the air.

". . . so be sure and tune in tomorrow at this same time, same station for another installment of The Becca Broccoli Show," Becca was saying as the show's closing theme came up.

Miss Voncille headed over and shut off the radio, leaned against the counter, and folded her arms. "Well, ladies, what did you think? My opinion is that it went very well, olive oil and all."

Both Maura Beth and Connie agreed that the show had been a success, but then Maura Beth offered up a sheepish grin. "I also think we had a very good time cutting up the way we did. There were even moments when I felt like we were schoolgirls whispering behind the teacher's back. I wonder if we would have said some of the things we said had Becca been here in person."

"Oh, it was all in good fun," Connie insisted. "I'm sure she wouldn't have minded. I thought Becca's program was full of wit, so it inspired us to react the same way."

"Absolutely!" Miss Voncille exclaimed. "I'm sure that's what Becca was going for—the humor angle to win everyone over to a slightly different point of view." Then Miss Voncille headed over and dramatically plopped herself down in her seat, putting her hands on the table. "Ladies, I have to confess something to you. Of course, I did want you here for breakfast and Becca's show, but I also had an ulterior motive. I thought maybe enjoying the show might bring us together even more than we already are, and I believe it certainly has with the way we've been laughing and talking. But there's something else I had on my mind and, well . . . it's just that . . ."

Maura Beth and Connie exchanged expectant glances, and Maura Beth finally said, "You've come this far, Miss Voncille. Follow through. What is it you wanted to tell us?"

"It's my relationship with Locke Linwood," she began, staring at her hands at first. Then she looked up and caught

Maura Beth's gaze. "It's been so long since . . . well, you know what I'm trying to say, don't you?"

Maura Beth reached over and patted her hand with a generous smile. "Since you've been with a man?"

Miss Voncille exhaled and briefly averted her eyes. "You librarians have good instincts. But, yes, that's exactly what I wanted to discuss with both of you. Frank and I were intimate, but that was way back in 1967. It seemed so easy then. All you heard from the media was how *free* love was supposed to be, I mean. What a lie! I think love is the dearest thing in the world—in the old-fashioned business sense of that word. What a price you end up paying for it whether you get to keep it or lose it! But now here it is another century. How do I . . . get back in the saddle again after all this time? How do I . . . free myself?"

"Connie, you're the married woman among us," Maura Beth said. "Do you want to take this?"

Connie looked briefly uncomfortable but soon drew herself up and patted her big hair—the latter gesture a sure sign that she was ready to tackle anything. "Well, the first thing I'd have to ask you, Miss Voncille, is how far your relationship with Mr. Linwood has progressed. Could you share that with us?"

"It's been very gentlemanly on his part so far, if you catch my drift," she explained. "I'm always ready to go out when he arrives. He has reservations at The Twinkle or somewhere else for us, and we talk politely over our dinner and wine. Later, when he walks me to my door, there's a gentle kiss on the cheek, and there are moments when it seems like something more should happen. But . . . it stops there. Or to be perfectly honest, I stop it there."

"Then you've never asked him in—for a nightcap, as they say?"

"No."

"Why not?"

"I—well, something tugs at me, and I end up thinking it would be disloyal to Frank."

Connie grew pensive, touching an index finger to her lips. "And have you ever ended up at his house?"

"Oh, he says he's not comfortable with that yet. But he insists he is trying his best to accept another woman being in the rooms he shared with his Pamela."

"Well, he is a fairly recent widower," Maura Beth put in. "Maybe it's easier for him to hold on to his memories of his wife and settle for something platonic with you. And maybe that's what he thinks you want—your memories of Frank and a gentlemanly escort."

Miss Voncille looked overwhelmed, putting her fingers to her temples. "Yes, I think you ladies must be right. Neither one of us has been willing to . . . saddle up."

"Do you think you could ever muster up the courage to let Mr. Linwood in for the . . . shank of the evening?" Connie proposed.

"That's such a colorful way of putting it," Miss Voncille replied, clearly amused. "Reminds me of a big, juicy leg of lamb." Then she grew more resolute, narrowing her eyes. "Maybe if I worked hard at it, I could try to let go. I keep a picture of Frank by the nightstand. It was taken just before he left for Vietnam. You can see the determination in his face, in the way his jaw was set, in the way he refused to smile and still looked contented with where he was about to go and what he was about to do. It's intriguing the way the camera can sometimes capture your soul on film. But in any case, I suppose I should remove it if I invite Locke into my emerald green bedroom . . . and he actually accepts."

"I would if I were in your shoes," Connie offered. "If it gets that far, you need to give the man at least a fighting chance to compete with all those perfect romantic memories of yours."

"And you don't necessarily have to go out of your way to explain the significance of all the potted palms, either," Maura Beth added. "Just go ahead and let him think you've gone a little mad. Lots of women have decorating fetishes. For instance, I've gone a bit crazy in my little apartment with a dozen shades of purple. But in any case, it's better than having Mr. Linwood be reminded of Frank everywhere he turns. It could definitely put a damper on things."

Miss Voncille clasped her hands together with an excitement in her voice that made her sound and seem much younger than her years. "Having girlfriends to talk to after all these years is so much fun. So much better than walking around this empty house talking to my palms while I water them. Therefore, I've decided to try and saddle up after our big *Mockingbird* to-do at the library is over."

"How brave of you!" Connie exclaimed. "And I'm so glad we could help out." Then she turned her head to the side, frowning in contemplation. "Ladies, I've just thought of something brilliant. Why should you be the only one with an escort at these literary outings, Miss Voncille? I need to get Douglas out of that damned boat of his and doing something interesting with me for a change. After all, this is my hard-earned retirement, too. So, I'm going to insist that he come to the *Mockingbird* potluck and book review. If he refuses to go along with such a simple and reasonable request, then I'll refuse to clean his unending stringers of fish. Now that'll put the fear of God in him!"

"Sounds good to me!" Miss Voncille replied. "And you know what else would be lots of fun? Getting Becca to bring her Stout Fella to the meeting. I think we'd all like to meet him since we've heard so much about him. Maura Beth, this would be a surefire way to grow our numbers!"

"Yes, it would," she answered, smiling broadly. "And growing our numbers is the most important thing we can do with this little club of ours. In fact, it's crucial. I only wish I had someone to bring."

Connie then gave Maura Beth one of her famous friendly nudges. "Oh, don't worry. Mr. Right will come along when you least expect it. I met Douglas at a charity auction, and we were bidding for the same piece of antique furniture. Well, he had quite a bankroll from being a successful trial lawyer, so he outbid me and I lost the sideboard. But it was only a temporary defeat because I liked the fact that he had the good taste to spend his money on such fine things. I thought he just might be a keeper, so I snared him in my web, and when I unraveled that big cocoon, the sideboard tumbled out with him, of course. It's sitting in our dining room out at the lake right this minute, and every time I use it for entertaining, I'm reminded of the crusty old adage, 'To the victor belongs the spoils.' "

"Then it's all decided," Maura Beth said. "I'll call up Becca and tell her to work on her Stout Fella, Connie will work on Douglas, and Miss Voncille, you'll show up with Locke Linwood in tow as usual."

Miss Voncille was almost giggling. "Oh, I'm so excited. I never thought I'd let myself feel this way again, and here I am actually considering inviting Locke into my jungle lair. But more as soft, sweet Melanie."

"Men like to think of themselves as the hunters in the game of love," Connie added, lifting her chin with an air of superiority. "But more often than not, it's we women who do the trapping."

7

The Perfect Man

Renette Posey was knocking insistently on Maura Beth's office door. "Gregory Peck has just arrived!" she announced with great enthusiasm, sticking her head in with a girlish smile. It was the good news they had both been anxiously awaiting.

Maura Beth shot up from her chair and clapped half a dozen times in rapid succession. "Well, where is he? I want to get my hot little hands on him right this instant!"

"You and me both!" Renette twisted her head around, looking back briefly. "Here comes the UPS guy in his cute brown shorts with the tubes. Wow! Just under the wire, huh?"

Indeed, it definitely fell into the category of close calls. Here it was the morning of the *Mockingbird* meeting, and the movie poster blow-ups of Gregory Peck as Atticus Finch were just now showing up. This, despite a guarantee from the online company that they would be shipped to The Cherico Library in two to three business days. But more than a week had passed, and there were no posters in sight. Maura Beth hated fooling with tracking numbers, but her sterling organizational skills and note-taking had paid off handsomely for her this time around. The tubes, it turned out, had been mistakenly bundled off to a library in Jericho, Missouri, thus creating the nerve-wracking delay. Murphy's Law, Maura Beth figured.

"Let's pull them out right away and see what we've actually got," Maura Beth instructed, after the UPS man had apologized profusely for the mistake and left quickly. "There were supposed to be three different poses."

Renette began tugging at the tape on one of the tubes, while Maura Beth sat behind her desk and took a pair of scissors to another. A few minutes later, all three black-and-white posters had been retrieved and unfurled. Though the order had gone astray, it was otherwise accurate: There was one pose of Gregory Peck as Atticus Finch in a dramatic courtroom scene; another of him as Atticus with Jem and Scout in her overalls standing in front of the little cottage they all called home; and a third of Peck as himself receiving the Oscar for his performance in *To Kill a Mockingbird*. Maura Beth was certain that these stills would create an ambience similar to the one the *Gone with the Wind* posters had.

"We'll back these with cardboard like we did for the other ones, and no one will be the wiser that they practically traveled all over the country before getting here," Maura Beth added with a sigh of relief. "I want everything to go smoothly this evening. With the two extra men showing up, Councilman Sparks will see that we're building up the club, and we can't be ignored."

"If you have enough food, I'll be happy to show up myself," Renette offered. "I had to read *To Kill a Mockingbird* my senior year in high school, and I still remember it pretty well. Even got an 'A' on my book report. I especially liked the part about the giant ham with the hole in it that saved the little girl's life."

Maura Beth looked especially pleased at the suggestion.

"Well, we won't have ham on the menu, but please come, Renette. I know we'll have more than enough to eat."

Then Maura Beth reviewed the menu sitting on her desk. For this second meeting of The Cherry Cola Book Club, Becca would be bringing her healthful version of chicken gumbo with tomatoes and okra; inspired by one of her latest shows, Connie would be throwing together a fresh golden bantam corn and red pepper salad; Miss Voncille was going to bake her delicious biscuits and offer her green-pepper jelly on the side; by popular demand, Maura Beth herself would repeat her chocolate, cherry cola sheet cake; and finally, honorary member Periwinkle had generously agreed to supply another gratis item from The Twinkle—specifically, her knockout tomato aspics with the cream-cheese centers.

"I know a lot of people think men will eat anything you put in front of them, but I've found that they can sometimes be hard to please," Maura Beth explained. "I think we'll have a good variety on hand tonight, though, and I bet Stout Fella will lead the way."

Renette seemed about to say something several times and finally got it out. "Should I bring a little dish, too? I could . . . thaw something?"

"Just bring yourself, sweetie. I expect a lively and unforgettable debate this evening."

Inside their opulent mansion out in the country, Becca and her Stout Fella were having heated words in their powder blue master bedroom suite around six-thirty that evening. She was applying the finishing touches to her face at her vanity, while he was pacing around the shag carpet in his bare feet, still half-dressed and mumbling things under his breath.

"This is a very important business meeting, Becca," he was saying, refusing to look her straight in the eye as he fumbled with his shirt buttons. "I can't help it if it came up at the last second. I've been trying to pin down Winston Barkeley for the last coupla months, and he wants to get together at The Twinkle tonight while he's in town. Maybe I can even close the deal. This is a premium piece of land for my next plat out at the lake, and it's going to be really high-end."

"As if there are a bunch of paupers out there now," she replied, briefly eyeing the touch of rouge she had just applied to her right cheekbone. "Sometimes I think all this conspicuous success is the worst possible thing that could have happened to you—Justin Rawlings Brachle. What more do you have to prove to the world?"

He snickered while pulling on his wide-load pants in front of their full-length mirror. "Hey, whatever I need to and with no apologies. There's more to life than winning a football scholarship, you know. Besides, you married me for richer or poorer, and I don't see you turning your back on the richer part."

"Oh, I've done my share as Becca Broccoli. You know as well as I do that I could go it alone if I had to. Not that I want to, of course." She caught her agitated husband's reflection in the vanity mirror as she carefully applied lip gloss, and his steady transformation into Stout Fella came sharply into focus.

She had called him on the weight gain and his eating habits early on. "We're going to have to buy you new clothes the way you're going—at the big, tall, and spiffy store, if it exists," she had said, trying her best to make light of it.

"That's not a bad thing," he had pointed out. "A well-fed husband is good advertising for your cooking show. Your listeners would lose faith in you if I were the gaunt, skinny runt of Cherico." And he had kept right on standing and making more "islands" of his ice cream, while taking second and third helpings of her scrumptious cooking at the dining room table.

"You need to slow down," she had warned on another occasion. "You act like food and time are in limited supply. You're always on that cell phone. I wish the damned thing had never been invented!"

"I sees 'em, and I calls 'em—just like I used to in the huddle," he had answered, making a joke of it.

But he was serious about cornering the real-estate market in Cherico before he was thirty-five, and he had done so with a succession of high-profile lake development projects. After that, his bank balance and his waistline had expanded simultaneously. Yet there were still vestiges in his fleshy face of the rugged, but handsome athlete who had swept bubbly Becca Heflin off her feet and down the aisle to the altar over a decade ago.

"The least you can do is accompany me to the library and have a bite to eat. You don't have to stay and open your big mouth after that. But everyone is expecting you to show up. They've been just dying to meet you," Becca reminded him. "You could end up being the star of the evening."

"And you set all of that up without my permission!" he fired back. "One night, I come home from work, and you tell me that we're going to one of your fussy 'ladies' night out' affairs at the library. You expect me to jump up and down?"

"I expect us to do something together once in a while, Justin. What's the harm in that?"

He didn't answer her, plopping down on the edge of the huge four-poster bed to pull his socks on. "For cripes' sake, these don't match!" he cried out suddenly, dangling the pair in front of his face. "One's navy blue and the other's black. You spend much more time on the radio than you do with our laundry. I told you to hire someone to help you around the house. Why do you object to our having servants? We can easily afford it!"

"I'm well aware of that, but let's argue one thing at a time," she continued as he headed toward his closet. "All I'm asking right now is that you go and at least meet my new friends. Won't you do that much?"

Momentarily, he emerged with a matching pair and then surprisingly gave in, nodding his head grudgingly. "Okay, okay. I'll put in an appearance to keep the peace around here. But after that, I'm off to The Twinkle to meet up with Winston. You can stay and yak about *To Kill a Mockingbird* 'til the cows come home and the early bird gets the worm."

"Now that's original commentary if I ever heard it," Becca remarked, rising from her vanity with a pert little smile firmly in place.

Connie was standing at one of her great room windows admiring the way the early evening sun played off the slack water of Lake Cherico in the distance. The horizon was tinged with orange and gold, except for wild brush strokes of coral that were doing their best to blot out what remained of the day's blue allotment. It was now quarter to seven, and she had spent the better part of the last hour luring Douglas out of his precious bass boat—which he had named *The Verdict*—and into shaving and showering mode.

"You smell like bait," she had told him, once she had him on the terra firma of the pier's faded planks and he had stowed his stringer of fish in the cooler. "Not that that's anything new. But I don't want everyone at the library to smell you coming. So, please, give yourself a thorough scrubbing."

Once inside, he had good-naturedly fallen to, even to the extent of singing in the shower. She could hear him trying to work his way through "Singin' in the Rain," although he was far from a Gene Kelly in the vocal department. Fishing most of the day had that effect on him, though. In short, he was in paradise. Connie, however, felt she had not yet punched her ticket, and she hoped that this *Mockingbird* evening would be the beginning of a shared retirement experience for them.

"I wouldn't mind seeing ole Justin Brachle again, now that I think about it," Douglas said out of nowhere, emerging from getting dressed at last and heading toward his wife with a snap to his step. He had chosen a silver guayabera shirt and dark slacks for the occasion, complementing the first waves of gray that had invaded his slightly receding hairline. "He did sell us this land seven years ago when we were first thinking of building the lodge."

Connie turned away from the window and the ongoing prelude to the sunset. "I told his wife, Becca, that I thought I remembered him as being quite a catch." Then she took in her own husband's still-trim physique, ending with the devilish smile that never failed to melt her in the bedroom. "Speaking of looking good, I don't think you've been this presentable since we left Nashville. And you smell divine! *To Kill a Mockingbird* be damned! I may have to attack you. What have you got on?"

He inched his sunburned but carefully shaven face closer to hers and lightly kissed her cheek. "Just a splash of Old Spice. I found a bottle in the bedroom closet. It was in one of those boxes we still haven't opened."

She put her arms around his neck and kissed him back. "Weren't you wearing that when we first started dating thirty-something years ago? That bottle belongs in the Smithsonian."

He pulled away and enjoyed a good laugh. "Not this one. I think Lindy gave it to me for Father's Day not too long ago. Maybe just before we moved down. She knows her old man's history, that's for sure."

"Not as well as I do," Connie added. "And I've begun to think you've given me up for the fishes. Maybe I should grow scales."

He narrowed his eyes and played at taking offense. "Okay,

I haven't been that bad, have I? I even managed to reread five whole chapters of *To Kill a Mockingbird* so I'd be up to snuff and wouldn't embarrass you at the thing tonight. It's been more than a few decades since high school, you know."

"Let's just see how it goes at the library. Then we'll talk," she said, managing a smile as she checked her watch. "We need to get there while the food's still hot. Or before Stout Fella eats it all."

Douglas looked puzzled. "Who?"

"Your Realtor friend, Justin. Oh, I explained everything last week. I'll remind you on the way there."

Miss Voncille got to her feet and smoothed out the wrinkles in her emerald green bedspread. She had been sitting beside her pillow, riveted to her beloved picture of Frank Gibbons on the nightstand for the past five minutes. "I'm going to hide you temporarily in the potpourri," she said out loud to the photo as she cupped it in her hands as if it were an injured baby bird. "The deal is, I may have company tonight, and I don't need you making me nervous standing guard the way you always do. But don't worry, I won't leave you with my scented hankies forever."

For a split second she imagined that her sturdy sentinel might just spring to life and answer her, giving her permission to change things up. But she knew only too well that she could not seek permission from anyone but herself. So she headed toward her chest of drawers, giving the picture a little peck before tucking it away among her many fancy sachets. "There!" she exclaimed, nodding proudly. "That's done. Onward and upward!"

As if staged perfectly by a theater prop crew, the doorbell rang, and Miss Voncille knew that her potential suitor was right on time. She drew in a hopeful, romantic breath and struck a graceful pose. An imaginary photographer would be capturing her at her best and bravest in that moment. After that, the sequence would be a simple one: She and Locke would have something to eat and drink while chatting amiably with the others; then seriously discuss the merits of Harper Lee's work; and finally Locke would escort her to her cozy cottage as usual. Only this time, she would not shrink like a wallflower from her intentions—

Locke Linwood's voice crashed in on her reverie from the other side of the front door. "Miss Voncille?!" He pushed the doorbell again. "Miss Voncille?!"

"Coming!" she called out, shutting the bottom drawer and rushing out of her bedroom like a teenager on her first date. "I'll be right there!"

From the moment she opened the door, she knew something about Locke had changed, and it wasn't just the single red rose he presented to her right off the bat. "For you, my dear lady," he told her, handing it over with the suggestion of a bow.

"My goodness, Locke!" she exclaimed, taking it and holding it briefly beneath her nose. "You've never brought me flowers before!"

"I still haven't," he said. "This is only one flower. But there could be more where that came from. I think you're getting sweeter every day."

Miss Voncille found herself blushing, and for a few moments she just stood there with her mind a perfect blank. Then she recovered nicely. "Well, I'm honestly trying not to be such a diva anymore. But where are my manners? Come on in, and I'll put this little beauty in a vase. And you can carry the biscuits out to your car for me. Let's head to the kitchen, shall we?"

After she had put the rose in water and pointed out the

foil-covered baking sheet full of biscuits that she had prepared, Miss Voncille retrieved an unopened jar of her green pepper jelly and dropped it into her shimmering, emerald green clutch. "Good. It just fits, and the color is a perfect match. I guess that's everything."

"Not quite," Locke said, momentarily putting the biscuits down on the breakfast table and nervously clearing his throat. "I've come to an important decision, and I wanted you to know about it before we headed off to the library."

"I'm intrigued. First a rose, now an important decision."

"Yes, well, I just wanted to say that I think I've finally come to my senses. I haven't let any woman inside my residence on Perry Street since Pamela's wake two years ago. But I know she didn't want the house kept like a museum. So this demeanor of mine has had nothing to do with you. It's all been due to my ridiculous defenses. As if keeping the whole world out could bring Pamela back to me. I have faith that she's gone on to better things." He paused for a big chest full of air. "So, if it's all right with you, I'd like to invite you back to my house after this to-do at the library is over, and we can have a nip of sherry . . . or something."

Miss Voncille could not suppress her laughter, a captivating mixture of delight and surprise. "Forgive me," she managed as she eventually regained control. "You're probably getting the wrong impression. I couldn't be more flattered by what you've just said to me. I've always been a big believer in great minds thinking alike."

Locke looked reassured. "Well, as long as you weren't laughing *at* me . . ."

"Not even close, believe me. All sorts of images were swirling around my head when you extended your generous invitation to me. Sachets, potpourri, scented handkerchiefs. Don't ask me to explain, just understand that I'll be thrilled to extend our evening together. Meanwhile, we need to get these biscuits and jelly to the library and put this party on the front burner."

Maura Beth was feeling on top of the world as she surveyed her busy lobby. As with the first meeting of The Cherry Cola Book Club a month earlier, the food was going over well, and everyone seemed to be getting along. It also appeared that Miss Voncille and Locke Linwood had chosen to keep largely to themselves, looking as if they were plotting something in a far corner of the room. While the others were either sitting or standing to savor what was on their plates, Stout Fella was living up to his billing and gobbling up his generous servings at what seemed to be a record pace.

"Who woudda thought corn and peppers would go this good together?" he was saying in between hurried bites of Connie's salad.

Becca gave him a skeptical frown. "For heaven's sake, Justin, I've been serving you Niblets for years. Same thing basically."

"Oh, yeah, you're right. But it's got something else in it."

Connie stepped up quickly. "It's the herbs. I put dill and rosemary in it. Gives it a little extra zing."

Stout Fella kept right on chowing down as if he were in a competitive eating contest. "Whatever it is, it's mighty good. I'll have another helping, I do believe."

For her part, Maura Beth kept right on circulating to engage her guests. Even Councilman Sparks seemed to be in a fairly sociable mood as she caught up with him near the Academy Award poster of Gregory Peck.

"Very warm, fuzzy shindig, Miz Mayhew. Maybe even award-winning," he told her while pointing to the blow-up. "Your numbers are growing slightly, I see. Emphasis on the slightly. By the way, who's the young lady over by the punch bowl?"

"Oh, that's one of my front desk clerks, Renette Posey. She's also my girl Friday when I need her to be. I didn't ask her to, but she seems to have taken over the ladling duties. She's probably a little nervous, being the youngster here tonight."

"Very sweet girl," he added, looking her over from a distance. "I see you've also gotten the wives to collar their husbands this time out. I never thought Justin Brachle would have the time to darken the doors of this library. He's the all-time wheeler-dealer of Cherico, and we're thankful he works his realty magic so well."

Maura Beth cocked her head. "As in lots more taxes to collect from wealthy homeowners?"

"Precisely."

"But not enough to keep the library open?"

Councilman Sparks gave her one of his most conspiratorial winks. "Don't worry, Miz Mayhew. I fully intend not to underestimate you. That's why I'm here tonight. By the way, I've been meaning to ask you: What shade do you officially call that red hair of yours? It's very unusual—even stunning, if I do say so myself."

"Oh! Well, I guess auburn would be the most traditional way of describing it," she answered, completely caught off guard. "An ex-boyfriend of mine at LSU once told me that I had a head full of good bourbon whiskey, but that always made me sound like the ultimate party girl, which I wasn't."

He wagged his eyebrows and smiled. "I've been noticing the way your hair changes in different kinds of light."

"Yes, it does do that."

"It looks one way in the sun and another way under the fluorescents."

Maura Beth decided to say nothing and nod her head.

"My wife's hair is brunette. It always looks the same everywhere."

They had reached an awkward pause, and Maura Beth decided she'd had enough. "Maybe you should get a job out at Cherico Tresses, Councilman. I think your comments would be much more appropriate there. So, if you'll excuse me, I'm going to continue to make the rounds."

She walked away without looking back, approaching the McShays and the Brachles. They were in the midst of friendly banter, and it was Connie who was holding forth at the moment. ". . . and I just love the way the light plays off the lake at certain times of the day, particularly around sunset. I could hardly pull myself away this evening." She gave Becca one of her nudges. "We must have you and Justin out for dinner soon around that time so you can see for yourself. I'll try and persuade Douglas to go out in *The Verdict* and catch some fish for us."

"Oh, we'd love to, wouldn't we, Stout Fella?" Becca replied.

He quickly swallowed the last of the corn and pepper salad he was chewing and nodded his head obediently, while Douglas flashed a sarcastic smile at his wife.

Maura Beth glanced at the front desk clock and decided to make an announcement. "Ladies and gentlemen, I think we'll begin our discussion in about fifteen more minutes. Meanwhile, please continue to enjoy this wonderful spread and each other's company."

"I intend to try a piece of your sheet cake next, Miz Mayhew," Stout Fella explained, stepping up and wiping the edges of his mouth with a napkin. "It looks mighty tempting from here, and Becca raved about it last time she came. Of course, everybody's dish was worth the price of admission. But after my cake, I'm afraid I'll have to make my manners to all you good folks and leave. I have some pressing business to attend to over at The Twinkle. But don't worry, Becca's staying for all this book bid'ness, and I'll be back to pick her up later. And don't let me forget to say again that all a' y'all are fantastic cooks. This was just delicious."

Maura Beth and the others offered up their group thanks and then watched him practically inhale his cake a few moments later. Finally, after guzzling a cup of punch and giving Becca's cheek a perfunctory peck, he headed toward the front door, dialing his cell phone all along the way.

"Isn't he incorrigible?!" Becca exclaimed to Maura Beth and Connie after he'd left. "Never even allows himself time to digest his food. He's the most driven person I've ever known in my life!"

"Connie told me about you nicknaming him Stout Fella," Douglas put in, "but I didn't really get it until he came over and shook hands with me when we first walked in. I did recognize him, of course, but I'm afraid it was a shock all the same. No offense, Becca."

"Oh, none taken. It is what it is. I just don't know what to do about it. He's completely turned up his nose at my new recipes. 'Fix it like you always do,' he complains. 'Stop taking things out. Make it taste like it used to.' I'm afraid he hasn't downsized an ounce."

On that note, Maura Beth decided to put an end to her kibitzing and get the literary portion of The Cherry Cola Book Club under way. "Ladies and gentlemen, shall we put away our plates, freshen up if we need to, and then delve into some Pulitzer Prize–winning prose?"

Maura Beth stood behind the podium ready to tackle the major theme of the evening: namely, "Was *To Kill a Mockingbird* one of the catalysts for the 1964 Civil Rights Act?" She did not, however, intend to open with such a ponderous question. She would lead up to it gradually, soliciting opinions from the members about the consequences of racism described in the novel. She expected the discussion would be far more substantial than the lightweight diversion that was Scarlett versus Melanie of a month ago. Her unspoken motto was: "Start simple, then step it up."

Instead, Councilman Sparks stole the floor right out from under her again. "If I might, Miz Mayhew," he began, "I'd like to pose a question here at the outset to all you good people—but particularly the men." He did not wait for her to acknowledge his request, pressing on like the polished politician he was. "I've been giving this a great deal of thought. Don't you feel that Atticus Finch is unrealistic as a character and a father? For instance, he's raising Jem and Scout by himself and always gives them the right advice and never seems to make any mistakes. He has the moral high ground on everything. I don't know any men like that, do you? Where are the typical male foibles? In fact, he has none."

It took every ounce of Maura Beth's restraint to keep from saying out loud: "I can see why Atticus Finch would be alien to a man like yourself." Instead, she gathered herself and asked for reactions from the others.

Becca was the first to respond. "I wish my Stout Fella was much more like Atticus Finch, even if the character is unrealistic. Justin knows his business and gets things done, but he doesn't leave much time for anything else. For instance, he hasn't made time to slow down and think about us having a family, and we've been married ten years now. If we have children eventually—and I do want to—do I think Justin will be an Atticus Finch? No way. I don't think men are like that in real life. So I suppose Councilman Sparks has a valid point."

Douglas, who had been fidgeting in his chair a bit, entered the discussion with a slight scowl. "Now, wait just a minute here. I'll admit we men aren't perfect. Neither are our women. But I always took care of my family. I love my wife and daughter and granddaughter. You don't have to be an Atticus Finch to do what you're supposed to do—or the right thing, as the case may be. Have you thought that maybe Atticus Finch is written that way to make us strive to be better men—and lawyers, for that matter?"

"Speaking of which," Councilman Sparks said, "don't you think the law profession has taken a turn for the worse since they allowed billboard and television advertising? Hasn't it cheapened everything?"

Douglas bristled, speaking up quickly. "I don't advertise, Mr. Sparks. Never will."

"But you do admit the existence of high-profile ambulance chasers?"

"Is that what we're here to discuss?" Douglas pointed out, struggling for control.

And then Locke Linwood spoke up while holding Miss Voncille's hand. "I'm not qualified to answer questions about lawyers, but getting back to the subject of the perfection of men, I can tell you for a fact that my Pamela had no complaints about me as a husband. Yes, we both made plenty of mistakes, but we hung in there and raised a family together. I don't know how much more you could ask of any man."

"Seems to me that what all of you are saying confirms my observation," Councilman Sparks added, his face a study in smugness. "Atticus Finch is the perfect man and lawyer, and the rest of us could never measure up. We all have our profound weaknesses, and I guess we have to try to overcome them. In short, Atticus is unrealistic, and we are real. But we shouldn't be made to feel bad if we can't achieve a fictional ideal for the ages."

Maura Beth realized she must step in soon to rescue the tone of the discussion, but Connie preempted her with an emotional plea. "I think we need to step back a bit. I didn't come here to gang up on the men, and I don't think I would appreciate it if they ganged up on me."

"I agree," Becca added. "Stout Fella drives me crazy, and I don't know how my life with him will turn out in the end, but God knows, I don't expect him to be perfect."

Maura Beth's cell phone vibrated behind the podium, causing her to start noticeably. Her body continued to tense up as she answered the call and listened to the very agitated voice on the other end, while the shocked expression on her face gave no doubt as to the serious nature of the message she was hearing. Then she snapped the phone shut abruptly, as if trying to punish the messenger, and said as calmly as possible: "Becca, I need to speak with you in private, please. If the rest of you will excuse us for a minute."

Becca rose from her seat quickly with a fearful tone in her voice. "What's the matter? What's happened?"

The two of them moved away from the podium and closer to the circulation desk where Maura Beth turned her back to the others for privacy, discreetly lowering her voice and blocking Becca from view. "There's no easy way to say this, but that was Periwinkle Lattimore at The Twinkle. It appears that Justin may be having a heart attack as we speak, and they're rushing him to Cherico Memorial right now—"

Becca lost control before Maura Beth could finish, her face overcome with panic and her voice going shrill. "Oh, my God! Somebody needs to drive me there. Who'll drive me? Who'll take me? He just can't be having a heart attack. That big gorilla is only thirty-nine years old!"

All the others reacted by jumping up and approaching the front desk, with Connie and Douglas being the first to surround Becca. "Stout Fella's having a heart attack!" she cried out, tugging at Connie's sleeve like a frantic child. "Will you drive me there? I don't have the car!"

"Of course we will. Don't worry," Douglas said, taking her gently by the arm. "And we'll stay right by your side."

Everyone in the room offered to do something helpful simultaneously, as the second meeting of The Cherry Cola Book Club dissolved in the face of the crisis. In the end, they all agreed that they would meet up at Cherico Memorial to provide whatever support they could for as long as they were needed. It might end up being a very long night.

8

Balloon Therapy

It was in the crowded, second-floor waiting room of Cherico Memorial Hospital a half hour later that Maura Beth put things in perspective. The Cherry Cola Book Club had switched its focus from snippets of prose to snippets from the ICU, where Stout Fella was being monitored for complications due to acute myocardial infarction. Everyone—including Winston Barkeley and Councilman Sparks, but minus the teenaged Renette Posey—had gathered for the vigil and were variously fidgeting in their seats, blankly turning magazine pages or standing around full of nervous energy.

All except Connie, who had become the liaison between the earnest young cardiologist, Dr. Oberlin, and the others. Each time he ventured out to give the latest update on Stout Fella's condition to a mildly sedated Becca, Connie was there for the helpful translation.

"They've given him a clot-busting drug called streptokinase to stabilize him," she was explaining to the group after the doctor's most recent visit, holding on to Becca's hand all the while. "Fortunately, the blocked artery in question is not the widow maker. The affected area of the heart is on the bottom. Once they're sure he can travel, they'll ambulance him to Centennial Medical Center in Nashville where they specialize in cardiac procedures. I know that facility well. It's one of the best in the country. I would love to have worked there during my career, but I could never quite pull it off."

Becca continued to grip Connie's hand tightly as she spoke. "I need to be there. How will I get up there?"

As he had at the library, Douglas reassured her. "Connie and I will drive you up when the time comes. We know every little nook and cranny of Nashville. We'll both stay with you until he's completely recovered, and we can even drive you and Justin back when the time comes. My brother Paul and his wife live up there and have plenty of room in their Brentwood house. I'll give him a call, and he'll put us all up. No problem."

"And Justin will recover," Connie added. "Dr. Oberlin says there are so many positive signs already. For one thing, Periwinkle's 911 call got him to the ER within minutes. Time is always of the essence with any heart attack. As we speak, I'm sure they've reduced the size of the clot. He has had a slight allergic reaction to the streptokinase, though. They haven't been able to remove the blockage completely, but he's got some blood flow back in the artery and that's the most important thing. He's in no pain at this point, so we can all take a deep breath and think our best, healing thoughts."

"And the rest of the blockage is why they need to take him up to Nashville?" Maura Beth asked.

"This is a very small, rural hospital," Connie continued. "They don't have the equipment or staff to do the next procedure he'll require. It's called a balloon angioplasty. They'll thread a small guide wire with an inflatable balloon from an artery in his leg to his heart. They monitor the whole thing with a camera. Then, once they've inflated the balloon—bam! No more clot!"

Despite her sedation, Becca rambled on a bit. "The doctor said the procedure was safe. But is it really? It sounds so dangerous and complicated. What if I lose him? Just tonight we had this silly argument over nothing and everything. I even told him that I could get along without him. Is this God's way of punishing me for such callous thoughts? Connie, please tell me the truth. Just how safe is this balloon thing?"

"Now, calm down, Becca. I've seen the procedure performed successfully so many times, I can't count," Connie said, stroking the back of Becca's hand. "It's far less intrusive than bypass, and the recovery time is usually a week or less. Some people are back at work in practically no time. This is a maximum recovery situation all around."

It was then that Periwinkle walked off the elevator with crisp authority, making straight for Becca and extending her hand solicitously. Hugs for Connie and Maura Beth soon followed, and she acknowledged the others with a smile and a nod. "What's the latest?" she asked, catching her breath. "I haven't been able to think about anything else."

Connie brought her up to date with a condensed diagnosis that only a medical professional could manage.

Periwinkle relaxed a bit from head to toe. "Well, I got to close up a little early. Nothing clears a dining room like someone on a stretcher." Then she brought herself up short. "Oh, I didn't mean to make light of the situation. Please forgive me, Becca. I run off at the mouth all the time."

"*Forgive* you?!" Becca exclaimed, her eyes widening in disbelief. "You've got it all wrong. I can't *thank* you enough for what you did, Periwinkle. Dr. Oberlin says the paramedics were there in record time. My Stout Fella probably owes you his life. How did you know what was going on so fast?"

"Call it instinct, I guess," Periwinkle explained, her gum noticeably absent for once. "Your husband called me over to the table and asked if I had some Alka-Seltzer or something for his stomach. He was drinking coffee with his friend over there, but he looked really pale and sweaty to me. I like to keep my restaurant on the chilly side during all this summer heat, so even then I started to wonder what was happening."

The tall, sportily dressed Winston Barkeley stepped up to add his own observations. "Yeah, I could tell something was wrong with him, too. He kept saying he had indigestion from the moment he sat down across from me. Said he'd eaten too much at a party he'd just come from. But I could tell the Alka-Seltzer wasn't helping much by the way he kept rubbing his chest."

Periwinkle nodded and continued, "Then he called me over to the table again and said he was really starting to feel much worse, like there were gears grinding somewhere inside. Well, that did it. I'm never pleased to see indigestion at my restaurant, but this was just way different from the usual drink water and belch, if you'll excuse my language. 'I'm going to call 911 right this instant,' I told him. 'I don't like what's going on here one bit.' So I pulled out my cell phone and the ambulance was at The Twinkle in . . . well, a twinkle, I guess."

Becca squeezed Periwinkle's hand a couple of times. "Bless you, Doctor Periwinkle, bless you. Make all the little jokes you want to."

"Oh, honey, believe me, it's just a part of being out there dealing with the public. You have to be on the lookout for everything and everyone. You're a hero one day—the next day, you're being sued for all you're worth when somebody slips on a piece a' lettuce."

Becca looked incredulous. "Has somebody actually taken you to court for something like that?"

"Not me, knock on wood. But it happened to a nice-looking fella I met at a restaurant supply convention once. Would you believe he ended up spending most of his savings having to defend himself against some spilled Thousand Island dressing that cost someone a broken leg?"

Becca managed to smile for the first time in a good while.

"Well, I'm just thankful my Stout Fella was at The Twinkle tonight. That cup of coffee he ordered was the best bargain of his life."

An hour later, only Connie, Douglas, Becca, and Maura Beth were maintaining the vigil in the waiting room. The others had headed home with the understanding that either Connie or Maura Beth would notify them of any change in Stout Fella's status. But the news was as good as it could be for the time being. With all vital signs stable, the doctors had decided that the patient would be ambulanced to Nashville within the hour for an angioplasty early the next morning.

"I know the last thing you want to do is leave this waiting room right now, Becca," Connie was saying. "But if Douglas and I are going to drive you up tomorrow morning, we need to get you home to do some packing, and we need to do the same. Matter of fact, why don't you just spend the night with us after we've picked up your things? Dr. Oberlin assures me there's no immediate danger now. Meanwhile, the three of us have got to get some rest for the trip."

Maura Beth backed her up with authority. "It's best you listen to her, Becca. Connie knows about these things."

But instead of agreeing to their advice, Becca suddenly began to tear up. "I know things are going as well as they can, but I just feel like this is all my fault. I'm the one that put all that weight on him. And then I teased him all the time about it, calling him Stout Fella."

"But you told us he embraced his nickname in the end. Even thought it made him a superhero in his own mind," Maura Beth said. "Don't beat yourself up like this. You pointed out to all of us how driven he's always been. I've never seen anyone eat so much food so fast in my life at the library tonight. No one was shoving it down his throat. You can't be responsible for that kind of behavior."

"You also said you couldn't believe he was having a heart attack at the age of . . . thirty-eight, was it?" Connie added.

"Thirty-nine, actually," came the sniffling reply. "His birthday was last month. I made him a big, fattening devil's food cake, and he ate the whole thing. Of course, if I hadn't baked something homemade, he would have gone out and bought a dozen éclairs from Hanson's Bakery and put candles on every one of them. That big dope and his sweet tooth!"

Connie smiled while once again assuming her medical professional persona. "There you are. But birthday goodies aside, you've got to understand that for someone to be that young and suffer an AMI, there have to be other significant contributing factors. Not just eating habits and weight gain, but issues like management of stress, blood pressure, and cholesterol levels have to be taken into consideration. This is by no means as cut and dried as it seems."

Becca furrowed her brow for a moment. "He's supposed to be taking cholesterol medication, but . . . I can't swear he does. But he does a lot of things he's *not* supposed to. I guess he's paying the price now."

"You can discuss all that with him after the angioplasty in Nashville when he's well on the road to recovery," Connie continued. "Meanwhile, I think we ought to check in with Dr. Oberlin and let him know we intend to join your husband up there."

It was only after she was told her Stout Fella was being prepped for travel and there was no more time for visitors that Becca finally gave in, and the vigil officially came to an end—at least in Cherico.

"What time do you think you'll be leaving tomorrow?" Maura Beth asked the McShays on the way down in the elevator.

They exchanged glances and then turned toward Becca. "Six-thirty okay with you? We can go up the Natchez Trace Parkway and be in Nashville well before nine," Douglas said.

"That's the way we've gone back and forth for our vacation time these past six years."

Becca offered no resistance, nodding slowly while briefly closing her eyes.

"Of course. You have no choice but to get up bright and early," Maura Beth observed. "And you might need something besides a cup or two of coffee to keep you focused on the way up."

Connie looked at her sideways. "What on earth are you talking about? Speed? Douglas and I have never gone there, and I worked many an all-nighter at the hospital to tempt me."

"Oh, don't be silly. It's nothing like that. I've just had this absolutely inspirational idea, and the closer you get to Nashville, the more excited you'll be about it," Maura Beth continued as the elevator doors opened. "I'd like for you to follow me and pop into the library after we leave the hospital. I promise this will only take a few minutes."

Douglas shrugged. "Okay, might as well. Nothing else has gone by the book this evening."

It was Connie who accompanied Maura Beth into the library once Douglas had pulled the car up in front of the portico, idling the engine with a drowsy, emotionally exhausted Becca slumped in the backseat. "I hope you're not going to offer us all the book club leftovers hiding out in your library fridge," Connie remarked. "If not, I can't imagine what you could possibly have up your sleeve."

Maura Beth laughed as she unlocked her office door. "Oh, I assure you, it'll make all of you feel better once you get to Nashville and get to visit with Stout Fella in his hospital room." She walked over to her desk and pulled open the bottom drawer. "Aha, I was right. My memory is not failing. I did put them in here." Then she handed Connie the big bag of balloons she had decided not to use for the *Gone with the Wind* meeting. "I'd hold off on blowing them up now, but they might make a terrific day-brightener when you walk in and say hello to Stout Fella. You can tell him they're from everybody in The Cherry Cola Book Club with their very best wishes for a speedy recovery."

Connie's face lit up as she stared down at the bag. "In honor of his balloon angioplasty, I presume?"

"His successful balloon angioplasty," Maura Beth emphasized.

"There's no other kind in my experience," Connie added. "Maura Beth, you come up with the cleverest ideas. Did they by any chance teach you that in library school?"

"I don't remember the course offering, actually. I think I must have an extracurricular type of brain."

They both laughed, and then Maura Beth leaned down and retrieved a ball of twine from the drawer. "You might also need this to tie the balloons off and string them together. You can make a balloon bouquet of sorts. I think you have to pay a fortune if you order them through one of those delivery services, but I'm going to set you up from scratch real cheap."

Next, she picked up a Magic Marker from a coffee mug atop her desk. "Here's something else you'll need. You can write, 'Get Well!' or whatever you want once you've blown them up. Just be gentle with the marker. I popped one of the balloons pressing down too hard once way back when, and I thought someone had shot me at point-blank range. Other than that, all you and Douglas need is a little carbon dioxide. But don't blow too hard, pass out, and conk yourself on the head. We don't need you in the hospital, too."

Connie gave her a heartfelt hug and pulled back. "I can't believe there's even the slightest possibility that you might be leaving us. Cherico needs more people like you. And I feel so bad that our meeting tonight got sidetracked. You went to so much trouble, and I was looking forward to getting my teeth into *To Kill a Mockingbird* again. Actually, I was proud that Douglas was, too. That sneaky man of mine had been reading chapters in between his beer and fishing expeditions. How about that? Maybe this retirement of ours will turn out to be fun for both of us, after all."

Maura Beth waved her off, smiling pleasantly. "Oh, I'm sure it will. And I can reschedule our *Mockingbird* discussion down the line. In fact, I fully intend to, even though we might have to take Stout Fella's recovery into consideration. I'm sure we'd want Becca to be a part of it."

"I just wish Councilman Sparks would stay out of your business," Connie said. "He found a way to almost get the girls fighting with the boys tonight, and he also went after the lawyers with a vengeance. I saw that exasperated expression on your face at the podium."

Maura Beth exhaled, unable to put that particular mischief out of her head. "I tried my best not to let it show too much. But don't worry about me. I'm not giving up so easily. Scarlett wouldn't have."

Connie turned to get a glimpse of the front desk clock. "Oh, it's almost ten-thirty. We have a lot of packing to do, so I better get going. And I'll give you a call tomorrow morning from the hospital as soon as we know something definite. Then you can phone the others, if you don't mind."

A minute or two later, Maura Beth stood outside the front door, waving to her friends as Douglas pulled away from the curb with a staccato honk. The prognosis for Stout Fella looked promising, and she was pleased with herself for coming up with the concept of balloon therapy. But as she went back in to turn out the lights before locking up and heading home, she could feel depression spreading over her like the precursor to an oncoming cold.

Recently, she'd read a very interesting and somewhat controversial book in the collection about chaos theory. She hadn't completely understood all of it, but the gist was that random events sometimes coincided to scotch the best-laid plans of the most organized and intelligent minds on the planet. She certainly wasn't about to hold Justin Brachle's heart attack against him, but that unfortunate occurrence, along with Councilman Sparks's concerted attempts at disruption, had effectively rendered the second meeting of The Cherry Cola Book Club less than successful.

It was time to rev things up a notch, to treat the book club more like a political campaign. Somehow, some way, people must cast their votes by walking their warm bodies through the front door of the library to take advantage of its services. Maura Beth's job was at stake, and there were people in Cherico who had stated to her face that they didn't give a flip about that.

9

Four-Letter Words

Miss Voncille and Locke Linwood had been the first to leave the vigil at Cherico Memorial once Stout Fella had been stabilized in the ICU. "I know you'll call us if you hear anything further," Miss Voncille had said to Maura Beth, who assured them that she would.

But after they'd climbed into Locke's Cadillac in the hospital parking lot below, an awkward silence overtook them both. They sat there for a while, listening to the muted sound of the engine and looking straight ahead with emotionless faces.

It was Miss Voncille who finally verbalized what they were both thinking. "Does what just happened change where we're headed?"

He continued to idle the engine and turned her way. "I assume you mean the physical address."

"Yes. Will you be taking me to your house on Perry Street or mine on Painter Street?"

He did not hesitate. "My invitation is still open."

But she posed another question instead. "Do you think we should have stayed longer? I hope the ladies won't think we abandoned them."

"We couldn't have done anything but sit there. The crisis seemed to have cooled by the time we left. We made our manners and showed the proper respect. I know who the Brachles are, but Pamela and I never socialized with them because they're so much younger. They're a different generation." He put the car in gear and started to pull out into the street. "I don't want to do anything tonight that will make you feel uneasy, so tell me which way to head."

"I'm still fine with your invitation," she said finally. "Go ahead and drive us to your house on Perry Street. I was looking forward to seeing it. And also seeing you in it."

They drove through the heart of a mostly deserted downtown, passing the always-spotlighted City Hall, eventually entering the oldest residential neighborhood of Cherico. Tree-lined Perry Street was its crown jewel, featuring a good many more restored Queen Anne cottages than Miss Voncille's fixer-upper on Painter Street on the other side of town. Here was where the Crumpton sisters, Councilman Sparks, and other well-to-do families resided, not necessarily side by side, but well within shouting distance of each other.

"The crepe myrtles are lush this year," Miss Voncille noted, making small talk during the short drive. "Especially the pink ones. Personally, I prefer the whites. I think they named them after Natchez in the southern part of the state."

He nodded enthusiastically. "I think I read that somewhere, too. And as you'll soon see, those are the only kind I have in my yard."

A minute or so later they had pulled into the driveway of 134 Perry Street, and the front porch lights enabled Miss Voncille to appreciate the sprawling, superbly manicured lawn, dotted with the crepe myrtles Locke had described. She had, in fact, driven the length of Perry Street over the years just to admire its perfection but had never had a reason to pay particularly close attention to Locke Linwood's house and grounds. She knew only that he and his wife lived there and religiously attended her genealogical lectures at the library, and that was the extent of her interest. Now, however, the ante had been upped, and the time had come for a sincere compliment.

"If your decorating is anything like your landscaping, I know I'm going to love your house," she said, as he opened the passenger door and helped her out.

"Pamela did all the decorating. Most all the furniture is from her family. She was an Alden from over in the Delta, you know, and they had all that soybean money," he explained as they headed in. "I just sold life insurance for my keep."

The living room they entered was as graciously appointed as Miss Voncille envisioned it would be: It included a spotless wool dhurrie on the hardwood floor, a mahogany linen press against one wall, an English bookcase against the other, a Victorian what-not in the corner, and an Oriental ceramic cat lamp on an end table beside a comfortable contemporary sofa. It was both eclectic and elegant, while at the same time calling to mind the museum-like quality that Locke had confessed to previously.

"Your wife had the touch," Miss Voncille said, her eyes roving around the room in awe. "This is just lovely. Puts my jungle to shame."

Locke shook his head with authority. "Nonsense. *Architectural Digest* is not for everyone." Then he gestured toward the sofa in front of them. "I'll give you the rest of the tour later. But first, why don't you have a seat, and I'll go get us those sherries we talked about?"

While he was gone, Miss Voncille passed the time studying the oil portrait of Pamela hanging beside the bookcase. It had obviously been done when she was very young—perhaps somewhere in her twenties—and it was easy to see why Locke had fallen hard. Here was a gently smiling woman with shoulder-length brunette hair and light brown eyes that suggested a benevolent prescience. They seemed to be looking off in the distance at something wonderful to behold.

"How old was your wife when that was painted?" Miss Voncille asked as soon as Locke had returned and handed over her nightcap.

He settled in beside her and took a sip of his sherry. "That would have been a year or so after we were married, so she was about twenty-five. She wanted one done of me, but I told her I couldn't sit still long enough. The truth is, I didn't want anything in the room to distract from her beauty."

"And nothing does," Miss Voncille remarked. "She aged very well, too, I always thought. I would never have known that—" She broke off, realizing just in time where she was going.

But Locke rubbed her arm gently as he finished her sentence. "That she was so ill there at the end?"

Miss Voncille sipped her drink and nodded.

"My Pamela was a trooper. She spent a fortune on designer scarves to cover up the chemo, and she did it with the same great style she used throughout this house. She wouldn't have made her exit any other way."

He rose from the sofa and headed toward the bookcase, pulling a letter out of a leather-bound journal. "I'd like to take the time to read this out loud to you. I only read it myself the other day, and it was what brought me to my senses regarding our friendship. Pamela wrote it while she was still pretty cogent, and the instructions on the envelope were that it was to be read by myself two years after her death. I kept it in a safety deposit box to avoid temptation, but above all, I wanted to honor her wishes, and I did. So, if you wouldn't mind indulging me?"

"Of course not, Locke. And I have to say again that you are the most constantly surprising man I've ever known. At my age, that's just so much fun, I can hardly stand it."

He smiled, resumed his seat on the sofa, and began:

My dearest Locke,

If you are reading this right now, I will assume that two things have happened: 1) You have lived two more years than I did, and 2) you didn't cheat and read this before I asked you to.

That aside, I want you to pay very close attention to what I'm saying. I know you only too well. In our many cherished talks near the end, we both agreed that you should go on with your life as best you could. We agreed that you should continue to attend "Who's Who in Cherico?" at the library; that you should do everything you could to support that sweet young librarian, Maura Beth Mayhew—she's just as darling as she can be, and she'll need all the help she can get with the powers-that-be, believe me; that you should get to know Miss Voncille Nettles better. She's just our age. Ultimately, I think you and she would make excellent companions, but you have to make the effort, Locke, as you did with me many years ago. I'm assuming you've done all those things. If not, just go ahead and do them now. Take the risk. Try again for love.

I also know that you have not changed anything in our house these past two years. You never were sloppy, so I'm sure you've kept it clean. You could probably charge admission and put our house on tour the way they do during the Pilgrimages in Natchez and Columbus and Holly Springs. But you and I know that won't happen.

It is my belief that I will be very busy with other

things during the two years you have been without me. I don't have readily available details at this time, but I want you to stop worrying about me and get on with the rest of your life. I will be very disappointed in you if you don't.

As the song says: I'll be seeing you.

Eternal love,
Your Pamela

Whatever words she had expected to come out of Locke's mouth, Miss Voncille considered these a universe away. She had to take a generous swig of her sherry to steady herself and give herself some time to think of what to say. But another quick glimpse of Pamela's portrait gave her just the inspiration she needed.

"It's almost like your wife was thinking of that letter when her portrait was painted so long ago," she observed. "Otherwise, I can't think of a thing to add to the sentiments she expressed."

Locke looked consummately pleased with her and himself. "Pamela was like that. She was forward-thinking, even though she wanted to know everything about people here in Cherico. That was why we first started going to 'Who's Who?' meetings. But it was the big picture that really interested her. Not just what came before, but what comes next? That's why having breast cancer never really changed her. She always thought it was part of something that would eventually make sense to her, and when I read her letter the other day after two years had passed, I teared up and laughed at the same time. She really knew me, and I have no choice now but to keep following through on what she's asked me to do."

Miss Voncille exhaled, enjoying the slight buzz from the sherry. "I assume the single rose was your idea, though?"

"That it was. Give me credit for some originality."

"Oh, I do," she said, inching closer to him. "As I've said to you several times, you're a surprising and original man."

The kiss that followed was gentle and brief but held the promise of more to come.

"So, here's a question for you—what's your opinion of four-letter words?" he said, pulling away slightly.

Her expression was skeptical but amused. "I don't use them. Well . . . not unless I hit my thumb with a hammer putting up a picture. You know how that goes."

"No, I meant the four-letter words that Pamela used in her letter," he explained with a mischievous grin. "She talked about *risk* and she mentioned *love*. Those four-letter words. Here we are getting ready to greet our seventies. Are we willing to take the risk of again losing someone that we love?"

For the first time all night, Frank flashed into Miss Voncille's head. She had put his picture away in a brave attempt at moving forward. If she became further involved with Locke, it would be impossible to predict how many years they might have together.

"It's been a while since I've risked anything in the love department," she answered. "You pose a very pertinent question."

Neither of them said anything for a few minutes, sipping their sherry for courage.

"So, where do we go from here?" he said, finally.

She turned to him with a sweet, reassuring smile. "I'd like to stay here tonight. Is that enough of an answer?"

"More than enough," he replied, matching her smile. And then they kissed again, this time lingering tenderly.

"Then by all means, show me the rest of the house," she added, pulling away with an expectant sigh. "It's gone unappreciated for too long."

10

All Good Things in Threes

The phone rang at a quarter to ten the next morning in Maura Beth's purple bedroom. The depression she had retired with the night before was still very much hanging over her, and she hadn't yet made a move to throw back the covers and get her day started. It all meant that she was going to be late for work, with Renette holding down the fort until she showed up. As a result, she picked up the receiver trying to make her "Hello?" sound like it wasn't the first word she'd uttered since opening her eyes.

"I didn't wake you up, did I?" said the familiar but discerning voice on the other end of the line.

"Oh, no, I've been up for an hour, Connie," Maura Beth answered, continuing to press the envelope.

"Well, I won't keep you in suspense. All is well. Stout Fella came through beautifully," Connie continued, her voice full of energy and optimism. "There were no complications, whatsoever. The artery was completely cleared, and there was no blockage in any of the others. He's been in his room most of the morning, and Becca is in with him now just beside herself with relief. It's the funniest thing you've ever seen. She alternately kisses him on the cheek and scolds him like a child for putting them both through all this. But he really loved your balloon bouquet! Douglas and I managed to blow up one of each color, and we even wrote a message or two with the marker without popping them. If I still sound a little winded, that's why."

Maura Beth suddenly felt like a schoolgirl waiting for a juicy piece of gossip. "Ooh, what did you write?"

"Well, I wasn't Dorothy Parker, you understand. 'Get well soon' was about it. But we told him it was all your idea, and he said to be sure and tell you what a big kick he got out of it. He also said he hadn't had anyone bring him balloons since he had his tonsils out as a boy. He says when he gets back and into the swing of things, he's going to come to every meeting of The Cherry Cola Book Club with Becca just to show his appreciation."

"That makes my day!" Maura Beth exclaimed. "Frankly, I didn't sleep well last night, worrying about how the procedure would go. And about our little book club, if you want to know the truth."

Connie made a sympathetic noise under her breath. "Well, the procedure part is looking real good now. The doctor predicts a full recovery if Stout Fella will just behave himself. Let's take the rest one step at a time. Meanwhile, you'll let everyone know the latest, won't you?"

"Will do. And you keep these good reports coming!"

After they'd hung up, Maura Beth yawned, stretched, and threw on her bathrobe. Then she trudged into her kitchenette, poured herself a glass of orange juice, and began making phone calls. Miss Voncille was the first person on her short list, but there was no answer at 45 Painter Street—which seemed odd so early in the morning. On the first try, however, she got through to Periwinkle, who was elated with the good news and prognosis, as well as properly supportive of Maura Beth's concerns about the future of the book club.

"All you have to do is reschedule, honey, and I'll help you promote it at The Twinkle, as usual," Periwinkle told her. "And this time, everyone'll show up hale and hearty without so much as a sniffle."

"Hope so," Maura Beth replied, trying her best to sound upbeat.

"Sure they will. I'll talk up your club like nobody's business, especially to all the cute fellas that come in."

Maura Beth ended their conversation with a resigned chuckle. "Yeah, well, I wish there were as many people out there—male or female—who like to read as there are who like to eat. You take care now."

Another call to Miss Voncille still found no one home; then Maura Beth took a deep breath as she dialed Councilman Sparks's office number. She really didn't want to talk to him at all, but temporarily shelved her equivocal feelings for him to do the right thing.

But when she told him the news, she discovered to her surprise that she needn't have bothered.

"Thanks for your call, Miz Mayhew, but I already know he's out of the woods. I phoned up there myself a little while ago and spoke to Becca. We certainly wouldn't want to see anything happen to Mr. Justin Brachle, what with all he's done for Cherico in recent years."

Maura Beth didn't try very hard to prevent a cynical tone from creeping into her reply. "Yes, I'm sure you're glad everything went so well. He'll probably be wheeling and dealing again in no time."

"Maybe not quite wheeling and dealing. His wife was more reserved. Her exact words were, 'He'll go back to work within reason, this time.' She also said he'll have to change some bad old habits of his for good. I imagine she's going to lay down the law to him now. But it's fitting that you called me anyway. If you can work it in, I'd like to talk to you about your future here in Cherico. Would it be possible for you to come to my office around four-thirty this afternoon?"

Maura Beth felt a spurt of adrenaline in her veins and reacted without even consulting her schedule. "I see no reason why I can't do that. But do you mind my being frank with you and sparing myself some anxiety? Will this be good news or bad news for me?"

"That's entirely up to you, Miz Mayhew," came the emotionless reply. "I look forward to seeing you then."

She hung up and closed her eyes. All sorts of paranoid scenarios swirled throughout her brain. Would she soon be looking for another job? Should she have been more proactive in sending out résumés long before the ultimatum because The Cherico Library was basically the dead end she didn't want to face? Four-thirty seemed an eternity away to find out what was actually going to happen, but she would try to make an ordinary day of it until then.

Temporary relief from the uncertainty came through in the form of a third phone call attempt to Miss Voncille, which finally worked like the proverbial charm.

"Oh, I'm so thrilled for him—and Becca, of course!" Miss Voncille exclaimed after Maura Beth had delivered the happy update. "I'll go ahead and call Locke right after we hang up. I know he'll feel the same way." There was an awkward pause highlighted by a sharp intake of breath at the other end, and Maura Beth could sense there was something more to come.

"Do you have a moment?" Miss Voncille added finally.

"For my most loyal library user and the consummate historian and genealogist of Cherico, I always have time."

"Thank God, there's more to me than that now," she began rather breathlessly. "I wanted you to be the first to know—and I want to delay this just the way the kids do these days, so here it comes now . . . wait for it . . . wait for it . . . I'm officially back in the saddle again."

"No!"

"Yes!"

"Was it in your jungle lair?"

"No, in his very formal Perry Street residence, if you please."

They both found themselves laughing like girlfriends, and Maura Beth said, "Oh, I couldn't be happier for you—and Locke, too, of course!"

"I feel so naughty. I was part Melanie, part Scarlett, and I just got home a few minutes ago."

"Scandalous!" Maura Beth exclaimed, picking up on the playfulness. "But it makes sense to me now, since I haven't been able to reach you for the last half hour."

There was another rush of air at the other end. "I guess the next step is for us to become a permanent item. We talked about it seriously, of course, and we're going for it. Can you believe it?"

"Of course I can."

"This is turning out to be quite a day so far," Miss Voncille continued. "Becca's husband on the mend, Locke and myself starting up at our age. I wonder what will happen next?"

Maura Beth sounded more upbeat than she felt. "Well, they say good things come in threes."

The first thing that seemed out of kilter to Maura Beth when she arrived for her four-thirty appointment with Councilman Sparks was the fact that his secretary, Nora Duddney, was missing and unaccounted for. There had never been a time when Maura Beth had entered his office that the blankest, dullest person in the universe had not been at her desk staring at her computer monitor, unable to utter more than two words of passable conversation.

"In case you were wondering, Nora is no longer with me," Councilman Sparks explained the minute Maura Beth walked in, apparently reading her mind. "Please, step into my office and make yourself comfortable." He went in and pulled out her chair and then seated himself behind his desk. "First things first. I think we're both pleased that Justin Brachle is doing so well."

"Yes. We had quite a scare last night, didn't we?" she replied. "But it looks like we're going to have a happy ending. All these advances in modern medicine never cease to amaze me."

"Good choice of words," he continued. "The happy ending part, I mean. We all want that, don't we?"

Maura Beth could only guess where he was going with that but played along as calmly as she could, despite her quickening heartbeat. "We do."

Whatever it was Councilman Sparks had on his mind, he was obviously in no hurry to reveal it. He used the awkward silence that ensued to tap his ball point pen on his desk in erratic, Morse code fashion. It soon became nothing short of annoying to Maura Beth.

"I do think we should be candid with each other today, Miz Mayhew. Or may I call you Maura Beth after all these years?" he said finally.

"Yes, to both," she answered, feeling as if his line of questioning was completely unnecessary. "I mean, yes, we should be candid, and, yes, you may call me Maura Beth."

"Good." He let that rest for an uncomfortable length of time and then resumed. "Maura Beth, we're about three months out from the afternoon I advised you to try and turn your library around. That means you have less than two months left. You've had no increase in your circulation figures, and despite your Herculean efforts, that little book club of yours with the cutesy name has a membership I can count on one hand and a thumb, if I'm not mistaken."

Maura Beth glanced down at the Persian carpet as she spoke. "You're not mistaken. People just haven't signed up like

I'd hoped they would. Maybe Cherico really isn't all that interested in literary things. Perhaps I miscalculated, but I don't want to give up yet. Tara wasn't built in a day."

He made a perfunctory effort to smile and then leaned forward, boring into her with his eyes. "Cut out the fiction and try to be realistic. I've always admired your spunk, and I've said as much to you several times. But this just isn't working for you right now. I never thought it would."

Somehow, she found the courage to verbalize her worst fears. "Are you firing me or asking me to resign?"

She was surprised to see him flash that smile of his. "Neither, exactly. I'd like to suggest an alternative to you. I think the library situation is hopeless even though your time is technically not up yet. However, with Nora now gone, I'll have an opening for secretary right here in my office."

Maura Beth slumped in her chair at what she considered to be a lukewarm proposition at best. She couldn't imagine doing anything with her life other than being a librarian. "So my future here in Cherico is to become your secretary and forget all my training?"

"I'm just trying to make the best of a bad situation," he insisted. "You'd be an asset to this office, and, frankly, anyone could see that Nora was not. I owed her father a few favors when I first got elected and was stuck with her up until now. Basically, she has the personality and IQ of a persimmon, but I'm established enough now that I don't have to worry about what her father will say or do about me firing her. But, you, Maura Beth, would make anyone who came through my office door feel welcome and special. I've seen how you handle yourself at these library meetings. But then, that's what I've always found most attractive about you. That glowing innocence of yours, the expectations you arrived with fresh out of school. It flows out of you like your beautiful red hair."

Maura Beth began to feel distinctly uncomfortable. "Aren't

you getting a little too personal here again? These odes to my follicles are getting old."

He tapped his pen on the desk again while mulling things over carefully. "I certainly don't mean to offend you, but let me put it this way. I didn't pay that much attention to you when you first came to Cherico. I approved your hire and forgot about it because the library has never been one of our priorities. But you have a way about you, and people took notice. Evie and I had dinner one night with Miss Voncille at The Twinkle, and all she did was rave about how cooperative you were with her 'Who's Who?' organization. I believe her exact words were, 'She's the sweetest thing to ever walk the streets of Cherico.' Of course, we knew she really didn't mean it the way it sounded."

Maura Beth's eyes widened even as she chuckled under her breath. "Thank goodness for small favors."

"My point is that you'd be a vast improvement over the nonentity who greeted my visitors, and with the money we'd save by closing down the library, your salary would take quite a healthy leap. You've worked hard these past six years, and you deserve more money for the effort you've made. But this is practically the only way I can reward you," he concluded.

"Not to mention that you had the time of your life sitting back in your chair and doing your best to keep things stirred up at all my meetings."

He rolled his eyes and screwed up his face for a moment. "Okay, I plead guilty to reading up on the classics to offer extremely literate criticism during sessions of The Cherry Cola Book Club. And by the way, I wasn't kidding when I said that Atticus Finch is the perfect man by any reasonable standard. Anyway, you have to know that Cherico isn't the center of the intellectual universe. The men folk talk college and pro sports all up and down Commerce Street, and the ladies complain about their husbands and children and exchange recipes at all the beauty parlors. I'd say literary criticism is way down the list of their topics to discuss. Do you really think you can ever pull this off?"

She touched her fingertips to her temples for a few seconds and then leaned in, staring him down. "More to the point, you haven't stamped the budget yet. I still have time to make the book club the talk of the town."

He nodded reluctantly. "Yes."

"Then I choose not to shrink from my ultimate goal. Like Scarlett, I shall valiantly defend my turf."

"You and your never-ending literary conceits!" he declared, cracking a smile. "And there's nothing I can say or do to change your mind at this time?"

"Nothing. I can't see myself putting people on hold for a living."

He stood up slowly, the disappointment clearly showing in his face. "Well, I have to say, it's a damned shame because I think the odds favor Cherico being without a library in the very near future."

"I'll just have to take that chance," she said, standing up and heading for the door.

He moved energetically across the room in time to open it for her. "I guess you will. Meanwhile, for the record, I'll stop trying to louse things up at your meetings. You really don't need any help in that department from what I've seen."

She turned back at the last second and managed to smile anyway. "Thanks for the vote of confidence."

11

Brainstorm in Brentwood

Milepost 327 along the Natchez Trace Parkway found Maura Beth driving across a two-lane bridge high above the Tennessee River, heading slowly northeast toward Nashville. It was now deep into the third week in September, and the first hint of fall color among the leaves of the hardwoods flanking the manicured right of way had begun to appear. Yet the green of the thick stands of pine and cedar still dominated as far as the eye could see. This impulsive escape from Cherico the morning after her showdown with Councilman Sparks was nothing short of liberating for Maura Beth, and she kept breathing in deeply as if she were sampling the bouquet of a fine wine. Occasionally, the fleeting glimpse of a deer or wild turkey at the edge of the woods or near a stone outcropping made her think she had died and gone to heaven. In a very literal sense, it reminded her that she'd had her nose in library books to the exclusion of nearly everything else far too long.

The decision to travel north by northeast for a change of venue came to her shortly after she'd returned to her apartment the evening before, collapsing on her sofa and virtually drenched in self-doubt. She had turned her back on security, which was certainly brave, but was it smart? Her first impulse was to call her parents in Covington—particularly her mother—or Periwinkle at the restaurant, or Miss Voncille wherever she could be found these days, but somehow she resisted. It wasn't so much that she was afraid of failing and going down in flames with the library. It was more that she was putting so much of herself into this ordinary little town of Cherico that had offered her a job straight out of school.

Of course, there were many other library jobs out there—some with far more responsibility, most that paid more money. But by some gradual, inexplicable process, she had gotten hooked on this particular position and this wildly diverse handful of people who had suddenly rallied to her side. They were beginning to mean more and more to her with every passing day, creating one of those alternative definitions of the word *family.* It all meant that making a big hit of The Cherry Cola Book Club was a challenge she fully intended to meet.

Then an idea flashed into her head with a clarity she could not ignore. What would be the harm in simply getting the hell out of Dodge for a day or two? She could put Renette in charge of the library, drive up to Nashville, visit with the McShays and the Brachles, and clear her head. She could run everything past all of them and even go to the hospital to bring Stout Fella another balloon bouquet, this time with something more original than "Get well soon!" to cheer him up.

So she put her doubts and fears aside, and reached Douglas at his brother's house. It did not take very long for her to wangle an invitation after summarizing all the drama that had taken place at City Hall.

"Sounds like you're living right on the edge there," Douglas told her. "But, by all means, come on up for a visit. We'd love to have you. My brother, Paul, and his wife, Susan, are empty nesters with three bedrooms gathering dust now, so they always have room for one more these days. I'll tell Connie and Becca you're coming. I know they'll be thrilled."

And that had sealed the deal. For Maura Beth, it was now Nashville or bust.

All the full-fledged, female members of The Cherry Cola Book Club except Miss Voncille were standing around Stout Fella's room on the fourth floor of Centennial Medical Center, daring him to pick a winner among all the new balloon bouquets they had blown up for him. Of course, the Magic Marker messages were the only criterion that really counted in this impromptu competition. At the moment, Stout Fella was milking it for all it was worth, and everyone looking on was amazed at his outlook and energy. Not even an AMI and subsequent balloon angioplasty had been able to keep him down for long.

Yes, it was true that his voice was not quite as strong as usual, and he had to pause now and then when he spoke, but there was no doubt in anyone's mind that he would recover completely just as the doctors had said he would.

"Hey . . . I'm sold on Maura Beth's . . . 'Good Health—Check It Out!' motto because it's got that library thing of hers going for it," he began, anchored to his bed by the tangle of lines monitoring his vital signs and the IV drips supplying his meds and nourishment.

"Thanks. And a little birdie told me you wanted to come to all my future Cherry Cola Book Club meetings once you get home," Maura Beth put in quickly. "I'll hold you to that."

He nodded her way and resumed, "On the other hand . . . who wouldn't like Connie's . . . 'No More Ice Cream Islands!' for the humor alone?"

"You do know that means no more standing around the kitchen with a spoon, digging in, don't you?" Connie said.

"Got the message, loud and clear. Nevertheless . . . I'm smart enough to remember who's gonna butter my bread for me . . . or probably not even let me have bread and butter anymore. So the winner is—ta da!—my wife and keeper, Becca Broccoli, for . . . 'I Love You, You Big Lug!' "

Becca leaned down carefully, finding a clear route to his cheek to plant a kiss, while the others laughed and lightly applauded. Then she pulled back and took several quick bows. "Thank you, thank you, one and all. Please, enough applause. This is so unexpected. I never thought I'd win among such fierce competition. And I want to say further that it will be my next goal to turn my Justin into a Medium-Sized Lug once again."

He smiled big and gave the entire room a naughty wink. "I promise to tow the line the best I can . . . but I just wanted to say that I'd like for everyone . . . to keep calling me Stout Fella . . . no matter how much I shape up. I keep telling Becca . . . that it makes me feel solid and sturdy. Hey, there's more than one meaning . . . to the word *stout,* you know."

Becca was rolling her eyes now. "Yes, we know all about that. You're Stout Fella, the Superhero, able to wrap up any real-estate deal with the lightning stroke of a pen."

He gave her a thumbs-up. "Now you're talking!"

"You'll just be writing a bit slower now, kiddo," Becca reminded him. "You'll get a crash course from me in taking your time whether you're eating or buying up all the land on both sides of the Tennessee River."

"But never fear. After you get released and we head home to Cherico, Douglas and I want to make sure you get a glimpse of the Batman Building downtown to honor your ongoing superhero status," Connie explained. "It's really the AT&T Building, but it's got these tall twin spires and a few other contraptions on top that make it look like Batman's mask. It's not quite the landmark Ryman Auditorium is, but it's pretty close. There now, that's a good reason to do what all the doctors ask you to do."

"To the Batmobile, Robin!" Stout Fella replied, enjoying a

laugh that turned quickly into a cough, and Becca immediately gave him his water to sip. "By the way . . . where is Douglas right now? No offense to all you beautiful ladies . . . but a man likes to talk to another man now and then."

"Oh, he's spending some time with his brother, Paul, but he'll be back to pick me up soon," Connie said. "Anyhow, don't worry. He'll be stopping by plenty before you get released."

Just then there was a knock at the door, and a mousy female voice announced the single word, "Nutrition." In walked a slight young woman in brown scrubs carrying a tray and smiling deferentially at everyone. "It's almost noon. Time for lunch. It's just a little something to eat—doctor's orders."

"Yeah, but I thought I was getting that . . . through one of these drips," Stout Fella pointed out, narrowing his eyes.

"You are, sir," she answered, nearly in a whisper. "But your doctor wants you to try a little broth, too. And some Jell-O, if you can manage it."

"Hey, I know I need to lose weight . . . but that sounds ridiculous!" he declared. "When do I start back on . . . meat and potatoes?"

"I'll handle him," Becca said, noting the sheepish look on the woman's face. "Here, let me take this from you, please." Whereupon the tray was transferred quickly, the woman scurried out, and Becca gave her husband a stern look.

"You practically scared her to death, you big bully. The poor girl was only doing her job."

"Never mind her. Hoo, boy!" Stout Fella exclaimed. "What have I gotten myself into? From my wife's home cooking to . . . this!"

Becca ignored the remark and uncovered the plate, inhaling the steam from the broth. "I think it's chicken."

He cut his eyes at her and smirked like a mischievous little boy. "I think *I'm* chicken."

"For heaven's sake, don't be such a big baby. If you could watch your artery being unclogged on a TV monitor from start to finish without flinching, you can certainly slurp up a tiny bowl of bland soup. Here, I'll even feed you." And she proceeded to do just that, while her husband made a gallery of ungainly faces even as he swallowed every spoonful guided toward his mouth.

It was out on the deck overlooking Paul and Susan McShay's vast backyard in the wealthy Nashville suburb of Brentwood that Maura Beth was getting ready to hold a brainstorming session about the future of the book club. That revved-up campaign she had envisioned would start here in earnest. The evening was still young and the air invigorating after a delicious menu in the formal dining room of baked chicken, smashed potatoes, and sautéed green beans that Susan had prepared for all of her guests. Now it was time to get down to business.

"I can only stay for about twenty minutes," Becca told Maura Beth as the gathering seated themselves around a rustic picnic table with their after-dinner drinks in hand. "Stout Fella is expecting me back at the hospital around eight, of course."

Then Douglas chimed in. "I'm going with her, and not just because she doesn't know her way around. Becca says Justin wants to shoot the breeze with me about the NFL, the college game, and other manly topics. So far, he says, they've refused to give him an injection of testosterone."

"You'd think this was just another day at the office, and his heart crisis had never happened," Becca said, waving Douglas off.

Maura Beth smiled as she quietly surveyed the friends she hoped would be sending her back to Cherico with a successful strategy to keep her library open. Connie, Douglas, and

Becca, she had expected to consult, but the Brentwood McShays were an unexpected bonus.

"You might like to know that Susan and Paul are still in The Music City Page Turners," Connie had told Maura Beth at the dinner table. "The three of us were almost half of the founding members, and we all know what it takes to make a success of one of these clubs. Douglas and I brought them up to date on what you're trying to do in Cherico, and they think it's fantastic."

One thing had led to another, and by the time the dessert of chocolate mousse with whipped cream and a cherry on top was served, Susan had committed herself and her husband to the confab out on the deck later on. "That is, unless you'd rather just have your Cherry Cola people only," she had added at the last second.

But Maura Beth had quickly reassured her. "Heavens, no! I need as much brainpower as I can round up!"

The Brentwood McShays certainly appeared to have the right credentials for offering intelligent advice. Paul was a taller, more distinguished-looking version of his brother and had recently retired from teaching psychology at Vanderbilt, while the stylish, model-thin Susan still ran her own crafts boutique at the Cool Springs Galleria south of Brentwood. The most important thing from Maura Beth's point of view, however, was that they were both fans of the printed word and would therefore be sympathetic to her cause.

"Time is growing short," Maura Beth began, officially opening the informal meeting. "The Cherico Library's days may be numbered unless we can drastically increase interest in The Cherry Cola Book Club. And also get more people to use their library cards." Then she offered a blow-by-blow of her most recent encounters with Councilman Sparks, but particularly his offer to take her out of the library business and appoint her his decorative gatekeeper.

"Something about that bothers me," Connie said. "Why doesn't he just shut everything down and let you go your merry way? Or should I say unhappy way?"

Maura Beth decided to hold nothing back. "The truth is, though, I'm not really unhappy. I want to make a go of my job in Cherico because I like the place. There are probably a thousand reasons I shouldn't, but I do. As for why he hasn't shut the library down by now to cut his losses, I don't know. That continues to puzzle me. But these local politicians are a law unto themselves."

"Would you like to have an ex-college professor's opinion?" Paul McShay offered, leaning in her general direction.

"Love to."

"I'm only going by a handful of things that happened to me during my tenure at Vandy," he began, after a sip of his port. "It doesn't mean that I'm right in my analysis, but what I'm about to tell you may have some merit nonetheless. There were a few young female students in my classes over the years who developed crushes on me." He turned and gave his wife a knowing smile and wink. "And I never kept any of that from Susan. I was determined to nip these things in the bud."

"I'm sure his nipping was effective, too," she put in. "A wife can usually tell if her husband is fooling around."

"Anyway, none of those young ladies ever got anywhere with me, but I got pretty good at picking up on the signals. Sometimes, they'd come up to me after class and tell me what a deep speaking voice I had and 'why didn't I go into broadcasting' and yada, yada, yada. Or other times it was how much they liked the clothes I was wearing—mostly the sweaters and ties that they didn't know Susan had picked out for me. I always thanked them for their compliments but otherwise played dumb, of course."

Maura Beth was frowning now, trying to follow the implications of his story. "What made you bring up the crush angle?"

He finished off his port and said, "Because that's my field of study. Psychology is all about predictable human behavior, and I listened carefully to all the emphasis you put on the comments your councilman kept making about your beautiful red hair. The way he carried on about it, and especially that line about your innocence that you said made you feel uncomfortable. It sounds a lot like my experience in reverse, but at a much higher level of expectation. I think it all probably means the man wants you around at all costs, despite this business about closing the library. It's a roundabout way of setting things up in typical male fashion."

The three other women sitting around the table, all of whom happened to be married, exchanged glances, and it was Becca who finally spoke up for them. "I have to agree with Paul. Regardless of what happens with the library, I think it would be a huge mistake for you to go directly to work for Councilman Sparks. You don't know what kind of pressure he could end up putting on you for—you know what."

Maura Beth bit her lip as she shook her head. "I can be such a naïve girlie-girl at times. The thought had crossed my mind that he might be hitting on me, but I didn't want to believe it."

"Hey, don't be so hard on yourself," Connie said. "You did the right thing. You turned him down and told him you were going for the gold. You have nothing to be ashamed of. The big question now is how to get that gold."

"Right!" Maura Beth exclaimed. "So now it's idea time. First step is to reschedule the *To Kill a Mockingbird* meeting and get into an honest, meaty discussion of Harper Lee's work. No more indulging the war between the sexes. At least Councilman Sparks has promised me he won't be doing that sort of thing anymore—that is, if I can take him at his word. But how do we get more people interested in participating?"

Becca waved her hand in front of her face a few times.

"*The Becca Broccoli Show* could go with the downsizing recipes full-time, for starters. And I could keep on pitching *To Kill a Mockingbird* as our upcoming food for thought in the club. Stout Fella could talk about getting his body in shape with my new recipes, and his brain in shape by reading and thinking about Harper Lee's work. I could invite my audience to come to the book club meeting to have a little bite and discuss literature with Becca Broccoli, Stout Fella, and everyone else. Just how far out were you considering scheduling this thing, Maura Beth?"

"A month? Maybe five weeks at the most? We can't wait too long, though, or we'll run up against the budget approval."

Becca nodded enthusiastically. "That should be enough time to get Stout Fella in some sort of reasonable shape—oh, and to get him to read the novel."

Then an inspired Connie stepped in. "I was thinking that Douglas and I could talk things up to all our new neighbors out at the lake. We're just now getting to know some of them. But people are pretty much the same all over. Everybody likes to eat, and you never know who likes to read until you bring up a few pop culture references. That's where you separate the TV watchers and moviegoers from the readers."

Maura Beth's face was suddenly alive with girlish excitement. "And I've just this second thought of something to run past Periwinkle when I get home." Then she took the time to explain The Twinkle and its congenial owner to the Brentwood McShays.

Susan briefly glanced at her husband after the testimonial to the restaurant. "Now that makes my mouth water—and on a full stomach yet. Looks like we're going to have to visit your brother and Connie more often than we'd planned. If nothing else, I want some of that tomato aspic with the cream cheese in the middle. And I bet I'd get so hooked, we'd probably even want to come back another time to take in a certain book review at the library."

Maura Beth clasped her hands together. "Are you saying you'd be willing to come for our *Mockingbird* session?"

"What do you say, Paul?" Susan added, winking smartly.

He thought for a moment and then leaned against his brother. "Let me check first with Doug, here. Think you could return the favor and put us up in Cherico now and then?"

"Done deal. Now that I think about it, I could use a fishing partner on *The Verdict*."

"Wow!" Becca exclaimed, checking her watch. "That was a productive ten or fifteen minutes, wasn't it? Now that all that's decided, I think it's safe to head for the hospital and let Stout Fella know about it."

"And I'll keep him from getting too antsy by predicting who I think will be in the Super Bowl this year," Douglas added, rising from his seat with a wink. "You know—the kind of stuff that only us men like."

Maura Beth took a deep breath as Becca and Douglas headed into the house. "I think I'll head back to Cherico tomorrow. For the first time in a while, I really believe The Cherry Cola Book Club has a chance to make a name for itself."

12

Shaking up the Bottle

When Maura Beth hit the town limits of Cherico upon her return from Nashville the next day, she couldn't believe how much it felt like home to her. It truly mystified her how that could be, since she had spent most of her life growing up in Covington and all of her college years at LSU. Yet there was no question in her mind that she was glad to be back, even after a mere couple of days away.

What was more, she was even happier to see *her* library. Funny, how possessive of it she had become ever since Councilman Sparks had cast it in those terms during the unveiling of his ultimatum several months earlier. She also now knew that she had officially embraced an either/or situation: Either she kept the library open through the book club and other measures, or she left town. As she and her friends had all agreed up in Brentwood in no uncertain terms, there would be no "working under" Councilman Sparks in any capacity whatsoever.

The informal report Renette had prepared for her boss's perusal on her first afternoon back was uneventful for the most part, but a couple of items took a bit of explaining.

"Exactly what is this notation here?" Maura Beth wanted

to know, pointing to the second scribble on the list as they reviewed it in her office. "What does 'V15 Damage' mean? Please tell me it doesn't have anything to do with the one and only Mr. Barnes Putzel."

Renette looked down at her lap while fidgeting in her seat. "Unfortunately, it does. We ran out of peanut butter crackers, and Mr. Putzel threw Volume Fifteen of the *Encyclopaedia Britannica* all the way across the room and broke the spine. It was actually the only exciting thing that happened all day."

Maura Beth covered both eyes with the palm of her right hand. "Oh, I knew there was something I forgot to do before I left. I meant to go down to The Cherico Market and buy some more crackers. I had even made a note to myself that we were running low. Well, did he do any more damage, or was it just Volume Fifteen?"

"Just that one. Do we have the money to replace it?"

Maura Beth flashed a sarcastic grin. "We barely have enough money to replace the crackers. I'll call his sister and tell her to write us a check." Then she moved down the list with her finger. "And what was this 'Complaint from Mr. Parker Place'?"

Renette had a guilty expression on her face. "I, uh, was really late putting out the most recent edition of the *Commercial Appeal.*"

Maura Beth shrugged. "Oh, I wouldn't worry about it. You put it in the newspaper rack eventually, didn't you?"

"Yes, of course. But Mr. Place told me he comes every day to go through the classifieds looking for a job, and he said he was annoyed that he had to wait three hours. I got sidetracked by some phone calls and stuff. He was polite about it all, but I could tell he was stressed out."

"What does this Mr. Place look like?" Maura Beth wanted to know, reviewing a mental slideshow of their regular patrons.

"Oh, we've both seen him in here a lot recently. He's that handsome black gentleman who's always dressed in a coat and tie. Only he says he's out of work now and comes to the library for job leads in the Memphis paper."

Maura Beth pursed her lips thoughtfully. "I tell you what. Next time he comes in, let me know. I'd like to talk to him. Do you know what kind of work he's looking for?"

"He didn't say."

"Well, you just keep an eye out for him, okay?" Then she ran down the rest of the list, looking up with a smile. "I think I understand the rest of this. All things considered, you did extremely well being in charge. Now, the next thing I want you to do is take some money out of petty cash and run down to The Cherico Market for those crackers. We've got to keep Mr. Putzel from destroying the rest of the encyclopedia."

For Maura Beth, it had come down to this: The *To Kill a Mockingbird* potluck and review had been rescheduled one week after Halloween, and The Cherry Cola Book Club had two weeks after that to build toward either the ultimate sizzle or a final fizzle. But the momentum that had been rekindled in Brentwood must not be squandered, and Maura Beth was so excited about it all that she was practically hatching schemes in her sleep. One that particularly intrigued her involved meeting Mr. Parker Place and finding out what his story was. Who knew? He just might turn out to be the perfect example of someone successfully using the library for job leads, and that also might impress and sway Councilman Sparks there at the end.

On Maura Beth's second day back from her Nashville trip, in fact, Mr. Place was ushered into her office by a smiling Renette, who had invited him over the minute he had finished with the paper. At close range, Maura Beth found him even more attractive than she had whenever she'd spotted him from a distance. His smooth, ginger-colored skin and generous smile made it easy to linger over his strong, angular features. In addition, there was a maturity about him that was both reassuring and titillating.

"My assistant tells me you're looking for work, Mr. Place," Maura Beth said, after they had exchanged greetings and other pleasantries.

"I am," he told her. "And I never thought I would be at this stage of my life."

"What do you do?"

Discernible pride was clearly evident in his smile and tone of voice. "I'm a pastry chef. And a first-rate one, too. I worked for nearly thirty years at the Grand Shelby Hotel over in Memphis making desserts fit for royalty. Provided the king or queen can practice moderation. What I make is good for your sweet tooth, not necessarily your figure."

Maura Beth chuckled briefly, but then there was a sharp intake of air. "Didn't I read in the *Commercial Appeal* that the Grand Shelby Hotel was torn down about a month ago?"

"Sure was, I'm sorry to say. It went belly-up in this economy, and they couldn't find a buyer for it. So they just tore it down and sold the land off for a parking lot. There's too much of that going on these days. Unfortunately, the hotel was also my home. I had a very nice, spacious suite all to myself on the second floor. So here I am back in my hometown of Cherico after all these years living with my mama until I can get back on track. I check the classifieds every day to see if there's an ad for anything up my alley. I have to say, I wish your library had a computer so I could go online and look for leads that way."

Maura Beth was unable to suppress her frustration at his last comment. "I wish we had one for the patrons, too. More than one, actually. But the City Council keeps turning down my requests for terminals. They're dead set against them, and I've asked for funding every year I've been here. It's just not a priority of theirs."

"That's a shame," Mr. Place answered, scowling momentarily. "If I was still in Memphis, I could use their computers, but down here, I guess I'll have to plunk down for one of my own. I have a little savings to tide me over until I find something that really suits me, though. I left this little town in the first place because there were lots more jobs in Memphis, you know. I'm a native Chericoan, as I said. Born over there at Cherico Memorial in the middle of a hailstorm fifty-four years ago. My mama always said I was a 'hail' of a baby—nine and a half ounces and bouncing all over the place."

Maura Beth leaned in and laughed. "That's cute. Your mother has a delightful sense of humor, and you do, too. I guess it runs in the Place family."

He slowly shook his head, smiling all the while. "Oh, we're not Places. We're Bedloes. I was christened Joe Sam Bedloe, but I changed it legally to Parker Place once I started working for the Grand Shelby Hotel. And yes, I had a good reason for doing that. When I was growing up, Mama gave me a Monopoly game one Christmas, and whenever my aunties would come over with my little cousins, we'd wear that game out. I liked all the names of the streets, particularly Park Place. It sounded so classy, and everybody knew it was where all the imaginary rich folks hung their hats. And if you could buy that deed and Boardwalk and put hotels up, you stood a great chance of winning the game, which I usually did. Made my cousins so mad every time. So here I am—Mis-ter Park-er Place of Cherico, Memphis, and Monopoly fame, pastry chef extraordinaire."

"It all has a nice ring to it, I must say."

"Yep, high-rent district all the way."

Maura Beth then flashed her warmest smile as she decided to tell him all about the book club. "While you're waiting for the right job to come along, maybe you'd consider joining us and coming to our next meeting in about five weeks? And why not bring your mother along with you? I'd love to meet her."

He looked as if he might be seriously considering her invitation. "Yes, I've seen your sign-up sheet. And I have to admit I have a little history with *To Kill a Mockingbird*. So does my mama." He rose from his chair and pointed to the front desk. "Maybe I'll just make my way right over there and sign up now."

Maura Beth could barely contain her delight. "That's fantastic, Mr. Place! And do you have a current library card?"

He told her he didn't as they headed out of her office.

"Well, let's go get you fixed up all around, shall we?"

That evening Maura Beth decided to have a late dinner at The Twinkle to tell Periwinkle all about her impromptu trip to Nashville, as well as the promotional idea that had come to her during the Brentwood brainstorming session with everyone. In fact, the two of them closed the place down, sending Lalie Bevins, the waitress, home to her family, before truly engaging each other.

"So what's this great concept you hinted at when I served you your grilled chicken and pineapple salsa?" Periwinkle began, finally taking a seat at Maura Beth's table after a hard night's work. "By the way, did you like it? It's the first time I've offered it. I don't want to get into a rut, you know. Expanding the menu is something I'd like to do."

"It was delicious, of course. Everything you serve always is." Then Maura Beth briefly outlined all the decisions that had been made in Brentwood before finally getting to Periwinkle's initial question. "Here's my concept. Why don't we cross-promote my library and your restaurant? I've come up with a perfectly brilliant way."

"I'm all ears."

Maura Beth went all girlish and giggly for a few moments. "We use library cards. If one of my patrons presents his or her library card to you when they order, they can get a free drink or dessert."

Periwinkle looked stoic and went silent for a while. "Hmm. I have to think about my margins, you know. What about half-price drinks or desserts?"

Maura Beth felt like negotiating. After all, it would surely be good practice for dealing with Councilman Sparks. "Two-for-one drinks or a half-price dessert?"

"You drive a hard bargain," Periwinkle said, extending her hand to shake on it. "But okay, it's a deal. I have more customers who prefer sweets over liquor anyway."

But Maura Beth kept on pressing. "I figure it makes my library card a more valuable commodity and encourages people to drop by The Twinkle even more than they do now. I'll have some new flyers printed up. I'm sure Connie will go along with it."

Periwinkle was chuckling now. "Okay, girl, you've sold me. You can let up. Besides, I only have two desserts on the menu—my sherry custard and my bread pudding. They're pretty cost-effective."

Then it flashed into Maura Beth's head that she had other work to accomplish at The Twinkle on this autumn evening, and Periwinkle's mention of expanding the menu had triggered it. "You know, I think it's ambitious of you to want to offer more dishes to your customers as time goes by. All successful restaurants do it, and The Twinkle certainly qualifies as successful."

"Yes, I'm doing better than I ever dreamed, and much sooner than I thought," Periwinkle admitted. "It's got my ex-husband, Harlan, green with envy that he let me get away. And what I have to say to him is, 'Tough pork chops!' "

"I love it!" Maura Beth exclaimed, enjoying a big laugh. Then she leaned in and gave Periwinkle her most studied gaze. "I know a way you can expand your menu right now and get raves in the process—no hit or miss dishes, no ifs, ands, or buts."

Periwinkle stopped her gum. "Now this I have to hear."

"No, I'm perfectly serious. Cherico is once again the home of the Memphis Grand Shelby Hotel's former illustrious pastry chef, Mr. Parker Place. The hotel was recently torn down and he's flat out of a job, but more importantly, he's dying to get back to work making his fabulous desserts for some lucky restaurant and its customers."

"And you know this how?"

Maura Beth recanted her morning visit with Mr. Place and went straight for the payoff. "Do you think you can take on a pastry chef? You said yourself you only had two desserts on the menu."

Periwinkle began mulling things over, but Maura Beth could discern the interest in her face. "I can certainly afford to take on a pastry chef, if that's what you mean," she said finally. "I guess it would just be a question of Mr. Place's salary expectations. I probably can't afford to pay him what the Grand Shelby Hotel was paying him."

"But you'll never know what he'll accept until you ask him."

"That's true. Girl, are you his agent or something?"

They both laughed, and Maura Beth said, "No, it just came to me a few minutes ago. I didn't even think of it this afternoon when he was sitting in my office. So, will you interview him and see what happens? I have his phone number from his book club sign-up today. I'll get it to you tomorrow."

Periwinkle nodded enthusiastically. "Sure, why not? I always like to think I'm at the top of my game."

"Baby, you'll get the job. Don't you worry," Ardenia Bedloe had told her son right before kissing him on the cheek and sending him on his way to the job interview at The Twinkle at nine-thirty in the morning. "That Miz Lattimore is crazy if you don't get it, good as you are. Nobody in Memphis ever fixed desserts as fine as you did!" Then she had drawn herself up as tall as her arthritis and seventy-five years of living would allow and waved good-bye to him at the door. "Hold your head up and your shoulders back!" she called out at the last minute. "You're a proud Bedloe, no matter what!"

And with that send-off to amuse and embolden him simultaneously, Mr. Parker Place drove from his family home on Big Hill Lane to the restaurant. He was thinking that Maura Beth Mayhew must be some sort of magician, getting back to him just a couple of days after their first meeting to tell him she had talked Periwinkle Lattimore into considering him for a position at The Twinkle. Though his world had come tumbling down around him in Memphis, thanks to the wrecking ball, it appeared he might be on the verge of constructing a new life for himself.

"What were your specialties?" Periwinkle was asking him once they had begun the interview in her cluttered office at precisely nine-thirty. Among the many good work habits he had acquired throughout his career, unerring promptness was near the top of Mr. Parker Place's list.

He took a deep breath and began a tempting recitation. "Crepes of all kinds, both cheese and fruit, Mississippi mud pie, grasshopper pie, carrot cake, red velvet cake, strawberry cake, caramel cake, éclairs, cupcakes of all kinds, macadamia nut cookies, dark chocolate chip cookies—"

Periwinkle held up her hand. "That's more than impressive, Mr. Place. Why don't I take a bite of the samples you brought?" She looked down at the éclair and the slice of grasshopper pie he had placed before her a few minutes earlier and settled on the éclair first. "What on earth have you put in there, Mr. Place?!" she exclaimed as she tasted his creation with ever-widening eyes. "It's heavenly!"

He leaned in smugly. "A little Amaretto in the filling."

"How did you know I love that wedding cake taste?" she continued. "Though why I have no idea. My marriage was a disaster!"

He gently pushed the pie plate toward her with a disarming smile. "Sorry to hear that, but maybe this will make you feel better."

Then she tasted the cool, green grasshopper pie, and he thought she might just swoon. "Ohhh!" Finally, she gathered herself. "My biggest gripe with mint is that it can be so overwhelming that you feel like you don't want to eat anything for another month. How did you manage to tame it like this?"

"Now that," he told her, "is one of my secrets I don't care to reveal."

She nodded enthusiastically. "I can respect that. I keep a few of my best tips hidden away on the pantry shelf myself."

Then it was time to get around to the details of an actual job offer, and Periwinkle predictably led with the issue of compensation. "Can you tell me how much the Grand Shelby Hotel was paying you there at the end?"

He said nothing, preferring to write a figure on a nearby Post-it note and hand it to her.

She looked down at it and smiled. "I must say I think you were worth every penny, judging by what I just tasted."

"Thank you."

Then she took another Post-it note and wrote down a figure of her own. "See if this will work for you, Mr. Place," she said, offering it to him.

He glanced at it quickly and caught her gaze. "Miz Lattimore, I'd love to come work for you whenever you say." Then he leaned forward, maintaining the intense eye contact. "My mama said you'd give me this job before I left the house. She's a great judge of character, you know."

"Tell you what," Periwinkle added, reaching across her desk to shake his hand. "I want you to bring your mother here for dinner real soon. It'll be on the house. Just think of it as a sort of signing bonus."

Miss Voncille glanced at the wall clock in her bright yellow kitchen and made a sour face. It was ten after two in the afternoon, one week exactly before the November *Mockingbird* meeting. "They're running late," she said to Locke, who was leaning against the counter nursing a small gin and tonic. "That's not like them."

He shrugged and began rummaging through the nearby dish of nuts she intended to set out for their upcoming bridge game with the Crumpton sisters.

"Why do men always do that?" she wanted to know, watching him poking his index finger around and feigning disapproval.

"Do what?"

"Pick out all the cashews and leave all the Brazil nuts."

Locke washed down the nuts with another sip of his drink and smirked. "For the same reason we date the prettiest girls in town if we can get them to go out with us. They're yummier."

"I'm not sure I like the sound of that too much," she added. "But at least it's consistent."

"Yes," he continued. "Also, cashews are compact, and

Brazil nuts are . . . well, always the size of Brazil." He decided to take a seat in the breakfast nook, and she joined him, bringing the nuts with her. "Playing bridge with the Crumpton sisters still seems like an extraordinary sacrifice on your part—or on ours, I should say, since I'll have to be in the room except when I'm lucky enough to be dummy. Please see if you can arrange for me to be dummy every deal. Those Crumpton sisters are the world's most acquired taste."

Miss Voncille looked exasperated and went after the last of the cashews herself. "I expect them to be testy if we cut off one of their legs, or even defeat one of their contracts, but if I can maneuver them into coming to the *Mockingbird* meeting in another week, it will help Maura Beth out immeasurably. We're all just trying our best to increase those numbers—day by day, week by week—right up until the last second. Maura Beth and Periwinkle really have that cross-promotional angle going, Connie's doing her thing out at the lake this Sunday with her seafood extravaganza, and Becca's been doing hers on the radio now with Stout Fella as her sidekick. I'm not about to be the only one who doesn't contribute something. And you have to be in on it for the simple reason that it takes four to play bridge."

Locke lifted his glass in tribute and took another swallow. "I must admit I never thought Mamie and Marydell would accept your apology about that crazy armadillo story of yours. Looks like they're back in the genealogy fold. Mind telling me how you managed it?"

"A strange form of flattery, if you must know. I told Mamie that I thought I must be showing the first signs of dementia with all that nonsense I made up. 'Clearly, you're the healthiest, sanest person in our class,' I went on. 'You'll outlive us all!' I laid it on pretty thick because it appeals to that unique morbid streak of hers. That's what we used to call her in high school, you know—Morbid Mamie. I think it started when our journalism teacher, Mrs. Lander, let her write an article for the school paper on poor Preston Durant's tragic death in a wreck. Oh, it was awful! His car stalled on the railroad tracks! After that, it got around that she had asked Mrs. Lander if she could write 'practice' obits for some of us. Apparently, something about it got her juices flowing. I only hope she doesn't drag our senior yearbook out of mothballs again."

Locke furrowed his brow. "Why? Would that be a bad thing?"

But the doorbell prevented Miss Voncille from answering his question. "Ah, there they are at last! Shall we go greet them and get the afternoon started?"

Unfortunately, Mamie Crumpton bounded through the front door out of the brisk weather with the yearbook of the Cherico High School Class of 1960 and her sister in tow. "This is why we're late," she explained, foregoing so much as a hello while brandishing the worn-looking annual over her head like some sort of sports trophy. "We got halfway over here and I realized I had forgotten to bring it. So I said, 'Marydell, we'll just have to turn around and go back.' "

Somehow Miss Voncille managed a careful, polite smile. "Why, of course you had to."

"I didn't know if you knew that two more of us had died last month," Mamie added, while Locke took the ladies' coats and hung them up in the hall closet. Then he gestured toward the long green sofa as both Crumpton sisters took their seats and settled in.

Miss Voncille sighed wearily, remaining standing beside Locke. "Who bought the farm this time?"

Mamie puffed herself up as usual and rattled off all the pertinent information. "It was Dexter Thomas Warrick, Jr. He and his family moved away a long time ago. I believe he was a basketball player back then. But a few weeks ago, he succumbed to a heart attack. I think some of these tall people have trouble with their hearts."

"I vaguely remember him," Miss Voncille said. "It continually amazes me how you keep up with all this. You must have runners all over the country."

Mamie was clearly proud of herself, completely missing the humor. "Oh, I do have my methods."

"So who was the second person to leave us?" Miss Voncille continued. "And then Locke will take your drink orders."

"Well, it was Katherine Anna Wilson. I think she went by Katie, or was it Kathy? I forget which. Anyway, she won Miss Home Ec her senior year. The obit didn't say what did her in—just that she passed away among family and friends. She wasn't in our crowd, though."

Miss Voncille was scowling in a genuine attempt to conjure her up. "Heavy girl?"

"Very much so. She wore dresses that looked like she'd wrapped a fabric bolt around herself. I wouldn't be surprised in the least if she won Miss Home Ec because she ate everything she cooked in class. That always made the teacher look good, you know."

Then it was time for the ritual. Mamie opened the yearbook and gestured to her classmate while locating the senior pictures of the dear departed. Both Locke and Miss Voncille moved around behind the sofa to take them in. "There they are. Both on the same page in the W's. Don't they look young as spring deer? Weren't we all back then? Ah, for the good ole days!"

Miss Voncille couldn't resist. "Yes, indeed! When we were all alive, each and every one of us!"

Locke gave Miss Voncille a playful nudge. "Let's see you, Voncille. Come on, Mamie, find her for me."

Mamie flipped a few pages and zeroed in on the picture with her index finger. "There you have her. Miss Voncille Deloris Nettles. I've always said you were a looker, Voncille."

Locke leaned down for a closer look and wagged his brows. "That you were, my dear. Of course, you still are in my book. Is Deloris a family name with that unusual spelling?"

"I doubt it. My parents just liked to be different. He was Walker Nettles, and she was Annis Favarel, and I have no idea where their first names came from." Miss Voncille finally exhaled dramatically, having survived the ordeal of Morbid Mamie and the yearbook yet another time. "Well, we've paid our proper respects now. Locke, why don't you see what the ladies will have, I'll get out the card table, and we'll play some bridge."

For the first time in their fledgling relationship, Miss Voncille and Locke were having a disagreement over something other than picking through the party nuts or which wine to have with dinner. A somewhat trying two hours of bidding, finessing, and drawing trumps had crawled by, but from Miss Voncille's point of view it had all been worth it. She'd gotten the freshly departed Crumpton sisters to agree to attend the *Mockingbird* meeting and even check out a few books in the interim for lagniappe. Mission more than accomplished.

"You were as obvious as they were clueless," Locke kept insisting. "It's true that I've never been your bridge partner, so I have no point of comparison. But I find it hard to believe that someone could renege, mismanage trumps, and overbid so many times in the same rubber. I wonder if they were wise to you but let you play on like that anyway. A win is a win is a win."

He began imitating her voice and gestures. " 'Oh, my goodness, I thought I had completely drawn trumps. Where did that come from, Mamie, you clever rascal!' And, 'Did I double your contract, Mamie? I wonder what I could have been thinking of with the hand I had?' And my absolute favorite, 'I shouldn't have bid a slam in no-trump without a stopper in spades.' Mamie ran the entire spade suit against us in that one. The only good thing about it was that I was dummy and didn't have to stay in the room to watch all the carnage."

"I had no idea you were such a sore loser," Miss Voncille said, watching him fold her card table and put it away in the hall closet.

He had an impish grin on his face when he emerged from his task. "And I had no idea you would go to such lengths to stay on the good side of your Morbid Mamie and her mousy little sister who only opened her mouth to bid. At least come clean and admit you played like a college student on a drinking binge."

She put her hands on her hips and turned her nose up. "I never drank when I was in college. Besides, what happened here this afternoon was only a game."

"Which you won, despite appearances to the contrary."

She finally gave in. "Very well, then, Locke Linwood. That was indeed the most atrocious rubber of bridge I've ever played in my life. But it got results, didn't it? I know Mamie Crumpton like the back of my hand. She loves nothing more than feeling like she's on top of the world, alive and kicking, while the rest of us are dropping like flies and playing beginner's bridge. This was the perfect afternoon for her—two senior pictures to shed crocodile tears over and two bridge opponents to trounce—with a little help, of course. Besides, it's all just part of my ongoing transformation from semi-curmudgeon to sweet little old lady."

Locke put his hand around Miss Voncille's tidy waist and gently pulled her toward him. "So, do you think they'll keep their word on everything?"

"Oh, I expect so. Even if you and I have to lose another

rubber or two of bridge to keep them happy and on track. And I also think explaining to them why they might be without a library soon didn't hurt one bit."

When Maura Beth walked into Connie's seafood extravaganza at her lake house the following Sunday, there was already a respectable crowd milling around, some with drinks, others with plates of grilled catfish and shrimp scampi in hand. In fact, the decibel level of the chatter was so high that Diana Krall's velvety recording of "It Could Happen to You" could barely be recognized.

"What a warm, rustic atmosphere!" Maura Beth exclaimed, as Connie welcomed her into what could only be described as the greatest of great rooms. It occupied the core of the house and sported rustic beams across a shed roof ceiling that was at least twenty feet high. The focal point of one wall was an enormous Tennessee sandstone fireplace, complete with crackling flames on this chilly autumn evening, while the other wall featured at least twenty framed snapshots of the most impressive fish Douglas had caught on Lake Cherico or in the Tennessee River itself. There was no denying that this was the lodge of a sportsman, definitely lacking a woman's touch, and Douglas quickly spirited Maura Beth away for a guided tour of his trophies.

"Now this one here is a thirty-one-pound striped bass I caught on a white spinner," he explained. "White does it for me every time. I just haven't had much luck with the yellow or the blue baits."

"That certainly is a huge fish," Maura Beth said, trying her best to sound interested.

"And this one next to it I caught on a pig 'n' jig," he continued. "Bet you've never heard of a lure like that."

"It sounds like a canapé."

Douglas snickered. "It does, doesn't it? Actually, there is a piece of pork rind on the hook."

"Now, Douglas," Connie said, stepping up to rescue her friend, "let's give Maura Beth a chance at the real canapés, shall we? She can come back and gawk at your fish collection later on. It's not going to swim away. You've seen to that." On the way over to the buffet table, Connie continued her rant. "Believe me, he would have told you how much every single one of those fish weighed and what bait he used to catch them all, if I had let him."

But Maura Beth was in no mood for criticism. "He's just proud of his pastime, that's all. Your husband is a sweetie, and you know it."

"Well, I have to admit, I always know where he is—out on *The Verdict* or at The Marina Bar and Grill every day. Meanwhile, you'll be pleased to hear that we have some of Douglas's family down from Brentwood joining the neighbors. Matter of fact, here comes someone now I'm sure you'll remember."

From across the room, Susan McShay ambled over with a smile and her cocktail in hand. "Surprise!" she exclaimed, giving Maura Beth a quick hug. "Paul and I decided we couldn't miss this. Connie's been talking it up so much."

They were all joined immediately by a robust young man who was in the midst of treating one of the shrimp on his plate as finger food. "You just have to be Maura Beth with that red hair and those blue eyes," he said. "Excuse me while I clean up my act."

She laughed while he found a spot on a nearby coffee table for his plate and wiped his hands on a napkin.

Then Susan made the introductions. "Maura Beth, this is my ravenous son and Connie's nephew, Jeremy. He teaches

English at New Gallatin Academy in Nashville, and he's been dying to meet you."

Jeremy extended his hand and said: "I just missed you when you were up in Brentwood before. I was chaperoning a field trip to the Grand Ole Opry, believe it or not. Nothing ties you up like a busload of eleventh-grade boys ogling rhinestones, big hair, and big—"

Maura Beth grinned at his widening eyes, while she stepped in to rescue him. "Voices?"

He laughed good-naturedly. "Did I mention I teach English and am awfully good at choosing my words carefully?"

"Well, if you'll excuse us, Susan and I will keep on circulating," Connie put in, giving them both a naughty little wink. "Please, you two eat and drink as much as you want."

Once Maura Beth had helped herself to a plate and a drink, and Jeremy had refreshed both of his, they found a couple of seats near the fire and settled in.

"Mom told me what you're trying to do with the book club down here, and I just couldn't pass up the opportunity to meet you. *To Kill a Mockingbird* is my all-time favorite Southern novel," he was saying after a swig of his beer. "I don't think it can ever be reviewed enough, and I make all my students do a term paper on it. It's a rite of passage in my classroom. Sometimes I describe it as a rite of passage for all true Southerners."

Maura Beth was content to let him do most of the talking while she took him in from head to toe. He was tall and dark haired like his father but had more of his mother's softer features, and she liked the fact that he enjoyed his food so much. However, he was no Stout Fella. Her assessment was that he was just about the right size—someone who might have leapt off one of the pages of her cherished journal of wishes.

". . . and it's so unusual for a novel to become an instant classic," Jeremy continued. "But *Mockingbird* was the rare exception. The problem now in teaching it is that we're so far away from that era of turmoil, and so much is taken for granted that was once a great struggle. There are still issues to resolve, of course, and I try to point them out. Getting my students to understand the novel in the context of its time is a tremendous challenge, but it's one I'm determined to meet."

Maura Beth finally put in a word. "Yes, I know what you mean. I think I'd like to make that the focal point of our big meeting in a couple of weeks. I want people to reflect upon the changes in the South since Harper Lee wrote the book. Of course, I wasn't around during all that civil rights turbulence."

"Same here, and I'm afraid my students are far more interested in technology than political history."

Maura Beth rolled her eyes and tilted her head. "Oh, yes. The cell phone thing, etcetera. It's all we can do to keep patrons from talking up a storm in the library. They hide back in the stacks and think we won't hear them gossiping and carrying on with their friends. It's so distracting. We have signs up everywhere, but they might as well be runes."

"Yep, those ringtones still go off now and then in my classroom despite the threat of detention. I'm afraid it's an addiction for some people."

"Sometimes I wonder what the future of communicating through books will be with all this electronic instant gratification," Maura Beth added. "There are those who feel that some readers will always want to hold a bound copy in their hands—something that they can put on a shelf and hand down to their children as part of our cultural heritage. And then there's the doomsday scenario which always favors books."

"Tell me about it."

"It's the one where if civilization falls apart and there's no technology left, you can still read a book lying in the grass munching berries or sitting up in a tree eating a banana."

"Never heard that one before," he said, tossing his head back as he laughed.

"That's because I just made it up. I have some other scenarios, too."

Now it was his turn to listen to her meanderings, and there was nothing but admiration on his face when she finished. "You really are a dyed-in-the-wool librarian, aren't you?"

"Guilty. I give my mother full credit for encouraging my love affair with books. She took me to the Covington Library when I was six and made me think summer reading was the only way a kid could have fun. That, licking cherry Popsicles to get a red tongue, and playing in the sprinkler to cool off."

The two of them kept probing, tackling various pop culture issues of the day and finding that they were in agreement for the most part. They would have preferred to be left alone entirely, but no matter where they moved throughout the great room, there was someone to hug or a hand to shake and always an introduction to be made.

"Jeremy, I'd like you to meet my friend, Periwinkle Lattimore," Maura Beth began, just as they had grown slightly uncomfortable from the warmth of the fireplace and claimed a couple of chairs farther away. "She runs the most successful restaurant in town, and if you haven't already, you must try her tomato aspic next time you go to the buffet table. They're those round red things that jiggle when you put them on your plate. But believe me, they're beyond delicious."

After a firm handshake, Periwinkle said, "Your Aunt Connie was thoughtful enough to throw this shindig on a Sunday. That's my only day off from The Twinkle." Then she leaned in to Maura Beth. "Oh, by the way, I've come up with the catchiest new slogan for my advertising, and I'm having it printed on the next batch of flyers, along with announcing

Mr. Place as my pastry chef. How does, 'Eat at The Twinkle—The Restaurant of the Stars,' sound to you?"

"Love it. Ties everything up neatly!" Maura Beth exclaimed. "Your decorations, the star quality of your food. It's a winner!"

"Next time I'm down, I'll have to give your restaurant a try," Jeremy added. "Maybe the weekend of the *Mockingbird* review."

Maura Beth's delight was unrestrained. "You'd come all the way from Nashville for that? Of course, I'm sure you'd be a wonderful addition to the discussion with your teaching skills and knowledge of literature."

"Wouldn't miss it, especially now that I've met the moderator."

Periwinkle gave him a thumbs-up and Maura Beth a wink on the sly. "Well, if you kids will excuse me, I'm starving. So I'm headed over to that seafood spread to see what kind of damage I can do."

No sooner had she left, however, than Connie began ushering over some of her neighbors for an introductory chat. Predictably, Maura Beth put the opportunities to good use.

"You and your husband must come and visit me at the library sometime, Mrs. Milner," she advised one couple, mustering every ounce of her charm. "I'm sure we can find you something of interest to put on your card. You do have one, don't you?"

The stylish matron hemmed and hawed. "You know, I—well, I believe I let mine expire. I'll have to check."

Maura Beth continued to press. "No problem, if it did. We'll get you a new one, and you'll show it next time you go to The Twinkle—oh, you do enjoy The Twinkle, don't you?"

"Why, yes, I think it's marvelous. I especially like all those stars spinning around and dangling from the ceiling. And the food is delicious."

"Those mobiles are creative, aren't they? You know, the owner, Periwinkle Lattimore, is here tonight," Maura Beth continued. "Anyway, next time you go there, you can present your library card and get two-for-one drinks or half off your dessert. And with the new pastry chef Periwinkle just hired, you'll have at least a dozen new scrumptious selections to choose from."

Mrs. Milner's eyes widened as she turned to her husband and smiled. "What a clever idea, George. We must take advantage of it!"

When the next couple confessed that they had seen *To Kill a Mockingbird* at the theater many years ago but had never bothered to read the book, Maura Beth was prepared. "Mr. Brimley, I don't know if I'd say that the movie was just as good as Harper Lee's novel, but it did take top honors in Hollywood. And I have several posters of Gregory Peck as Atticus Finch to remind myself of that illustrious fact. Meanwhile, I'd love to have you and your wife attend our review at the library, have something delicious to eat, and give us your opinions on the subject in general. Connie's left a stack of flyers over by the buffet table with all the information."

During the lull that followed, Jeremy excused himself when he spotted his mother energetically motioning to join her across the way. Meanwhile, Miss Voncille and Locke Linwood showed up, spilling the good news about the Crumpton sisters and the bumbling bridge game that had won them over.

"As Locke has been reminding me constantly," Miss Voncille explained, "I was completely, but I trust not transparently, incompetent in my play. I've never had such a good time losing."

"Excellent work," Maura Beth said, shaking her hand vigorously. "As I keep telling my clerks, nothing less than standing room only will do for The Cherry Cola Book Club this time around."

"Locke and I are getting an awfully good feeling about this," Miss Voncille replied. "Everyone in the club is certainly doing their part." And then they were off to join the crowd at the buffet table.

But it was when Jeremy finally returned from the visit with his mother that Maura Beth realized the evening would end up being about far more than the library's future.

"Mom wanted a blow-by-blow of how it was going with you," he told her. "She said she was getting tired of trying to read our lips and body language from a discreet distance. Typical mother, huh?"

Maura Beth flashed a smile and couldn't help batting her eyelashes coyly. "And what did you tell her?"

"I said that I wanted very much to see you again and that I hoped you felt the same way. And I didn't mean just for the *Mockingbird* review."

At first Maura Beth said nothing, playing at building the suspense, but she couldn't sustain it for long. "When you have a weekend free of field trips, please give me a call. I think I'd like to discuss everything under the sun with you."

Then they both just stood there, locking eyes and letting that and their smiles do all the talking.

Becca's contribution to promoting The Cherry Cola Book Club had been going splendidly in the weeks since the brainstorming in Brentwood, even if it was a constant hassle to keep Stout Fella focused on the over-the-air role he had been assigned. This particular frosty October morning was no exception.

"Just one more week on the air, sweetheart," she was saying

to him as they enjoyed their healthful breakfast of cereal, fresh fruit, yogurt, and coffee at the kitchen table.

He glanced at his watch and groaned. "Why couldn't you have gotten you an afternoon radio show? I'm so tired of getting up at six to get to the station on time."

"It's part of the price you have to pay for being a radio personality," she quipped, after swallowing a spoonful of her Cheerios and sliced bananas. "And you, my dear husband—minus all that weight you've lost so far—are helping my program and Maura Beth's library at the same time. You can catch up on your sleep later, and, believe me, I'll see to it that you do."

He leaned back in his chair and briefly glanced down at his significantly reduced girth, the result of the nutrition regimen and exercise program that had been prescribed for him before he'd come home from Nashville over a month ago. "It still seems like apples and oranges to me. I mean, a Pulitzer Prize–winning novel and weight loss don't exactly go together. Unless, you get so caught up in reading it that you forget to eat."

Becca took a sip of her coffee and chuckled softly. "That's a cute idea for a diet. And who knows—it just might work. But you've finished *To Kill a Mockingbird* now, and you said you really enjoyed it."

"Yeah, it's hard to imagine that things were really like that at one time. Kinda opens your eyes."

Becca pointed her index finger in his general direction. "Now you've got it. That's what Maura Beth wants us to concentrate on during the meeting. How much things have changed here in the South since the novel came out. So if one of my listeners comes up to you and compliments you on sticking with my downsizing program, you just shake up the bottle and get all bubbly about The Cherry Cola Book Club."

She swallowed more Cheerios and continued, "Now, have you gone over this morning's script yet?"

He dug into his pocket and pulled out a sheet of paper. "Yes, ma'am. If you'd like to rehearse it with me right now, your Stout Fella aims to please."

She put down her cup, glanced at her own copy on the table, and gave him the go-ahead with a nod. "That's more like it. Okay, we'll skip over my intro—yada, yada, yada. 'And how are we feeling this morning, Stout Fella?' "

He began a line reading that was short on enthusiasm but technically correct. "Why, hello there, Miz Becca Broccoli! I'm feeling on top a' the world, mostly due to your downsizing regimen. So, what delicious recipe are we gonna fix up today for all the good folks listening out there in our beloved Greater Cherico?"

"This one's a real crowd pleaser. How does a honey mustard turkey burger strike you?"

His energy level picked up a tad bit, if only because it was difficult to deliver the next line without sounding excited. "Bam! Pow! It knocks me out! But here's the big question: Is it a lot of trouble to prepare?"

"That's the beauty of it. It's quick and easy and guaranteed to help get and keep you in shape. By the way, Stout Fella, I know our listeners will want to know how many pounds you've dropped since we started you on our 'Downsizing with Comfort Food' regimen."

At last, his sincerity broke through. "Twenty big ones and counting in a little more than five weeks, and I have to say, I don't miss an ounce."

"Wow! That's quite an achievement. But my Stout Fella has also been improving his mind. As I've been telling you, he's been reading *To Kill a Mockingbird* for the November 6th, seven-o'clock meeting of The Cherry Cola Book Club in the library. And now he's finished it and ready to review it with his fellow Chericoans."

"Yes, I am, and I just wanted to say how much fun I've had getting back into reading. You can, too, by using your library card. Let's shake hands, have something good to eat, and talk about it on November 6th, why don't we?"

Becca gave him a thumbs-up for the enthusiasm he was finally showing. "Great suggestion, Stout Fella. But for now, why don't we get those turkey burgers started by listing all the ingredients you'll need? First, of course, you'll want to pick up some lean ground turkey at your supermarket. Be sure it's fresh, and remember to leave time to thaw it if you buy it frozen. You want your meat to be pliable when you form your patties. Next, some seasoned salt, pepper, paprika, bread crumbs, honey mustard—"

Stout Fella's cell phone suddenly buzzed on the kitchen counter, and he jumped up to answer it, cutting short their rehearsal. Despite the early hour, Becca knew it would be pointless to continue. He was talking to whoever was on the line in his real-estate, negotiating voice that had returned full force scarcely a week after his hospitalization.

But at least she had gotten him to take all his medications regularly, chew his food more slowly, get more rest, and go for those thirty-minute walks the doctor had recommended. Leaving nothing to chance or indifference anymore, she had wisely chosen to accompany him so it wouldn't feel so much like work; and she'd dropped a couple of pounds herself in the process.

"I don't care who that was at this ungodly hour or how close you are to a deal," Becca admonished after he had hung up, clearly on one of his negotiating highs. "You and I are still due at the studio in twenty-five minutes."

"Yes, ma'am," he answered. "Can't disappoint my public. And for the record, I'm nowhere close to a deal yet."

She finished her last bite of cereal and gave him a warm smile. "As long as you take your time."

He returned to the last of his yogurt and then looked up with a quizzical expression. "Do you think all these plugs you've been giving the book club will actually work?"

"Judging by the e-mails I've been getting, I have to say it looks promising. Some of my listeners say they'll drop by and see what all this hoopla is about. But one lady said she didn't know the library was still open. That's not good. I'm not about to tell Maura Beth about that one. So my opinion is that we can't plug away at this enough."

In the weeks leading up to November 6, no one in the club worked harder at promoting the *Mockingbird* event than Maura Beth did. Picking up on her theme of an under-the-radar political campaign, she explored every nook and cranny of Cherico with her flyers and unflagging charm. She was out of the library more than she was in, but the ever-dependable Renette always covered for her beautifully, and the small cadre of loyal patrons never knew the difference.

On one of her appointments at her trendy salon, Cherico Tresses, Maura Beth talked up a storm to her tall, blond stylist with the edgy, geometric cut, Terra Munrow, after getting permission to leave a stack of flyers on the faux-marble front counter. To be sure, this was not your grandmother's beauty parlor, given over largely to henna and blue rinses. The clients were mostly younger women, many of them single and therefore still searching for a suitable partner. Perhaps, Maura Beth reasoned, a decent percentage of them might also be readers.

"My goodness," Terra told her favorite customer as she applied a towel to her dripping-wet red hair. "I've never seen you so excited before. You haven't talked that much about the library since I started styling you, but now you can't seem to stop. This book club must be a real big deal."

Maura Beth waited for the towel to come off and then kept at it. "Now, Terra, I've heard you say many times that you just love those Wednesday night potluck dinners at the Methodist church. We've got some delicious dishes at our book club, too. But you also told me once that you liked to read romance novels. I remember telling you to check out our selection at the library, but you've never come in."

Terra exhaled and began combing out Maura Beth's hair. "My schedule is so hectic. But, you know what, I think I'll come in on my day off and check something out. You're one of my best tippers. I owe you the courtesy."

"And what about the book club?"

Terra giggled as she took her scissors in hand. "Why not? Truth is, I used to read a lot more than I do now. Then my grandmother kinda made me feel guilty about reading romance novels all the time. She claimed those covers with the shirtless men and the women spilling out of their bras, as she so graphically put it, were bad news, and they would rot my mind."

"Bodice rippers and lusty busties."

Terra jerked her head and blinked. "What?"

"In the library business that's what we call the books you just described," Maura Beth explained, enjoying herself thoroughly.

"That's news to me. I just liked them for the fantasy of it all."

But by the time Maura Beth had walked out of the salon freshly coiffed, she was reasonably certain that Terra Munrow would resume her career as a reader and maybe even join the book club as a bonus.

On another occasion, Maura Beth was equally effective proselytizing at The Cherico Market, where she already had her flyer tacked to the community bulletin board just inside the automatic sliding doors. But she wanted to go a step further and decided to go all out with the portly but affable manager, James Hannigan, who had special-ordered many holiday food items for her over the years. She also began to wonder if the relatively sparse use of the library might just be on her more than she cared to admit when she realized she had never once invited Mr. Hannigan to patronize her library. Well, it was way past time to do it.

"Mr. Hannigan," she began one afternoon, seated in his office overlooking the aisles filled with shoppers and their carts below. "I wanted to ask you about your P.A. system, if you don't mind."

"Of course I wouldn't mind. What did you want to know? Is the music too loud? I realize it sounds like elevator music," he replied, clearly puzzled.

"Oh, no. The music is just fine. Just wondering if you'd be willing to use the P.A. to help my library," she told him. "You already know about The Cherry Cola Book Club because you've been generous enough to let me post my flyer here. But I'd like to ask you to go a step further. Would it be out of line for me to request that someone in the store read the flyer to the shoppers several times a day over the intercom?"

Mr. Hannigan raised his eyebrows but looked more amused than anything else. "As in, 'Attention, shoppers!' That sort of thing?"

Maura Beth matched his pleasant expression and lighthearted tone of voice. "Any way you wanted to handle it would be fine with me. We're just trying to let everyone know about our next meeting because we need a healthy attendance. Frankly, the future of the library could be at stake."

"I had no idea," he said, his demeanor darkening considerably. "But let's just put it this way, Miz Mayhew. You're one of my best customers, particularly around holiday time, so if you think these announcements over the P.A. would do you some good, then let's go ahead and start 'em right away."

"That's very generous of you, Mr. Hannigan. I can't tell you how much it means to me," she answered, handing over another of her flyers. But she wasn't finished yet. "And maybe at the tail end of the announcement about the book club meeting, you could mention to the customers that flyers were available at the checkout counters?"

He laughed big, his entire body shaking for a brief moment. "You're as tough-nosed as one of my route salesmen, Miz Mayhew. But in a delightful way. Don't worry, I'd be happy to help you out here."

"I couldn't ask for more than that. Except maybe your attendance, too."

He cut her off with a playful wink. "I'll see what I can do about juggling my schedule. I'll even talk to the wife." Then he pushed a notepad and pen across the desk in front of her. "Meanwhile, as long as you're here, you might as well give me your special-order list for Thanksgiving and Christmas since they're not very far away. I assume you're in the market for another free-range turkey?"

She smiled warmly and began writing. "Among other things. It's the time of year I like to splurge."

"We'll get everything to you as usual," he added. "I also have something I'd like to share with you. Most everyone here at the store knows you—all the cashiers and the clerks, the deli people, too. You're one of our favorite customers, and we have a special name for you."

She momentarily abandoned her list and caught his impish gaze. "Don't tell me. I bet I can guess."

"Go ahead, then."

"Something to do with crackers?"

"You got it. You're the Peanut Butter Cracker Lady."

They both had a good laugh, and Maura Beth revealed everything about Mr. Putzel and his behavior.

"I'll share that with the store, Miz Mayhew. Maybe everybody that works for The Cherico Market will show up for your book club meeting."

"I've heard rumors from a certain source," Councilman Sparks was saying to Chunky Badham and Gopher Joe Martin, as the three of them gathered in his office for a last-minute strategy session the day before the *Mockingbird* meeting. "Of course, I'll be attending the book club to-do as usual. But I want both of you working that library full-time tomorrow night, too. It shouldn't be a problem for you. There'll be plenty of food to eat and lots of folks to talk to. What I want you to be on the lookout for is where people are actually from. It should be easy enough to find out if they live here in Cherico or somewhere else. We need to see if these rumors are true that Miz Mayhew may be bringing in out-of-towners to pump up her numbers and give us a false impression of the library's popularity. Not that we'd be fooled."

Chunky frowned. "What about license plates?"

"What about them?"

"Should we inspect all the parked cars and see if there are any from different states?"

Councilman Sparks took a moment and then cleared his throat. "I want you to stay in the library to circulate, Chunky. There's no point in your roaming the streets at night. Someone may think you're about to steal their car. Besides, a license plate is nowhere near as conclusive as a direct question."

"What about if I ask them if that car with the Alabama plate outside belongs to them?" Chunky continued.

Councilman Sparks was unable to keep from rolling his eyes. "Again, not as direct as asking them if they live in Alabama. Or Tennessee, or anywhere else in Mississippi, for that matter. Either they live in Cherico, or they don't. Either they're regular library users, or this is just a bunch of smoke and mirrors on the part of Miz Mayhew and her fellow travelers."

Chunky busied himself writing things down, while Gopher Joe entered the fray. "What kind of rumors you been hearing?"

"Oh, that this book club meeting has gotten to be the talk of the town. All the little people seem to be excited about it. Also, that there might be a bus coming down from Nashville. I have to hand it to Miz Mayhew. She doesn't give up easily, men. She's been out there beating the bushes."

"Can we eat as much as we want?" Chunky said, having finished his note-taking duties.

"Yes, Chunky, you can go for seconds and thirds if you like. Just remember to also use your mouth for a few questions. Listen, I don't want you two going around frightening people or making them think they're being investigated or something. For God's sake, try to be subtle."

"Gotcha!" Gopher Joe exclaimed, while Chunky settled for nodding his head obediently.

Councilman Sparks dismissed his cohorts and then buzzed his new secretary in the outer office. "That'll be all for today, Lottie. See you on Monday morning bright and early."

"Yes, sir," she answered promptly.

He could picture Mrs. Lottie Howard throwing on her warm coat, padding down the hall and out into the chilly weather. She was a pleasant enough woman, certainly more animated than Nora Duddney had ever thought about being, and she had come highly recommended from friends. But she was also plain, middle-aged, prone to be forgetful, and addicted to abbreviating his messages with cryptic abandon. Above all else, she was a far cry from the first impression that Maura

Beth Mayhew and that wild red hair of hers would have made on anyone walking through his office door.

This was a tough one to take on the chin; firing the listless but reasonably efficient Nora Duddney only to end up with someone who had turned out to be quirky, obstinate, and a hundred other adjectives no businessman ever wanted to deal with in his daily routine.

13

Friends of the Library

The weather decided to cooperate on the day that had been so long in coming. To be sure, it was chilly the way early November often is, but there was no threat of rain to give people an excuse for staying inside their homes and not venturing out in "all that stuff." Maura Beth was happy to have at least one given amid so many unknowns. For instance, would all of Connie's lake house neighbors make an appearance as they had said they would? Would the Crumpton sisters renege after their tainted bridge victory? How many of Periwinkle's customers who had taken flyers would be inspired either to get a library card or attend the potluck and review? What about Becca's diligent radio promotion? Or the many businesses Maura Beth had visited personally to stir up interest?

Then there was the New Gallatin Academy field trip that Jeremy had thrown together over the last couple of days. He was still waiting on last-minute approval from the headmaster. There was also some concern on the part of a few of the parents about the overnight expenses they would incur and the matter of the school being willing to share those with them. If the final decision went Jeremy's way, twenty-one schoolboys from Nashville would be attending the *Mockingbird* event as part of his inspirational "Living the Classics in the Real World" program.

In fact, Maura Beth was a nervous wreck all morning waiting for Jeremy's phone call. She paced around her purple apartment holding her journal in her hand, having already revisited page twenty-five three different times. She truly believed that this was the most important juncture of her life to date.

When the phone finally rang, she jumped like an armadillo in highway traffic and picked up the receiver in the kitchen with great trepidation. "Hello?" she managed, her face looking as if she were tiptoeing around a coiled snake.

But it wasn't the voice she was hoping to hear. "Hey, it's me," Periwinkle said. "I've got good news. Mr. Place is bringing his mother, Ardenia, with him tonight. She's delightful. I treated them both to dinner a few days after I hired him."

"I'll look forward to meeting her, then."

"How are you holding up, honey?"

Maura Beth knew better than to play games with her friend. "I'm about to lose it waiting for Jeremy to call me about the bus trip. I thought you might be him when you called."

"Sorry about that. But you just listen to me. You told me that you were trying to make the transition from a Melanie to a Scarlett right after that first club meeting. So you be strong and don't fade into the wallpaper. That's strictly for wallflowers."

Maura Beth managed a much-needed chuckle. "Thanks for the reminder. You're the best."

Another hour passed and still no call from Jeremy. It was all she could do to keep from dialing him up, but she focused on Periwinkle's advice instead. "If you can't sit still for this little detail, how are you going to manage the entire evening when it rolls around?" she told herself out loud as she stood in front of her full-length mirror.

Then, another phone call, producing another spurt of adrenaline. This time it was Becca.

"You won't believe this. I'm having unexpected trouble with Stout Fella and his wardrobe," she explained, her exasperation flowing through the line.

Maura Beth briefly held the receiver away from her face and then frowned. "What do you mean?"

"He's acting like a prima donna today. I want him to wear the new three-piece suit I just bought him. Of course, all his old clothes just hang on him. Anyway, he wants to wear his old cowboy clothes from back when he went out line dancing three times a week at The Marina Bar and Grill. He had all of them taken in by a seamstress down at Hodge's Department Store without even telling me. He thinks it'll show off his new athletic frame better. I reminded him that he was still very much a married man, and he said he was just doing it to promote our show more effectively. Really, Maura Beth, there's no one like him."

"Look at it this way, Becca. He'll have plenty of opportunities to wear that suit when he negotiates all those big real-estate deals of his. Meanwhile, why not go ahead and let him be Roy Rogers or Tex Ritter for the evening? Just make sure he doesn't bring a horse into my library. I don't have the budget for the cleanup."

Becca's tension immediately dissolved into laughter. "Maura Beth, you always have the right answer for everything. Cowboy shirt, boots, and jeans, it is, then. And I'll make him keep Trigger in the stable."

They both chuckled, said good-bye, and hung up, but Maura Beth stared at the phone for a minute or two with something that felt a lot like resentment. Was Jeremy ever going to call?

Finally, he did, and Maura Beth could tell by the tone of his "Hello, sorry this has taken so long," that the news was not going to be good. "The majority of the parents thought it was too expensive," he continued, "and the headmaster said we just didn't have the money to send one of the buses down there for—his words here—a 'glorified book report.' Translation: *That* kind of travel money is reserved for the football team's road games."

"I'm so disappointed," Maura Beth said. "We're not off to a good start with our attendance."

"Maybe if I'd thought of it a little sooner and had more time to talk to the parents. Anyway, there is a bit of good news in all this. Three of the families want their boys to attend. So they've ponied up for hotel rooms over in Corinth, and I'll be driving down in a few hours with three of my students and one set of parents as chaperones. I know six is a far cry from twenty-one, but it's better than nothing."

There was a hint of relief in Maura Beth's sigh. "You're absolutely right. You went out on a limb with this ambitious project, but we'll have a good time no matter how many people show up."

After Maura Beth hung up, she paced around the apartment for a while, unable to sit still and calm herself. Having a good time was hardly the goal here. That could easily be done at any bar or restaurant. So much more was at stake, and she began to doubt the effectiveness of her untiring campaign with many of the local businesses. True, the first person had yet to walk through the door of the library, but she couldn't help projecting how many actually would. Numbers flew out of her head and swirled before her eyes. Twelve? Too few. Fifteen? Still not enough. Twenty? The beginning of respectability. Thirty? Was that even possible?

No matter what Periwinkle had said, it was hard work becoming a Scarlett.

* * *

The hours leading up to seven o'clock were as unsettling as the original ultimatum from Councilman Sparks had been several months earlier. Maura Beth spent most of the time in the library lobby, arranging tables, chairs, and posters with Renette Posey and Emma Frost, but no configuration seemed to satisfy her.

"Everything has to be just right," she was telling her clerks after the latest round of musical chairs. "And this isn't it."

Renette walked toward the front door and then turned around, making a frame of her hands. "It's the same semicircle we had last time—only a little bigger. It looks just fine when you first walk in."

But Maura Beth was still shaking her head. "I'm going by instinct here, ladies. Something tells me we need to think even bigger tonight. We only have fifteen folding chairs out there right now. Let's double that, okay? If we have empty seats, we have empty seats. But let's don't get caught scrambling if we're lucky enough to have overflow. It won't look professional, and the last thing I want tonight is to come off like I don't know what I'm doing."

So the three of them dragged more chairs out of the storage closet in the back and began making a double row in front of the podium. Finally, everything was laid out so that it passed muster, and Maura Beth sat down in one of the folding chairs beside her cohorts for a breather. "I've already called everyone who's bringing food and reminded them that they need to be here no later than six-thirty." She consulted her checklist. "Let's see, we have Becca and her grilled chicken breasts with avocado and salsa for those watching their weight; Connie with her fish of the day à la Douglas and *The Verdict,* as she calls it; Miss Voncille and her famous biscuits and green-pepper jelly; Susan McShay with her killer potato salad that she swears by; Periwinkle with éclairs, courtesy of the culinary skills of

Mr. Place; and I'm bringing my sheet cake again. Plus, we'll have Becca's cherry cola punch with lime. I think we're all set."

Momentarily, Emma Frost excused herself and headed home to her family, but Renette remained, and it was apparent to Maura Beth that she had something on her mind. She kept biting her lip and cutting her eyes this way and that but was still saying nothing.

Finally, Maura Beth decided it was time to put her at ease. "Did you have something you wanted to tell me?"

Renette straightened up a bit and exhaled. "Well . . . yes. Maybe it's not so important now that you've said that the bus isn't going to be coming down from Nashville. But the other day, Councilman Sparks came by while you were at lunch, and he asked me how things were going. I could tell he meant the *Mockingbird* meeting, of course. And I told him that everything was fine and that we were hoping for a big crowd."

"So?"

"It's just that I got a little carried away and let it slip about the field trip that Mr. McShay was working up at the last minute and that there might be a bus full of schoolboys coming down to boost our attendance. Even while I was talking to him, I could hear myself doing that singsongy thing in my head—you know, 'I know something that you don't know.' But it seems I couldn't wait to tell him. Then he got this weird expression on his face, and he goes, 'Interesting.' That's when I felt that maybe I had said too much. And then today when you told me that the bus wasn't coming, I thought I might have had something to do with messing things up."

Maura Beth quickly reassured her with a couple of pats on the shoulder. "Believe me, you had nothing to do with it, Renette. Don't worry too much about our illustrious councilman and his sidekicks. It's always been up to us to keep the doors of this library open, and tonight's the night we can make that happen. But in the future, I'd only offer to check out the councilman's books for him—that is, if he ever comes around for that. Nothing else."

Renette gave her boss a grateful smile. "Yeah, I'll remember that next time." Then she hesitated as her expression grew slightly more serious. "There was something else I wanted to tell you. It's strictly good news, though. I've talked two of my girlfriends into coming with me tonight. We've all been rereading *To Kill a Mockingbird* to get ready so we don't come off as a bunch of teenaged airheads. So I just wanted you to know that I'm doing my part."

This time Maura Beth gave her a big hug. "You've always done your part, sweetie. You're the best front desk clerk and assistant I've ever had. But don't tell Emma—you might hurt her feelings."

"No, of course not. Emma's a dear. She's just not a reader."

Then Maura Beth sat back and took a deep breath. "Well, we're just a couple of hours away from our defining moment, I think. I'd like nothing better than to clone myself so I could wish us good luck."

Maura Beth had taken it upon herself to greet people inside the front door of the library, playing the gracious hostess starting around a quarter to seven. It was also going to be her way of keeping an accurate head count for the eventual showdown with Councilman Sparks, who was already sampling the buffet. As it happened, it was Renette and her girlfriends, Deborah Benedict and Liz Trumble, who were the first recipients of her hospitality.

"Help yourself to food and drink over there, young ladies," Maura Beth said after the introductions. "Renette, you'll show them the way, won't you?"

"Of course." Then she leaned in to whisper in Maura Beth's ear. "I see lots of people eating and drinking already."

"Those are all the book club members, a couple of their relatives from Nashville, and the councilmen," Maura Beth whispered back. "Don't get too excited yet."

After another couple of minutes had passed, Jeremy sauntered in with his three New Gallatin Academy students and the parents who were chaperoning.

"Let me introduce these studious young men who would do any teacher proud," he announced. "We have here just champing at the bit to express their literary insights—Mr. Graham Hartley, Mr. Vernon Garner, and Mr. Burke Williams. We also have Burke's parents, Charles and Louise Williams, who are here to enjoy the evening."

Maura Beth made her manners to the contingent, and Jeremy finished all the hoopla with a peck on the cheek for her. "As I told you over the phone, six is better than nothing," he managed out of the corner of his mouth.

She pulled away slightly for her best smile. "You and I will talk later, Mr. Jeremy McShay of New Gallatin Academy."

By five to seven, no one else had appeared, however, and the sweat began to bead across Maura Beth's forehead. Surely the handful of people who had shown up so far were not going to be the extent of the turnout. Perhaps people were caught in traffic. She nearly laughed out loud at that one. What on earth was she thinking? There was no traffic in peaceful little Cherico. Never had been, never would be.

Seven o'clock arrived, and Maura Beth continued to grasp at straws. Maybe the rest were just going to be late. Yes, fashionably late. That had to be the answer.

Then, finally, one minute past seven, more warm bodies. In this case—the Crumpton sisters. They made a grand entrance, indeed, with Mamie leading the way as usual. They were both overdressed for the occasion in floor-length ball gowns and matching clutches—Mamie in gold and Marydell in silver—

giving the unmistakable impression that they had shown up principally to preen and be admired lavishly and often.

"Why, look at all this excitement! I had no idea there'd be so many people here," Mamie began, surveying the lobby and striking a dramatic pose just inside the front door. "I thought this would be more like our 'Who's Who?' meetings. Just a few of us hardy souls with a taste for genealogy and the twists and turns of local history. But Marydell and I are pleased to alter our Sunday evening routine to lend a hand, aren't we, sister dear?"

"Oh, yes," came the answer, along with a predictably weak smile.

Even before Maura Beth had a chance to reply, however, Councilman Sparks stepped up to intercept the sisters by executing a pretentious little bow in front of them and then taking each of them by the arm. "May I have the honor of escorting such a delightful pair of ladies?"

"It seems you've assumed the honor before asking," Mamie fired back. "But exactly where are we going?"

"To the buffet table, perhaps?"

Mamie gently pulled her arm away and looked him straight in the eye. "Durden, I believe I'd like to catch my breath first. Perhaps find a nice seat for the proceedings."

"Then let me at least assist you with that," he continued.

"Enjoy yourselves. Thanks so much for coming!" Maura Beth called out, watching them all move away and shaking her head. She knew quite well that Councilman Sparks was nothing if not deferential to money and social position, particularly when it lived on his street and contributed to his former campaigns.

Then, a trio of women whom Maura Beth did not recognize entered with wide eyes and a hint of confusion in their faces. One was young and slim with her brown hair pulled back in a ponytail, while the other two were matronly and somewhat overweight.

The slim woman spoke up immediately. "Hi, there. I'm Donna Gordon, and these are my friends, Paula Newhouse and Bettye Carter. Sorry we're late. First, we couldn't locate the library, and then we had trouble finding a parking space. We had to walk here from two blocks away."

Maura Beth quickly introduced herself, maintaining a smile while her mind raced. Of course. That was probably why people were showing up late. No off-street parking. And Councilman Sparks had turned her down two years ago in no uncertain terms when she had inquired about creating a parking lot next door.

". . . and we found out about your program because we're all fans of *The Becca Broccoli Show,*" Donna Gordon was saying when Maura Beth focused in again. "Not a show went by when she didn't mention you. We thought it might be something fun and different to do. We hadn't thought about the library in years."

Maura Beth beamed. "Well, I'm so pleased you decided to come. Meanwhile, if you'd like to meet and chat with Becca, she's the short blonde standing next to the big guy in the cowboy boots over at the buffet table. And, yes, that's her Stout Fella in all his downsized glory."

The trio thanked her and headed over, making all sorts of excited noises under their breath.

Maura Beth began to feel more comfortable. The head count had risen to fourteen, not counting the club members and the councilmen. Could a respectable number be far behind?

In fact, a steady succession began to stream in. Terra Munrow was all possessive smiles introducing her boyfriend with the conspicuous but undecipherable tattoo on his neck. "This is my

Ricky I've been telling you about, Maura Beth. Do you have any books he could check out about motorcycles since he's a biker and all?"

"We sure do. I'd be happy to help you locate them any time you come in, Ricky. And by the way, Terra, we probably have a romance novel or two with guys on motorcycles in the plot."

"Doubly righteous!" Ricky exclaimed while raising a fist in the air; then the two of them were off to the buffet table.

But nothing compared with the group of ten led by James Hannigan that showed up next from The Cherico Market. Once again, as Maura Beth had surmised, finding convenient parking spaces had been the culprit for their tardiness.

"We all ended up two streets over. I kept hoping you wouldn't start without us," Mr. Hannigan concluded.

"I wouldn't have dreamed of it."

Then Mr. Hannigan leaned in with another of his friendly winks. "Good. Because we wanted to support our Peanut Butter Cracker Lady at all costs. And it turns out I've got some readers in the store. They just haven't made the time to find their way to the library before. Guess you lit a fire under 'em with your book club to-do."

When The Cherico Market contingent had finally dispersed, Maura Beth realized that the head count was inching toward thirty. They were probably going to need more chairs—and quickly. So she temporarily abandoned her station and hurried across the room to enlist Renette's help.

"Put down your plate for now, sweetie," she told her. "We're going to be scrambling around after all. Quick, think. How many more chairs do we have in the closet?"

Renette squinted for a moment, moving her lips as she counted. "I think six, maybe seven of the folding. Oh, but we have eight more with the soft cushions in the meeting room."

"Good catch!" Maura Beth exclaimed. "I forgot about those."

"If this keeps up, looks like you'll get your standing room only wish," Renette added as they headed toward the closet.

Nor was Maura Beth's urgency unwarranted. At least a dozen more people came through the front door. Among Connie's lakeside neighbors, the Brimleys and the Milners kept their promises to attend. Then Mr. Place walked in with his mother, who was a bit on the fragile side but still had kind, sparkling eyes.

"I'm Ardenia Bedloe," she said to Maura Beth while extending her hand and smiling graciously. "I know you're not confused by that because my son told you all about changing his name, but I just wanted to thank you for introducing him to Miz Lattimore down at The Twinkle."

"Oh, my friend Periwinkle is deliriously happy with all those delicious pastries he makes. His éclairs have been wowing everyone this evening, including myself."

Mr. Place thanked her and then suddenly spotted Miss Voncille across the room. "Mama, I'd like to go speak to someone over by the food table and introduce her to you after all these years. She's the lady standing next to the white-haired gentleman."

Ardenia trained her thick glasses in the direction of his index finger. "Who is she, baby?"

"Miss Voncille Nettles, my history teacher that first year Cherico High was integrated."

"Oh, yes," Ardenia replied, a smile exploding across her face. "I remember now. You liked her best."

"Please go on over and make yourselves at home," Maura Beth added. "I'm sure she'd be delighted to see you both. And help yourselves to the food and drink."

Among the last six or seven people that showed, two more

cited Becca's radio program as their inspiration, while the others credited a flyer from such businesses as The Cherico Market, The Twinkle, Cherico Tresses, or the library itself. Happily, The Cherry Cola Book Club was going to be playing to a full house.

Councilman Sparks took a dim view of the party going on full-blast after he had finished schmoozing the Crumpton sisters. Everyone present was eating, chatting, or laughing the way people do on New Year's Eve or some other carefree occasion. It particularly annoyed him that the library suddenly seemed to have discarded its perennial "just growing mold" personality.

Momentarily, Chunky intruded on his leader's pique. "Man, this sure is a helluva lot a' people in here!"

"It doesn't look good from our point of view," Councilman Sparks replied under his breath, making sure that no one was within earshot. "I'd guess there are between forty and fifty people in this room. We've never had a budget hearing when that many people showed up."

Chunky leaned in and responded in a half-whisper. "I know you told me not to, but I checked out the license plates around the library anyway. Didn't see but a couple from out of state, both from Tennessee. Davidson County, I believe it was. But there was a bunch from other Mississippi counties. I can rattle off the different ones if you want."

"And no bus anywhere to be seen," Gopher Joe added.

"Oh, never mind all that now. Both of you just go get something more to eat and try to mingle."

Something told Councilman Sparks that he had better monitor the situation closely, however, so he kept both of his charges within an approachable radius. As it turned out, his concerns were definitely warranted.

"Hi!" Chunky said, immediately approaching one of

Renette's girlfriends even before he'd helped himself to a plate of food. "What's your name and where do you live?"

The ordinarily extroverted Deborah Benedict shrank visibly from his directness, managing an imitation of a smile. "I might ask the same of you."

"Well, I hope you voted for me. I'm E. A. Badham, one of your city councilmen. But folks call me 'Chunky' most of the time," he continued, while patting his bulging belly. "I guess you can see why."

To her credit, Deborah did not pull away further, but neither did she answer his questions. "Well, then, Chunky, I think you should help yourself to more of this delicious food I'm sampling here. I've seen you make several trips already, if I'm not mistaken."

The lurking Councilman Sparks soon intervened, giving Deborah a nod and a perfunctory smile. "If you'll excuse us for a second, young lady." Then he pulled Chunky aside and lowered his voice. "Change of plans. You and Gopher Joe just concentrate on stuffing your faces. Forget the socializing. I don't know what I was thinking."

There was no denying, however, that most everyone else had the knack of socializing down pat. Especially Maura Beth. From afar, Councilman Sparks watched her flitting around the room with such ease that he actually had to turn away at one point. The library was pulsating with an energy it had never possessed before, and it was all due to the outside-the-box efforts of this unusual woman who just refused to go away. More importantly, it would be difficult to shut down her pride and joy with all this to her credit.

"Are you sure you want to do this?" Maura Beth was saying to Becca. They had managed to slip away into the privacy of the meeting room, closing the door behind them shortly before the actual review was about to begin. "Of course I'd be delighted to have you and Stout Fella here doing cooking demonstrations together every month. We need to get as much activity going in the library as possible."

Becca exhaled and thought one more time about what she had just proposed. "I know it'll help you out. And Stout Fella promised even before he got out of the hospital in Nashville that he'd do his part, too."

Maura Beth gave Becca a thoughtful glance. "So what do you think you should call these meetings?"

Becca took her time before a dramatic intake of air. "How about 'Becca Broccoli in the Flesh'—you know, for those who just can't get enough of the radio show?"

"I certainly like your idea of becoming visible after all those years of just being a voice on the radio."

"You know what gave me the idea?" Becca said, smartly raising an eyebrow. "It was all the conversations I've just had at the buffet table with some of my fans. They kept saying over and over how thrilled they were to see me in the flesh. One of them—I believe her name was Donna—said that putting my face with my voice made me seem all the more real. So I thought, 'Why not meet more of my fans in person and help the library at the same time?' "

Maura Beth was nodding enthusiastically now. "I bet it'll work out great. The only thing I'll need to do is make sure you don't conflict with 'Who's Who?' and Miss Voncille. We don't want to start a turf war, but I have to admit the idea of people fighting over using the library is something I've been wanting for a long time."

Becca smiled pleasantly and then reached over to gently grasp Maura Beth's hand. "There was something else I wanted to say to you. I've been meaning to for a while. You don't know how much it meant to me—and especially Stout Fella—that you came up to Nashville to visit us in the hospital when you did. That entire balloon thing you invented just brightened our days and nights, and we needed something out of the ordinary to get us through it all."

"Oh, it was nothing," Maura Beth insisted, breaking her grip and waving her off. "I think that little trip helped me out as much as it helped you. I needed to clear my head."

"But there was more to it than that," Becca continued. "I was such a mess when Justin had his heart attack and I thought I might lose him. But all of you rallied around me and kept me going. Connie was the reassuring voice of medical authority, and she and Douglas piled me into the backseat of their car and wrapped me up in a blanket of kindness all the way up to Nashville. His brother and sister-in-law in Brentwood were just as soothing to me, and then you inspired all those balloon bouquets. I remember turning to Stout Fella one evening as he was propped up in bed and saying, 'Nothing bad can happen with all these pretty, playful things floating around us. No one's ever sad at a children's party.' "

Then the two women hugged. "That's the sweetest thing anyone's ever said to me," Maura Beth told her. She glanced at her watch and gave a little gasp. "But I think we need to get started. Our big moment has finally arrived."

After Becca had made her initial announcement about the upcoming "In the Flesh" meetings at the library to the delight of her fans, Maura Beth took back the podium and opened the program in earnest.

"I trust all of you have enjoyed plenty of this delicious food, courtesy of various members of The Cherry Cola Book Club," she began after introducing herself. "It's one of the perks you'll enjoy if you join us, which we hope all of you will do. But the time has come for us to tackle our Southern classic novel, *To Kill a Mockingbird,* written by Harper Lee and published in 1960. As everyone surely knows, this was her only work, but it won the Pulitzer Prize for her, and the film version won several Academy Awards, including Best Actor of 1962 for Gregory Peck." She paused to point toward the Gregory Peck posters and waited for a ripple of female sighs and buzzing to dissipate before again consulting her notes.

"For those who are visiting us for the first time, we do things a bit differently here in The Cherry Cola Book Club," she continued. "Anyone can summarize a plot and express emotions like admiration, disapproval, or even indifference as a result. Such is the subjective nature of literature. But we prefer to relate that plot to our own lives or even wider issues. So I'm going to suggest that we discuss *To Kill a Mockingbird* tonight in the context of the changes that have occurred here in our beloved South since its publication. That said, do I have a volunteer to go first?"

Jeremy's hand went up immediately. "If you don't mind, I'd like to propose that one of my students begins this discussion with a poem he wrote right after reading the novel."

"I think that would be a lovely beginning," Maura Beth replied, stepping aside and smiling at the fresh-faced New Gallatin Academy contingent sitting on the front row in their navy blue blazers and red ties.

"Ladies and gentlemen," Jeremy continued while getting to his feet. "I'd like to introduce to you Mr. Burke Williams of Nashville, Tennessee."

There was polite applause as the lanky young man with big ears and a deferential demeanor rose and took his long strides toward the podium.

"Thank you," he began, after taking his notes out of his pocket. "Before I read my poem, I'd like to say a few words. My teacher, Mr. McShay, told our class all about The Cherry Cola Book Club, and I wanted to be here no matter what. I know I'm only sixteen and don't know much about the real world, but after I'd finished reading *To Kill a Mockingbird,* I felt like I at least knew a little something. I live in the new millennium, not in the 1930s when the novel is supposed to take place, or even in the 1960s when it was published; but *To Kill a Mockingbird* was like a time machine for me. It enabled me to understand what life was like for a wrongly accused black man like Tom Robinson. I understood how things worked back then and how easy it was for justice to be swept under the rug. So, this is my poem in honor of what *To Kill a Mockingbird* did for me."

He cleared his throat and looked up from his prepared speech. "I know this part by heart." The audience laughed gently and he acknowledged them with a grateful smile. "Okay. Here goes: 'On *To Kill a Mockingbird*,' by Burke Williams:

The Southern town of ancient birth
Lies prostrate and fervid under summer's sun;
The children of Atticus play in the yard,
Engrossed in the realms of fantasy and fun;
Then the tranquil streets grow frigid with anguish
As a man of color struggles to live
Under the wing of Atticus's justice—
Of all the benevolence one man can give;
The wrath of prejudice flows through the veins
Of those who would try the innocent man;
And here, as o'er earth, life's chances unjust—
Despite brave attempts to fashion a stand;
But yet as the stars on the face of God's sky,
Subtly as sweet scents of roses in bloom,
The town slips again into everyday life,
Forgetting the storm and the tears and the doom."

The polite reception of a few minutes earlier became healthy applause, and the young man blushed, hanging his head at first.

But Jeremy's hand signals urging him to lift his chin had an immediate effect, and Mr. Burke Williams accepted his moment in the sun with an ingratiating, boyish smile.

"That was beautifully done, Mr. Williams!" Maura Beth exclaimed, after he had resumed his seat and the reaction had finally died down. "Your insights show a great deal of maturity."

Before Maura Beth could ask for another volunteer, however, Mr. Place stood up, gently waving his hand. "If you don't mind, Miz Mayhew, I have a little something I'd like to contribute. Could I speak next?"

"Of course, come right on up."

Once he was comfortable behind the podium, Mr. Place caught his mother's eye with a smile and began. "Ladies and gentlemen, although Cherico is my hometown, I didn't know what to expect when I left Memphis after losing my job as a pastry chef at the Grand Shelby Hotel. I'd been working at that for decades and would have retired at it up there, too. But you may have read that the hotel went out of business and was torn down recently. So that brought me back home to live with my mama for a while until I could find another job."

He paused to acknowledge first Maura Beth and then Periwinkle with nods and hand gestures. "I found one a lot quicker than I thought I would, thanks to Miz Mayhew here and Miz Lattimore sitting right there on the front row. In case some of you didn't know, I'm now the pastry chef down at The Twinkle. As we like to say here in the South, 'Y'all drop by and see me sometime, ya hear?' "

A spate of warm laughter erupted, and Mr. Place wagged his brows until it tailed off. "So that brings me to our topic tonight—how things have changed here in our South since *To Kill a Mockingbird* appeared. I saw the movie when I was a boy. That's what I want to talk to y'all about next. It played here in Cherico at the old Starbright Theater on Commerce Street, which as we all know, got torn down a while ago. You have to go somewhere else to see movies these days. At the time, my mama made extra money for us by babysitting for white families, and she'd take me with her now and then. I made friends with the son of one of those families. You good folks might remember the Wannamakers over on Painter Street? Since I got back, I found out they don't live here now."

That produced a buzz of recognition among the crowd, and Mr. Place waited for it to die down. "Anyway, I became good friends with Jamie Wannamaker, who was about my age, and we played together out in his yard, doing things that little boys do together like catching fireflies and hide-and-seek. Then, my Mama saw where *To Kill a Mockingbird* was coming to the Starbright. That was back when the *Daily Cherico* was still in business, and she read an article all about it in the paper. She told me, 'Baby, I'm taking you to see that movie. I believe we both need to see it!' "

Mr. Place paused and smiled thoughtfully, shaking his head at the same time. "I didn't understand at the time why she felt that way. Now, of course, I do. But the world is full of strange coincidences, I've found out. Don't know why they happen, but when they do, there's always a lesson to be learned, it seems. Turns out, the very afternoon my mama took me to see *To Kill a Mockingbird* at the Starbright, Miz Wannamaker decided to take Jamie to see it, too. Back then, everybody bought tickets at the booth in front, but only the white people got to go in that way. The coloreds, as they called us back then, went around to the side door to enter the colored section. Some of you might remember that it was much smaller than the white side, but there was a thin wall separating the two."

Again, there was a ripple of noise throughout the audience. "I'll never forget what happened next. Jamie said to his mother right after he'd spied me, 'Oh, this'll be so much fun. We can all sit together.' And she had to tell him that he couldn't sit with me, and I couldn't sit with him, and you could tell she didn't want to go into an explanation of the white and colored thing—just that there'd be a wall between us. Then Jamie started crying, and he wouldn't stop. It was the strangest thing. I was the one who felt real bad for him. I was the one comforting him. You see, I'd been to the Starbright before, and I knew where the coloreds were allowed to sit. So I said, 'Jamie, maybe we can't sit together, but we can be right next to each other. We just have to pretend the wall isn't there.' And he said, 'But how will we know where to sit if we can't see?' And this is what I came up with. I decided that we'd move slowly along either side of the wall, row by row, and make a pounding noise each time. When we'd both found a seat we liked on the edge, we would pound five times. Fortunately, both our mothers didn't make a fuss and let us do it. But I've never forgotten all the trouble we had to go to just to pretend we were together. Today, anyone can go to the movies over in Corinth or up to Memphis, and they don't give a hoot about anything, not even how much noise you make. I sure wish they'd crack down on that—and the prices you have to pay for candy and popcorn."

That produced some much-needed laughter. Then Mr. Place continued, "So it's my belief that *To Kill a Mockingbird* helped tear down that wall in the theater between the whites and the coloreds. Everywhere else, too. That book and that movie helped to make all the fair play we take for granted now possible, and that's pretty much what I had to say here tonight. That, and it's good to be home again in Cherico with my mama and a great job. And don't forget to come by and sample my pastries at The Twinkle. Even if you're on a diet, treat yourself once in a while."

A round of applause even more vigorous than that for Burke Williams erupted, as Mr. Place headed back to his seat, nodding graciously all the way.

"Thank you for that interesting and heartfelt testimony, Mr. Place!" Maura Beth exclaimed. "So much food for thought along with good food to eat."

Then Miss Voncille stood up. "I think all this has inspired me to contribute something, too."

"By all means, step up. We welcome what you have to say."

Miss Voncille approached the podium with gusto as Maura Beth stepped aside. "I had no idea I would be saying anything tonight. I'd made up my mind just to sit and listen. But as young Mr. Williams was talking, I realized that I, too, had a story to tell. It's about my long career as a schoolteacher here at Cherico High. Looking out into the crowd tonight, I can see many familiar faces that I taught. Only, some of the names seem to have changed. When you were my student, Justin Brachle, Stout Fella had yet to see the light of day. And your wife, Becca Heflin, was a few years away from her alter alias of Becca Broccoli on the radio. Then there's Edward Badham, who now goes by the name of 'Chunky,' I believe; and 'Gopher Joe' sitting right next to him is the former Josephus Martin. Of course, I must point out Councilman Durden Sparks, who decided to leave his name alone."

Everyone mentioned was nodding and chuckling, and Miss Voncille paused briefly for a breath. "But let me not forget Mr. Parker Place, who went by the name of Joe Sam Bedloe when I taught him. He was, in fact, a member of my very first integrated classroom, and a very good student he was."

Mr. Place smiled big at his former teacher and gave her a neat little salute. "And you were a great teacher, Miss Voncille. Tough, but great. But I don't remember being all that good a student in your history class. I had trouble remembering dates."

"But you were attentive, and you tried hard. Anyway, none of that is really the main point," she continued, returning his smile. "I wanted to confess something here in public for the first time. I remember the fall Cherico High was getting ready for the first wave of integration. Of course, all of my fellow teachers were white, and some of them were very apprehensive, including myself. Mrs. Johnnie-Dell Crews was the most vocal in the teachers' lounge. 'I don't know what to expect,' she would say all the time while we were having our morning coffee and doughnuts. 'Do you think there'll be any trouble with the coloreds?' "

Miss Voncille seemed a bit hesitant to continue but finally gathered herself. "That was the way people talked back then, and it was definitely on our minds. So I'm here to confess that there were moments when I allowed myself to succumb to my worst fears, and I'm not proud of it. There were those at the time who thought the world would come to an end because Cherico High was going to be integrated. But the world kept on spinning when it finally happened. I found that I had worried needlessly, and when I got students in my class like Joe Sam—I mean, Mr. Place—I felt ashamed that I had doubted myself and my ability to teach even for an instant. Helping him learn was what it was all about—the same goal I'd always had for every student I ever taught."

Mr. Place raised his hand, almost as if he were back in the classroom, but did not wait to be called on to speak. "Miss Voncille, I can tell you what it was like from my point of view, if you'd like to hear it."

"Please tell us, Joe Sam—oops, there I go again. Sorry, I just can't seem to get used to all these name changes."

He waved her off. "Don't worry about it. Anyway, I was just as nervous as you and the other teachers were. My mama sitting right here next to me tonight said to hold my head up high, be calm and respectful no matter what anyone said to me or called me, and to do my best, but I was still scared. There'd been killings and bombings in the state in the years leading up to integrating the school, so that was always in the back of my mind. Nothing terrible like that ever happened to me or my family, thank God, but we had friends in other parts of the South that had some close calls. But the thing I remember most from my first day was the way you smiled at me when you called the roll in homeroom and came to my name, Miss Voncille. There was something about the way you said, 'Joe Sam Bedloe?' that made me feel just like the other students. You pronounced it so it didn't stand out, like I had always been around. Like I belonged there. It made me relax and pay attention from then on to my lessons, not some worst-case scenario running around my head."

Miss Voncille nodded approvingly. "Yes, it was a time for putting out feelers for all of us. But even though my subject was history, I read *To Kill a Mockingbird* when it first came out and Miss Nita Bellows in the English department had recommended it to me so highly. Looking back on it, I'm convinced that reading it before integration actually occurred a few years later helped prepare me for the changes to come. I believe the novel is full of a certain prescience in that way. My final thought is that *To Kill a Mockingbird* seems to be saying to you, 'This might have been the way things were at one time here in the South, but these words will see to it that they don't stay like that much longer.' "

"And I think we would all agree things have changed for the better," Maura Beth pointed out. "Your analysis is certainly well-taken. Does anyone have a further comment or angle to discuss?"

"I like the prescience angle," Jeremy added from his chair. "I've always told my students that the novel was an instant classic when it was released. What that really means is that it tapped into something that had been on a lot of people's minds over the years and verbalized it precisely. I believe it prepared the country for the turmoil to come, as Miss Voncille and Mr. Place have expressed in a very personal way. It was a novel both very much before its time and right on time."

Miss Voncille nodded graciously and said, "I can't top that." Then she stepped away from the podium to generous applause.

Mr. Place rose again briefly once Miss Voncille had resumed her seat. "My mother, Mrs. Ardenia Bedloe, would like to say something at this time."

"By all means," Maura Beth said, gesturing graciously in her direction. "Would you like to take the podium?"

Ardenia shook her head. "I believe I'll stay right here, if you don't mind. My arthritis has been acting up lately."

"Then please go right ahead."

"Well, when I was growing up in this town a long time ago now, I wasn't allowed to check out books in this very library. I wanted to. I wanted to read more fairy tales and look at more picture books after I'd finished with the ones Santa Claus brought me for Christmas, but I couldn't get a library card. Nobody in my family could. That was before Miz Annie Scott came in the sixties and way before *To Kill a Mockingbird,* even. So to be here this evening enjoying the food and the company and feeling so welcome the way I do is the sweetest thing in the world to me. I don't believe I thought things would ever change back when I was a little girl, but they have. They really have."

Maura Beth felt something catching in her throat as she responded. "Thank you, Mrs. Bedloe. I'm sure everyone here appreciates your candor. As for myself, I've been working very hard to make this library an integral part of Cherico for everyone. This book club is my most comprehensive effort yet. I've been library director for six years, and in many respects I now consider myself a Chericoan. But there are things some of you probably don't know. If we still had a newspaper, you likely would have gotten wind of it by now. But since we don't, I feel it's my duty to inform you that this library is in real danger of being closed down at the end of the year. It should come as no surprise to hear that Cherico is not exactly swimming in money, and our City Council will have to make some tough decisions in the years ahead. One of them may be to stop funding the library and use the taxpayers' money elsewhere."

Maura Beth's revelation was creating quite a stir throughout the gathering, causing Councilman Sparks to rise from his seat. "Unfortunately, what Miz Mayhew has just said is correct. The library is a huge drag on our budget, and we'd like to put that money to better use by creating an industrial park to attract new jobs to the community."

"But if I may continue, Councilman," Maura Beth said, careful to keep a pleasant tone in her voice, "what I wanted to emphasize was that this event tonight proves that the library can be a much more valuable community asset than it has been for many decades. If it can regularly accommodate groups like 'Who's Who in Cherico?' and the proposed 'Becca Broccoli in the Flesh,' and, of course, The Cherry Cola Book Club, it is performing a useful service. Over time, that usefulness will expand and become more essential, and the taxpayers will more than get their money's worth. Those who support the library for these and other purposes such as student research after school hours and adults hunting for job leads should make their views known to Councilman Sparks and City Hall as soon as possible."

"What about right now?" Miss Voncille put in quickly, waving her hand energetically.

Knowing better than to cross her, Councilman Sparks deferred. "Go ahead, then, Miss Voncille. Speak your piece to us."

"I will do just that, Durden. You can't brush aside us library users so casually. I've had a wonderful ally in Maura Beth

Mayhew for my 'Who's Who?' organization from the day she arrived here in Cherico. Yes, Annie Scott was cooperative, too, but she was never as pleasant about it the way Maura Beth has been. Annie always acted like I was bothering her, intruding on her precious time, whereas Maura Beth has given me the respect a devoted daughter would have."

Surprisingly, Mamie Crumpton was out of her seat. "My sister and I always look forward to coming to the library and hearing what Miss Voncille has to say. We enjoy the sense of continuity. Our parents were big library users. And, Durden, a little birdie told me not too long ago that you were seriously considering this library closure. Of course, I was shocked, and you might as well know that such a move would not be without consequences, I assure you."

Councilman Sparks dropped his trademark smile as he responded. "I understand and respect what you're saying, Mamie, but these club functions can easily be accommodated elsewhere, and, I might add, with more space available in the homes of private citizens, to name at least one alternative. Tonight, this library appears to be bursting at the seams, but it might also be considered something of a dog and pony show. Emphasis on the show. I think we all know very well that the library usually just sits here collecting dust, your genealogy meetings excepted."

Maura Beth intervened, feeling the anger rising in her blood but managing to steady herself. "With all due respect, Councilman, I think what has been discussed here tonight so far has been substantive. We've brought some very diverse elements of the community together to reflect upon their shared history and, by the way, just have an old-fashioned good time together. How many things can you say that about? I think The Cherry Cola Book Club has a promising future, and I trust it will take place right here."

Surprisingly, it was Becca who took the floor next. "If I

could just say something. Mrs. Bedloe triggered some pleasant memories for me. I'm so sorry she couldn't come to the library and use it in her day, but I could and did in mine. My mother enrolled me in summer reading every year, and I had a ball. At the time, Miz Scott gave out blue ribbons if we read so many books between the first of June and the end of July. If you fell short, you still got a red ribbon. Let me tell you, I still have every ribbon of every color I won tucked into one of my scrapbooks up in the attic somewhere. It would be a shame not to let Cherico's current crop of children earn those kinds of memories during all the summers ahead of us."

But Councilman Sparks would not back down. "I don't want to come off as the bad guy here, Miz Brachle, but the library is just not an essential service. There are other departments that everyone here would agree we can never do without, such as police, utilities, water, sewage, and fire protection. On the bright side, if our proposed Cherico Industrial Park does bring in industries the way we hope it will, maybe then with more taxes to collect we can consider reopening the library down the road."

"But closing it isn't a done deal, is it?!" Donna Gordon exclaimed out of nowhere. "My friends and I were looking forward to coming to Becca Broccoli's demonstrations, and we were even going to start checking out some cookbooks. We browsed through the stacks before the meeting got started and we really liked the selection."

"Yeah! You can't cut us off just when we're getting started!" Terra Munrow complained. "I spotted some off-the-wall hairstyling books I'd like to read, and my boyfriend found a motorcycle repair manual he wants to check out when he comes back tomorrow to get his library card. Please don't dangle the library in front of us and then snatch it away!"

Locke Linwood got to his feet next. "And I want to say

that The Cherico Library and I go back a long way. When I was a little boy, I was hooked on all the Hardy Boys mysteries. I checked out and read every one because at the time I thought I wanted to be a detective when I grew up. Of course, I ended up selling life insurance instead, but I never forgot the sense of wonder and adventure that those books instilled in me. And the library helped sustain me later in life when the sailing got a big rough." Then he sucked in air and lifted his chin with authority. "When my dear wife got terminally ill a few years ago, I checked out as many books as I could find on being a caregiver. I did what I could for her all the way to the end. I'd like to think that the answers I found would always be available to others in their time of need."

Locke's testimony inspired James Hannigan to stand up. "He's right, you know. When my mother passed away, I was having a tough time accepting it. It was so traumatic for me because she died unexpectedly in her sleep. But then my pastor suggested that after I'd finished praying, I go to the library and see if they had any books on dealing with grief." He paused to gesture at Maura Beth. "And Miz Mayhew, you had several for me to choose from. I checked them all out, and as I read them, I began to see that other people had gone through this and come out at the other end ready to get on with their lives. I was able to make my peace, and I accomplished that with a little prayer and my library card. That's another reason I was so eager to help you out."

Maura Beth finally stepped into the respectful lull that followed. "I'm fighting back tears when I say that everything I've just heard from all of you defines what a library is and what it does for a community. All of you are true friends of the library. I'm not sure you can put a price on that, Councilman Sparks."

"Perhaps not," he answered with no trace of his customary arrogance. "But the City Council has to consider the big picture in running this town. Next year's budget will be finalized exactly two weeks from tomorrow. Money is tight, and we're looking for ways to funnel more of it into Cherico. We've had the industrial park on the front burner for some time now, but we'll make our final decision on the library at that time. All of you are welcome to attend."

For a few seconds, Maura Beth felt like she'd lost the battle. This was not the way it was supposed to happen. How could anyone not be impressed with everything that had gone on in the library tonight? She had expected a clear decision in her favor and was temporarily at a loss for words.

But Miss Voncille had no trouble expressing herself. "I'll get a letter and e-mail campaign going, Durden Sparks. I'll rustle up a list of my former pupils and put them on the job. Then you'll have to keep the library open!"

"Miss Voncille," he replied in a tone that was semi-conciliatory, "I have not made my decision yet, and all opinions will be welcomed as the Council reviews the matter. But have you considered that the town of Cherico can do everything a little better with more revenue flowing in? Meanwhile, using library money to pay for movie posters of Gregory Peck seems a bit extravagant to me."

Maura Beth motioned for Miss Voncille to resume her seat and was somehow able to conjure up a smile. "You seem to have covered all bases, Councilman Sparks. But I want it noted as a matter of public record that Connie McShay, the treasurer of The Cherry Cola Book Club, paid for those posters of Gregory Peck with her own money. They didn't cost the library a cent. So now, if you don't have any objections, I think we'd like to wind up our discussion of *To Kill a Mockingbird*."

"Of course," he answered, turning to head toward the door with Chunky and Gopher Joe. "We're at cross-purposes regarding the library, but I'm sure we both want what's best for Cherico. Now, if you'll excuse us, please."

Maura Beth watched the three of them leave the building,

while the Scarlett side of her that she had been cultivating so meticulously seethed with frustration. "Just don't count me out!" she exclaimed finally.

"I never have!" Councilman Sparks returned just before making his exit.

Some of the crowd moved forward to chat with and console Maura Beth, but the words seemed to blend together after a while. One remark stood out, however, when Jeremy said, "I truly wish I could stay a little longer to help you figure out what to do next, but I have to drive the boys over to the hotel in Corinth. Burke Williams wanted to say something to you before we left, though."

The lanky young poet approached Maura Beth shyly, barely able to look her in the eye, but his message struck home. "I hope you don't think this is out of left field, Miz Mayhew, but I keep thinking about the character of Boo Radley in *To Kill a Mockingbird.* How he quietly saved the day there at the end when everything seemed so desperate, I mean. Maybe someone or something like that will happen for you and your library so you'll stay open."

Maura Beth gave him a hug and smiled as he blushed crimson. "Thank you for that, young man." Then she pulled back and turned to Jeremy. "And thank you for bringing these bright young students of yours to The Cherry Cola Book Club. To know that they exist, caring about literature the way they do, gladdens this librarian's heart."

Most of the people left shortly after the unexpected showdown between Councilman Sparks and Maura Beth, but the Brachles, McShays, Locke Linwood, Miss Voncille, and Periwinkle had remained for an impromptu strategy session. Mr. Place wanted to participate as well, but his mother had grown a bit weary, so he understandably drove her home after wishing the core of the book club the best of luck.

"We've got City Hall on the defensive," Maura Beth was explaining to the group gathered around the meeting room table with their serious demeanors in place. "But we can't let up. All of that testimony we heard tonight on the library's behalf was terrific and reassuring, but what we need now is signatures. I say we circulate petitions to keep the library open and then present it to the City Council. Those signatures represent votes, and if I know anything about politicians, they'll pay attention to that when they ignore everything else."

Connie was the first to come on board with enthusiasm. "Absolutely. And we have the perfect starter list, since we asked everyone to write their names, phone numbers, and e-mail addresses on the bulletin board sheet. They can be our first contacts."

Maura Beth smiled and shook her head at the same time. "Well, not quite, Connie. Our patron list will be our first call. But tonight's list won't be far behind."

The suggestion gathered further momentum. "I could put up one petition at The Twinkle," Periwinkle added. "And we could ask the other businesses that have been helping us out with the publicity to do the same."

Maura Beth brightened further. "I bet James Hannigan will make more P.A. announcements for us at The Cherico Market. He's a sweetheart, and he really rounded up his troops tonight. I nearly cried when he told that story about his mother."

"Same here," Becca added. "But we'll publicize the petitions on the show, won't we, Stout Fella?"

"Yes, ma'am," he answered in his most playful tone.

"And I was serious about contacting my former students,"

Miss Voncille added. "I've kept in touch with some of the ones that never left Cherico."

"Every signature counts," Maura Beth answered.

"Was it just me, or did y'all think that Councilman Sparks might have softened up there at the end?" Douglas wanted to know.

Maura Beth looked amused and caught his gaze, every inch a Scarlett sizing up a formidable situation. "Douglas, that man is a piece of work. I've dealt with him for six years now, and he has agendas coming out the wazoo. We can't go by what he said tonight because the truth is, I've never seen him not get his way. He's hell-bent on creating that industrial park for his greater glory, so it's my opinion that we need to impress him where he lives and breathes. And that, my friends, is with the votes he prizes above everything else. Those signatures are our best shot at keeping this library open."

Locke Linwood pounded his fist on the table for emphasis. "I'm all in. I can contact all my former life insurance customers here in Cherico. You know, I was pretty good at selling policies all those years."

"Go for it, Mr. Linwood!" Maura Beth exclaimed, giving him a wink.

Connie and Douglas exchanged glances, and he said, "We don't know that many people, but we'll keep our neighbors in the loop. They were interested enough to show up tonight, so I don't see why they won't help us out with this. They could certainly network with their friends who care about the library."

"You just design those petitions, and I'll have them printed up for you," Connie added.

Maura Beth took a deep breath while she quickly scanned the room, admiring her very own fearless army of library soldiers. That was yet another course they should have taught in library school—Introduction to Going to War for the Patrons. "I couldn't ask for more support, but we simply can't fail in this. When that budget is approved a couple of weeks from now, the library must not be removed as a line item." There was momentary silence, but then Maura Beth summed it all up. "We're The Cherry Cola Book Club, and we're just not going to let that happen."

14

Two Weeks and Counting

The instant Maura Beth opened the front door of the library the next morning, she found herself entertaining a dark premise. What if all the petitions they were about to circulate failed to excite people or made no difference, no matter what? In that case, this carefully cultivated turf of hers would suddenly become alien terrain. It would no longer be hers to manage and manipulate, to try and improve, or simply to inhabit with professional pride. Six years of hard, mostly thankless work would then be discarded like dead flowers in a vase of stale, discolored water.

But when she plunked herself down at her desk a few minutes later, she chided herself out loud for her pessimistic ramblings. "You, Maura Beth Mayhew, are being most un-Scarlett-like today. Have you no confidence in your ability to pull this out of the fire and keep the enemy at bay?"

Perhaps the long-distance conversation she'd had with her mother when she'd gotten home from the confrontation with Councilman Sparks the evening before had coaxed her doubts out of hiding. "Come on home, honey, just come on home," her mother had said in response to hearing about the possibility of Maura Beth losing her job. "You can find something better down here where you're closer to your family. We've all missed you so much. Just pack your bags and come back where you belong. You know we'll take care of you."

Maura Beth had long known that William and Cara Lynn Mayhew had never approved of her moving to North Mississippi, especially when she had told them what she would be earning. Apparently, it had never occurred to them that they should be thrilled she had gotten a directorship on the heels of her graduation, applauding her moxie.

Instead, "We'll send you money anytime" had been their initial mantra; followed by the overly dramatic, "Don't worry about getting by. No child of ours is going to clip coupons and go to thrift shops."

Except for the rust-colored sofa—which she had not asked for—and the brass bed—which she had—Maura Beth had resisted financial assistance from her parents. Cherico was her big chance to prove herself, to make a mark on her own. Now she must bear down harder than ever if she intended to achieve the goals on page twenty-five of her college journal.

She had, in fact, just hung up with Connie about the logistics of putting the petition together when Renette knocked at her door and asked to speak with her.

"What's on your mind?" Maura Beth said, once Renette had taken her seat.

"It's what happened last night at the book club meeting," she began, hanging her head. "I never realized politicians could be so scary."

"Dealing with Councilman Sparks in particular is never easy," Maura Beth explained. "Don't let him upset you, although I realize you haven't had as much practice as I have."

But Renette started tearing up anyway. "It's just that if the library does close down—well, I know it will be hard on you.

I've seen how much running this library has meant to you. I've seen how hard you've worked at it, and it's inspired me to be the very best front desk clerk Cherico's ever had. Plus, I'll never find a boss as good as you are if I have to get another job."

Maura Beth quickly explained the decision to create the petitions and then moved to Renette to give her a warm hug. "That's sweet of you to worry about me, but you may not even have to do any job hunting. But if the worst happens and you do, you'll probably find a boss that's even better. Now I want you to run to the ladies' room and dry your eyes. After all, we're still up and running, and you're the first impression our patrons get when they walk into the lobby. We don't want them thinking you've been up all night crying. Oh, and get those girlfriends of yours to come in and sign that petition in the next two weeks. And tell them to tell their friends, too."

Renette smiled even as she sniffled. "When are you going to put it up on the bulletin board? Seems like every minute counts."

"Connie McShay is having it printed and copied later today," Maura Beth told her. "She'll be dropping by to tack it up. Then the countdown begins."

After a couple of hours had passed, Maura Beth was pulled away from her petition networking by another knock at her door. "Come in," she announced, wondering if Renette needed further reassurance.

But it was loyal, matronly Emma Frost who appeared instead. "Excuse me, Miz Mayhew. I know I'm prob'ly intruding, but Renette called me up this morning to tell me what went on here last night. I'm sorry I couldn't come, but my husband has a real bad cold, and I don't want it to go into the flu. We just can't afford to have him miss any more workdays. So I had him all bundled up last night, stuffing him with my best home remedies. I know it's not my day to be here, but I just couldn't let this news about the library pass without coming in to say something to you."

"I completely understand. But have a seat for a minute." After Emma had pulled up her chair, Maura Beth continued, "I trust Renette didn't tell you that the library was definitely being closed."

Emma worked her hands into a nervous tangle as she spoke. "Well, I sorta got that impression. And I know we've had our share of days without a soul showing up, but I need this job in the worst way to help my family make ends meet. Do you think we really will be shut down?"

Maura Beth gave her an engaging smile, realizing that this was definitely an occasion to bring out the best of both Melanie and Scarlett as she had once promised to do. "You have faith, Emma. We'll do everything we can over the next two weeks to prevent that from happening with the petitions we're circulating. Meanwhile, there's something you can do to help. Tell all your family and friends to come to the library and sign that petition to keep it open. You march straight home and get things started."

Emma thanked her for the pep talk and left, after which Maura Beth sat back in her chair with a sense of accomplishment. She and her staff must keep it together and plug away at the end game. In fact, every member of The Cherry Cola Book Club must meet that challenge without flinching.

Connie and Douglas McShay were sitting in front of their great room fire discussing their efforts on behalf of the library exactly one week before the budget approval.

"There's got to be more we can do," Connie was saying, frustration creeping into her voice. "We've got everyone we know out here covered, but that's only half a dozen people.

Maybe a dozen if the Brimleys, the Milners, and the Paxtons follow up with a few of their friends."

Douglas gave her a little hiccup of a chuckle and wagged his brows. "Surely you're not suggesting we go around badgering strangers at their front doors like Jehovah's Witnesses?"

She punched his arm playfully and snickered. "No, but Maura Beth actually *is* going door-to-door on Commerce Street. I offered to help, but she insisted she had it covered. Meanwhile, Becca and Stout Fella are mentioning the petition every day on the radio show, Miss Voncille and Locke Linwood say they've heard from lots of her students and his customers, and—"

"Okay, okay, I get it," Douglas said, holding his hand up in surrender. "Listen, it's not like we haven't pitched in all along. We've paid for posters and flyers and printing up the petition and that monster seafood party we had out here. I don't think you should be beating yourself up as if you've done nothing."

Connie shrugged with a pleasant smile. "I'm not really. I just want to collect as many signatures as I can for Maura Beth." Suddenly, she snapped her fingers and bore into him with her eyes. "Of course. The Marina Bar and Grill. At last, something useful will come of your haunting that place."

"Haunting? Come on, I go for an occasional beer, that's all," he insisted.

"Do they like you out there?"

He drew back in disbelief. "Uh—yeah. I'm not the Creature from the Black Lagoon. Although I felt like it sometimes in the courtroom."

"I've been thinking about that since we retired here," she began, gently rubbing his arm. "I guess all this fishing really does help you forget some of the legal stunts you had to pull over the years."

Douglas looked suddenly uncomfortable, and he did not

answer her for a while. "I suppose you could make a case for that. A guy can put up with only so much stress in his life, you know; and it's not like you didn't have plenty of it in the hospital day and night."

"Yes, I did."

"And you've always had your books to read to keep yourself on an even keel, right?"

She nodded dramatically, widening her eyes. "Going to the library to check out my novels has always been my great escape. I get to explore someone else's mindset for a while. It's a very sane exercise. More people should try it."

"So what do you want me to do out at The Marina Bar and Grill?"

"Ask the owner if you can put up the petition, at the very least," she began. "And then talk it up with your drinking buddies. Well-lubricated people are more apt to listen to what you have to say."

He gave her a little smirk. "Or forget it."

"Never mind that. Don't you guys bond watching football games and other sports out there all the time?"

Douglas laughed out loud. "You make The Marina Bar and Grill sound like one of those tree houses that little boys build where little girls aren't allowed. There are wives and girlfriends on the premises. Women fish, too."

"I can't believe you just said that!" she exclaimed, turning to face him directly now.

"Why? You don't believe me? You don't think women can bait hooks?"

"Don't be absurd. Of course I believe you. It was the perfect segue for something else I wanted to discuss with you. It's about the details of our retirement. I feel like we're leading two separate lives again, just the way we did in Nashville when we put everything we had into our careers. This was supposed to be a new start for us."

"But I think last night at the library went well for us," he pointed out. "Maybe not at the end there for Maura Beth with Councilman Sparks jumping down her throat the way he did, but you and I had a good time together, didn't we?"

"That begs the question. We still spend most of our time apart. You're out there with your beer and your fish, and I'm here inside waiting for you to get your fill. The truth is, the rain brings you in more often than the sound of my voice does. If this is the way it's going to be, I'd rather go back to Nashville where I had Susan and Paul and so many other friends to do things with."

Douglas turned to her with a puzzled expression, briefly shutting one eye. "I thought you considered these Cherry Cola people your friends. You've just finished saying how much helping Maura Beth means to you. Matter of fact, I think we've both made some nice new friends in the book club. Paul and Susan like them, too."

"They are our friends, and I'm thankful for them and the things we've done together. But they can't fill up all of my days or any of my nights. We can only expect so many visits from Lindy and Melissa or Susan and Paul. You and I have to manage the rest of the time together. Since we moved, it's almost like retiring has given us permission to stop working at our marriage."

He folded his arms and made a brief hissing sound. "I don't think I'm such a slouch in bed, if that's what you're implying."

"I'm not talking about that," Connie said, throwing up her arms in frustration. "Your true passion now is fishing, and that wall of photos across the room is proof. Retiring down here has made me realize that I come second."

"Now you're really exaggerating," he said, the annoyance clearly evident in his voice. "But if you truly think that way, then let's talk about what we can do to turn that particular perception around."

Connie straightened up, patted her hair, and surprised him with a pleasant grin on her face. "I thought you'd never ask. Here's what I'm proposing. I know you'll never be a reader the way I am, and two people can't read together anyway, except to sit in the same room and turn pages in silence. So, why don't you teach me how to fish? You've always said you needed a partner out there in *The Verdict*. Why not have a good time with your wife? I'm not too old to learn new tricks."

He jerked to attention, almost as if he had been pricked with a needle. "You're serious? You'd actually be willing to learn about different baits and lures and how and where to cast? You know there's so much more to reading the water than most people think."

"Well, I have to start somewhere. Maybe we'll both be reading together after all. Then we can negotiate what else we can do with our retirement from my point of view."

He put his arm around her shoulder and squeezed it affectionately, followed by a sweet little kiss. "I can handle that. So, being the reader that you are, can you tell me if we're back on the same page again as husband and wife?"

Connie chuckled softly even as she pulled back. "I'm going to say yes, but with an important caveat."

"And what's that?"

"You take over cleaning what we catch and keep for a while. I'm so over fish guts, it's not funny."

"You got it," he said without a moment's hesitation. Then he extended his hand and they shook on it firmly. "Meanwhile, I'll take one of the petitions out to the lake this afternoon to Harlan Lattimore. Why don't you come with me and make friends with a few of the women? Who knows? Maybe some of them will even be readers, and you can talk best sellers."

* * *

Locke Linwood and Miss Voncille were comparing notes, sitting side by side on his living room sofa. It was a mere three days to the budget approval, and they were counting up their successes.

"Okay, that makes a total of sixteen of my life insurance customers with Vince Langham and his wife promising to drop by the library to sign the petition," Locke was saying, puffing himself up proudly. "You have to realize that a lot of my clients have died off, so this is a pretty good response in my estimation."

But Miss Voncille was far less sanguine, disdaining the humor he was trying to inject. "But sixteen is a just a drop in the bucket. Even if you add the twenty-three students who've responded to me positively. That's barely forty people. I wanted to do a lot better for Maura Beth, and frankly, I'm disappointed in my students. Maybe some of them didn't like me as well as I thought."

"You've been in a pessimistic mood all this week about this, sweetheart. Please don't revert to type and channel that nitpicky schoolmarm of yours again. I thought you'd banished her for good," he contended. "We can only do what we can do."

"I think you're being a little nitpicky with me yourself," she snapped back.

"Perhaps I am. Sorry." Then he rose from the sofa and headed over to the bookcase where he again retrieved Pamela's letter from beyond the grave. "I think we both might be in need of a little inspiration again." He resumed his seat and ran his finger halfway down the paper. "Go ahead and read it out loud starting right there. It shows you just how prescient my Pamela really was—why, she may even have been clairvoyant."

Miss Voncille scanned the page quickly and began:

> *"We agreed that you should continue to attend 'Who's Who in Cherico?' at the library; that you should do everything you could to support that sweet young librarian, Maura Beth Mayhew—she's just as darling as she can be, and she'll need all the help she can get with the powers-that-be, believe me—"*

"Stop right there. You can't tell me that that doesn't give you goose bumps, knowing how long ago it was written."

Miss Voncille looked up from the letter, staring over at Pamela's mesmerizing portrait. "I have to agree. It's definitely uncanny the way everything has converged to make her words seem as if they were written this morning. Hats off to you and your foresight, Miz Pamela."

"My sentiments exactly. And it's my further opinion that this is a sign we'll succeed with this petition and that this is the right thing to do."

"I'd certainly like to think so."

"I believe there's more to this world than we could ever imagine."

Miss Voncille considered for a moment and then raised an eyebrow. "I know this much. You just can't give up on your life because it gets hard and bad things happen to you. Eventually, something good that you've earned from hanging in there comes along. Like a sweet, chivalrous Southern gentleman fresh from his morning shave."

"I'm happy to resemble that."

They both leaned together in laughter, but she let go of the moment quickly. "I'm still wondering if this petition will sway Durden Sparks in the end, though. I've known him most of his conceited life, and I've never seen him not get his way."

Locke nestled his shoulder against hers again and then shot her a dismissive look. "There's always a first time, and this may very well be it."

Then Miss Voncille sighed dramatically. "Do you think I should call up Morbid Mamie and make sure she's put her John Hancock on our petition yet?"

Locke gave her a thumbs-up. "Not only that, but invite her and her sister over here for what will be our revenge game of bridge. I still have a bad taste in my mouth from last time."

Jeremy McShay's daily phone calls and e-mails from Nashville had kept Maura Beth energized during the two-week petition countdown. Their conversations hadn't lasted all that long but had served to keep their burgeoning emotional connection alive and well, while their e-mails had contained the ordinary details of his life at the school and hers at the library. It particularly pleased Maura Beth that he was always the one to initiate the contact in the old-fashioned manner she had always projected both in her dreams and in her journal. She couldn't get enough of his thoughtful pursuit and made a habit of concluding each and every communication with her very own signature phrase: *Keep those cards and letters comin', folks!*

Finally, though, all the long-distance flirting gave way to the day before the budget approval. Just past three o'clock that afternoon, Maura Beth had set out from the library on what she considered to be the most important journey of her life. The butterflies in her stomach felt more like a swarm of bees as she reached Commerce Street on foot, but she did her best to disguise her anxiety with an unwavering smile as she entered Audra Neely's Antiques to pick up her first petition.

"Here you go," Audra said, smiling brightly while handing it over from behind a counter crowded with everything from music boxes to ceramic figurines. "I talked you up every time someone came in."

"Thank you so much," Maura Beth replied, not particularly surprised by the revelation. She had conjectured that the women who fancied the stylish Audra's cutesy boutique approach to antiquing were among the more sophisticated in Cherico and likely to be sympathetic to the cause.

Then came the surprising downer. "I only wish I could have collected more for you, Miz Mayhew. Business has been a little slow lately. It's the economy, you know."

Maura Beth glanced at the sheet and counted the signatures. "Well, you got fifteen for me, Audra, including your own. That's fifteen I didn't have before I came in. And we'd love to have you make an appearance at City Hall when the final decision on the library is made."

Once she was out on the sidewalk again, Maura Beth drew her overcoat closer to her body against the brisk November breeze. Those fifteen signatures were now registering as a nasty chill at the bone. What if all the petitions turned out to be so disappointing?

The Vernon Dotrice Insurance Agency a few doors down was next. As Maura Beth had discovered, the dynamic and very dashing Vernon had bought the business from Locke Linwood when he had retired a few years back. Furthermore, he had been double-teamed by Locke and Maura Beth herself with e-mails, phone calls, and personal visits, and was now thoroughly behind the valiant attempt to keep the library open.

"Hope this helps," Vernon told her once they were seated inside his office. He handed over two copies of the petition with an impish grin and waited for her reaction.

"You're kidding?!" she exclaimed, scanning the paper with her eyes bugging.

"No, ma'am, I'm not. Seventy-five beauties—signed, sealed, and delivered. Hey, Mr. Linwood sold me a very solvent concern here. I took what he gave me and turned it into an even bigger goldmine." He paused and gently wagged a finger. "Just one caveat. You might want to check my list against Mr. Linwood's to make sure there are no duplicates. I don't think there will be, though. I'm pretty sure all these signatures are customers I've won over since I bought the agency—and their spouses, in many cases. That's what really got the numbers up."

"You must be the only game in town, then," Maura Beth added, still a bit dazed by his results. "If I ever need life insurance, I promise I'll look you up."

"You do that, Miz Mayhew. You know your way here. And, by the way, I'll make it a point to drop by your library now and then. I don't want to be just a signature on a piece of paper."

"We'd love to see you in the Council Chambers tomorrow, too."

"I'll see what I can do about rounding people up."

An ecstatic Maura Beth felt her marrow warming again as she popped into Cherico Ace Hardware next door to greet the store manager, Harry Weeks. But she could tell by the evasive look on his wide, bearded face that this was probably going to be another Audra Neely's Antiques' outing.

"I'm sorry, Miz Mayhew," he told her, taking the petition down from his bulletin board and handing it to her. "I guess people in the market for a hammer and nails don't go to the library much. Apples and oranges?"

Maura Beth glanced at the six signatures he'd collected for her but was careful to give him her brightest smile. "Thank you for putting it up for me, Mr. Weeks. That's all I could ask. If you get a moment, drop by the Council Chambers tomorrow around nine-thirty."

As Maura Beth made her way one block over to The Cherico Market, she bucked up anyway. Her instincts had told her from the beginning that she wouldn't find much of an audience at the hardware store, but she couldn't imagine that James Hannigan, his employees, and customers wouldn't come through for her.

"There she is!" Mr. Hannigan exclaimed as the automatic doors parted for her, and she walked in eagerly anticipating some good news. The two embraced warmly, and a couple of the cashiers stopped their grocery scanning long enough to smile and wave.

"I hope you're having a special on signatures today," Maura Beth told him, zeroing in on the sheets of paper he was holding in his hand.

"We outdid ourselves," he said, leaning in and presenting three separate petitions to her.

She gasped in delight, feeling as if she'd just received an early Christmas present. Two of the sheets were completely filled, while the third sported only a few empty lines.

"Two-hundred and sixty names, to be exact," he explained. "Count 'em."

She held them against her overcoat and sighed. "I'll take your word. But it's lovely. Just lovely."

"Frankly, I don't think my customers could resist the little announcement I kept making over the P.A. system," he explained, puffing out his chest. "I've still got it memorized. Wanna hear it?"

"Absolutely!"

"Well, first I did the 'Attention, shoppers!' opening because they always perk up when they hear that. 'What's on sale?' they think right away. Then I said, 'If you or your spouse or your children or any other member of your family swears by the library for any reason whatsoever, you'll want to be sure and sign our petitions on the bulletin board to keep it up and running. That's right, your Cherico Library could be closed for good starting the first day of January if you don't stand up to be counted. Books are the only thing about the library that should be shelved! Sign today!' "

Maura Beth gave him another quick hug. "That's so clever, and it obviously worked."

He blushed and gave her a shy smile. "Well, I do write all the copy around here, and it's not bad if I do say so myself."

"As far as I'm concerned, you're the Shakespeare of the supermarket."

Things were definitely looking up, as Maura Beth thanked Mr. Hannigan, reminded him of the time the budget approval would take place, and walked back to the library to complete her rounds—this time in her car. She had to drive over to Cherico Tresses and then out to The Marina Bar and Grill to pick up those petitions. But she would not know the final total until Periwinkle closed her doors that evening. Then she could add the library signatures to those collected at The Twinkle and by other members of the club such as Locke Linwood and Miss Voncille. That, and continue to solicit warm bodies in the seats for the actual budget approval.

But when all was said and done, would it be enough to force Councilman Sparks to do the right thing tomorrow morning?

15

Standing Room Only

As usual, Councilman Sparks did not know what to make of the latest message Lottie had left in the inbox on his desk. It was a mere fifteen minutes before he was about to head down the hall for the budget approval. "CCBC SAYS SRO"—she had printed in big block letters on his notepad. At the moment, however, further clarification would have to wait until she returned to her post in the outer office—most likely from one of her frequent trips to the ladies' room.

When she finally showed up a few minutes later, Councilman Sparks was hardly calm and collected as he blocked the door frame while holding her mysterious note in his outstretched hand. "What the hell does this mean, Lottie? You've got to give me a break from all these abbreviations. It took me half the afternoon in your absence last week to decipher that we were out of printer solution when you left me a message that read, 'OOPS—NEED REORDER.' "

"I'm sorry, sir," Lottie replied, although she hardly sounded contrite. "I thought I had mentioned it to you earlier that day. The out of printer solution, OOPS part, I mean."

"Never mind that. What does this latest hieroglyphic of yours mean?"

He moved aside so she could sit down at her desk, whereupon she started thumbing through some notes she had made to herself that morning in his absence. "Oh. They called around nine before you came in."

He took a deep breath to steady himself. "Who are *they?*"

"The Cherry Cola Book Club," Lottie explained at last. "You've been so involved with them lately, I thought you'd understand my abbreviation."

He was frowning now. "You mean Miz Mayhew—of all people?"

"Yes, it was her."

"Then why didn't you just write—" Once again, he realized he was fighting a losing battle and retreated from this latest argument on her terms. Then he made a mental note to ring in the New Year by advertising for a new secretary. He'd endured this comedy of errors long enough. "I'll settle for SRO. What does that mean?"

Lottie had an almost triumphant look on her face, obviously proud of stumping her boss one more time. "Standing room only. Miz Mayhew said that you should expect a full house for the budget approval. She was on her cell phone and already in her seat waiting, she said."

"Those people never give up," he mumbled as he rolled his eyes. "They've tacked up petitions all over town. But I checked out a couple on Commerce Street like the hardware and the antiques store, and I wasn't impressed with what I saw." He checked his watch while narrowing his eyes. "Anyway, it's time to put all this foolishness to bed, Lottie. You hold down the fort while I give Miz Mayhew and her entourage the bad news."

Maura Beth had not exaggerated when she had spoken to Lottie Howard and told her that there would not be an empty seat in the Council Chambers. All seventy chairs were occupied, and there were at least a dozen more people standing against the wall in the back of the room. As for her Cherry Cola Book Club friends, they were all seated with her on the front row. They had taken no chances and shown up thirty minutes early to ensure maximum physical presence, particularly that all-important eye contact with the councilmen as the budget process unfolded.

There were other friendly faces that Maura Beth was pleased to see among the crowd: James Hannigan, Audra Neely, Vernon Dotrice, Emma Frost, Terra Munrow—even the Crumpton sisters. But there were many others she did not recognize, and she assumed that they were the rank and file of citizens they had managed to reach with their campaign to save the library. That had to be a hopeful sign as the session got under way.

However, Maura Beth noted, as the tall, severe-looking City Clerk, Mrs. Benita Porter, began her robotic reading of each budget item, glaciers had been known to move faster in their trek to the sea.

"This is like listening to a recitation of the phone book," Connie whispered to Maura Beth out of the side of her mouth. Mrs. Porter was taking forever working her way through the Sanitation Department budget, then had hit a snag regarding the question of how much money to allot for road salt during the upcoming year.

"Nobody knows how much snow we'll get," Chunky Badham was pointing out. But he was not about to let up. "Last year, we got three big snows and that ice storm. My wife even had enough to make snow ice cream for me. Plus, I like to have gone off the road and into a ditch during that one we had last January. And it was because we didn't have enough road salt to put out where I live in the Netherfield Community. Now I realize we only have about twelve people out my way . . ."

He kept droning on and on, and neither of the other two councilmen saw fit to interrupt him.

Maura Beth felt her annoyance registering as an adrenaline rush. Here they were going on about how much extra road salt to purchase, while threatening to do away with her library entirely was waiting in the wings. She began playing mind games to calm herself. Which would the good people of Cherico prefer: a sprinkling of salt or books to read? In any case, an extra thousand dollars was finally appropriated for road salt, and there were no objections from the citizens attending, putting the stamp of approval on that specific budget item.

Utilities came next, and Maura Beth caught Councilman Sparks's gaze as Mrs. Porter waded through that particular appropriation. There was an unusual smugness to his handsome features, and her instincts were telling her that he intended to send her packing. But she held inside the folder on her lap the ultimate defense against such a decision—the voice of the people.

Finally, after what seemed like hours, Mrs. Porter announced, "The Cherico Library."

To Maura Beth, those three words felt like bullets penetrating her flesh. She played another game in her head and breathed deeply. Would she end up suffering a fatal wound or live to order and process books for another day? Being in the line of fire was the pits. "Here we go," Maura Beth whispered to Connie, and the two of them gave each other a reassuring smile.

Councilman Sparks rose after Mrs. Porter had reviewed the costs of running the library for another year, line item by line item—a total of $85,000. "It is our intention," he began, "to redirect this money to a new project for Cherico. It is our belief that you, the taxpayers, are not getting your money's worth with our library facility. We further believe that using this money to prepare land just north of town for industrial use will attract new industry and good-paying jobs to Cherico, thus increasing our tax base and improving our infrastructure. At some time in the future, perhaps we will then have collected enough money to improve and reopen the library. But it is the City Council's decision to close the library as of December 31st and begin preparations for the industrial park. We will now entertain feedback from you, the taxpayers."

As other hands and voices were raised all over the room, Maura Beth shot up immediately, brandishing the folder she had been so jealously guarding. "Councilman Sparks!" she exclaimed, taking no chance of being overlooked.

"Miz Mayhew?" he replied, refusing to match her urgent tone and careful to maintain his smile.

"On behalf of many of the taxpayers of Cherico, I would like to present to you today this folder of petitions requesting that the City Council keep The Cherico Library open. I have taken the time to check the names and addresses of all the signatures on these various petitions and have found them to be residents of our town, each and every one. No made-up or dead people, no jokes, no fakes. These are the taxpayers you represent, and as you will see, I have calculated and compiled the total number on all the petitions for you. Eight hundred and three people have expressed their desire to see The Cherico Library stay open. These signatures came mostly from various businesses around town, all of which are well-known to you, as well as the library itself. Those eight hundred and three signatures represent almost half the number of registered voters in this town—one thousand six hundred forty-five, according to public records."

Councilman Sparks was having trouble keeping his smile in place. "That doesn't necessarily mean those eight hundred or so are all actually registered voters. Some of them could even be children or teenagers."

"That might be true," Maura Beth returned. "Although I

think the underage signatures would probably be limited to the library. But in any case, children and teenagers grow up to be voters, Councilman. You above all should know that. Surely that's not going to be your argument against these signatures."

His smile had completely disappeared now. "Hand me your folder, please."

She reached over and gave it to him, taking a moment before continuing. Here was Scarlett at her best, daring anyone to take advantage of her.

"Furthermore, I'd like to say that the library's present budget is hardly adequate, even for a town of five thousand. But as the director, I'm not asking for an increase or a raise—only to continue to do my job for the people of Cherico. We've initiated a number of events recently that have this town buzzing about the library. I hardly have to remind you of that since you've attended some of these meetings, such as The Cherry Cola Book Club. I urge you and the other councilmen not to turn your back on what is fast becoming a popular and valuable community resource."

"Listen to her, Durden!" Miss Voncille exclaimed, rising to her feet. "You can postpone that industrial park or find some other way to fund it. My parents always told me that there was some slush fund hanging around from the days the library started up originally. I believe there was some question as to what really happened to some of the money the women of the town donated at the time. Wasn't your father on the Council back then? Being the historian that I am, I'm also quite sure that no one has ever bothered to look into that whole matter. As the saying goes, they just let it ride."

Councilman Sparks had gone from being supremely confident to actually looking uncomfortable for all the chamber to see. "Give me a few minutes, please," he told her, sitting back down and thumbing through the petitions Maura Beth had presented to him. Then the folder was passed around to his cohorts. Finally, after the trio had huddled for a good five minutes with their backs to the crowd, Councilman Sparks turned and rose again, his best campaign smile restored to full glory.

"It is the decision of the City Council to postpone the industrial park for another year and to fund The Cherico Library for the corresponding year—"

Enthusiastic applause and cheering erupted across the room. Maura Beth jumped up, embracing Connie and Miss Voncille, who were sitting on either side of her, and the rest of the book club did the same with one another along the front row.

"If I might continue!" Councilman Sparks cried out, and he had to repeat himself to gain the floor before the commotion died down. "Over the next year, we will be monitoring the library in hopes of seeing increased circulation figures and use of the meeting room facilities by the citizens of this town. It is to be understood that we will be reviewing funding of the library at this same time next year. For the time being, however, we cannot go against the will of the people in this regard."

"Thank you, Councilman," Maura Beth said, nodding his way.

"Please remember that this is a one-year reprieve, Miz Mayhew. There are no guarantees."

"I understand that. Or rather, Scarlett understands that."

She watched him struggling to keep his face from turning sour. Ever the politician, however, he somehow managed. But Maura Beth's smile was genuine and full of the thrill of victory. Above all else, she had played the game and won.

16

A Family Feast

Maura Beth was staring at the clock in her kitchenette and feeling like a million dollars. In less than ten minutes, she would be seeing Jeremy's smiling face at her door, putting an end to their separation of more than two weeks. The time had come to celebrate the library's recent victory over City Hall, and Jeremy was driving down from Nashville on this crisp November Saturday afternoon to help her do just that.

He was on time precisely at three, as she expected a responsible schoolteacher would be. Being late for anything in that profession was a big no-no. When she opened the door to him in her lavender dress, the first words out of his mouth were, "You look amazingly beautiful!" He was standing there dazzled by her with a bouquet of gardenias in his hand.

Maura Beth smiled and took the flowers, briefly inhaling their perfume as she admired his New Gallatin Academy navy blue blazer and red tie. "So do you, and so do these. Come on—I'm going to put them in water."

They headed over to the kitchenette together, and she pulled a large clear vase out of one of her cabinets. "What made you think of gardenias?" she continued, sticking the vase under the running faucet. "I absolutely love them. They're so delicate."

"A conceit from an English major, I guess," he explained, shrugging his shoulders and looking utterly charming in the process. "Gardenias, like women, bruise easily, but that never takes away their beauty or their fragrance."

She smiled brightly as she finished arranging the flowers and found a spot for them on the counter. "No wonder your students like you so much. I would have loved to have had a teacher like you."

Jeremy pointed to his watch and wagged his brows. "We better scoot. We don't want to be late."

Once they were on their way, Maura Beth shifted into an even more flirtatious gear. "I wanted to tell you just how much all your calls and e-mails have meant to me these past two weeks. I was under such pressure, I don't think I could have made it through without you. Today, I was half expecting you to show up in shining armor."

He drove for another quarter mile or so toward town before turning briefly to snap his fingers. "Darn it! I knew I forgot something!"

She reached over and gently rubbed his arm several times. "Never fear. The flowers did the trick just fine."

They had reached Commerce Street now, and Jeremy began searching for a parking space. "Small town, not much parking," he observed as they passed The Twinkle. They waved to Becca and Stout Fella as they were walking down the sidewalk toward the restaurant for the grand celebration.

"They obviously found one somewhere around here," Maura Beth answered. "I don't mind walking a bit, do you?"

He turned the corner and was immediately rewarded with a space on the right side of the street. "Not at all. We can get a head start on working off this wonderful feast Miz Lattimore has fixed for all of us."

"This is where it all began a few months back," Connie was saying as she and Maura Beth were sitting at one of The Twinkle's corner tables sipping their wine. "I remember dashing in to pick up my aspics that blazing June afternoon and mentioning The Music City Page Turners to you."

"Ah, yes," Maura Beth mused. "We almost became The Cherico Page Turners, didn't we? By the way, you must bring your granddaughter down sometime from Memphis. I'd like very much to meet the little sweetheart, since she ended up changing our name."

"Lindy almost came down with her for our meeting last Sunday, but Melissa wasn't feeling well at the last minute. Some bad cough that just wouldn't go away," Connie explained. "But don't worry. We've got plenty of time now for her to shake your hand and take full credit."

Periwinkle headed over to the table with the bottle of good Merlot she was offering to the group, lingering briefly. "Are we all still sufficiently wined up here?"

"I think I'd like another swallow or two," Maura Beth said, feeling on the wild and wooly side.

Periwinkle poured a little more into her glass and wagged her brows. "I see your adorable designated driver not having any over there across the room. Are you and Jeremy definitely becoming an item?"

Maura Beth gave Connie a conspiratorial glance and said, "We're going to be working at it, I think. So you can retire your camera phone."

"No way, Jose. I'm still looking, remember?"

A few minutes later it was time for every member of The Cherry Cola Book Club to take their seats around the big table Periwinkle had configured out of two smaller ones. "Mr. Place and I will join you after we've served the first course," she told them.

Maura Beth perked up and ran her tongue over her lips. "Icepick salad?"

"What else would I serve?"

"Now you're talking!" Douglas exclaimed. "I think we've practically lived on that since we moved down here."

"I can vouch for that," Connie added. "I wish The Twinkle had a delivery service."

"Not a bad suggestion. I'll think about it," Periwinkle said, nudging her gently.

Over Periwinkle's entrée of grilled salmon with dill sauce, the conversation turned toward the next meeting of The Cherry Cola Book Club.

"I don't suppose we've selected our next novel, have we?" Miss Voncille inquired.

Maura Beth's sigh clearly contained a hint of frustration. "How could we? We never seem to be able to finish the one we're reading. Something earthshaking always happens and sends us to the exits. But I think things will settle down now. Anyone got a brilliant suggestion?"

Connie was first up. "Something by Eudora Welty? Or have we put Harper Lee to bed?"

"I think we've had enough of *Mockingbird,*" Becca observed. "Not that it wasn't overflowing with drama and portent from the very beginning."

"Sorry about that," Stout Fella added.

"No, no, no," Maura Beth continued, wagging a finger. "Your little incident, if you will, brought us all closer together."

Becca put down her fork and chuckled. "You might even say our friendships ballooned from there."

There was laughter all around; then the subject of the next

novel resurfaced quickly. "Seriously, though," Connie offered, "what about Eudora Welty? We had quite a session up in Nashville with *The Robber Bridegroom*. Specifically, is it or is it not a fairy tale?"

"I definitely like that theme," Maura Beth replied. "What do the rest of you think?"

"Sounds good to me," Locke Linwood put in while Miss Voncille nodded approvingly.

One by one, the others agreed to the choice, and Maura Beth declared that the subject of the January session of The Cherry Cola Book Club had been decided. "And this isn't exactly a prayer, but may we get through it without interruption this time around."

Then slices of one of Mr. Place's scrumptious desserts, Mississippi mud pie, came out to put an exclamation point on the meal.

"I can see myself getting addicted to this," Jeremy was saying after his first bite. "Kudos to you, Mr. Place."

"My pleasure," he returned, smiling graciously.

As everyone was finishing up their pie and coffee, Maura Beth rose from her seat with her wineglass in hand. "I don't know why we didn't do this before the appetizers, but I'd like to make a toast, please." She waited for the group to stand up and hoist their glasses before continuing. "I can't tell you how grateful I will always be to all of you for your generosity of spirit in standing behind me and the library. The thing is, I truly believe that we have already become more than just an ordinary book club. We've gotten involved in each other's lives in ways that we would never have expected—and without even half trying. It just seems to have evolved naturally, as if something we don't fully understand has been driving it and making sure that we all stay connected. You're like a real family to me." She surveyed the table once more and smiled. "I've been told I can go to a long-winded, hammy place at times, and I hope I haven't overstated my case just now. But I think the future looks so much brighter than it did last week, and I want to thank you all again from the bottom of my heart for helping to make it possible."

Everyone leaned this way and that to clink rims and sip, and there were lots of cheerful responses such as, "It was our pleasure," and "I couldn't have said it better myself," to go around.

"And, Periwinkle," Maura Beth continued after all the commotion had finally died down, "you outdid yourself this afternoon with this very special dinner. So, long live both The Cherry Cola Book Club and The Twinkle!"

There was more clinking and sipping; then Periwinkle added the capper, gazing around with great pride at all her fanciful spinning mobiles. "The one and only Restaurant of the Stars!"

"I'm already settled in with Aunt Connie and Uncle Doug at the lodge for tonight, but they told me they weren't coming straight home," Jeremy explained as he and Maura Beth drove through town in the general direction of the lake house. "There were a few logs blazing when I left to pick you up. Would you like to sit and watch them turn to soot together for a while?"

She reached over and patted his knee a few times. "I think I'd like that very much."

"I know that I don't want to rush things," he continued, "but I've always liked telling stories by the fire, ever since I was eleven having a blast at summer camp on Lookout Mountain. It was always chilly after nightfall up there, and it was easy to imagine monsters lurking in the woods as the counselors would try and scare us with their spooky voices and tall tales.

I remember everything from deranged farmers on out-of-control tractors to maniacal lumberjacks running around the forests sawing people in half while they were sealed up tight in their sleeping bags. None of us slept a wink after that one. I guess boys grow up with a lot more visceral thoughts in their heads."

Maura Beth had a resigned expression on her face. "I'm afraid my experience at summer camp was a lot tamer. Just us girls allowed, and the most daring thing we ever discussed was makeup and who was being allowed to use it. Or who wasn't and why. The whole summer was an all-out 'my mother is a monster' vent, so in that respect, there was a bit more drama than I first remembered."

They drove on along the two-lane road that wound its way to the lake from the outskirts of town. There was a full moon rising ahead of them, filling up the windshield with such luster and swollen size that it appeared the night had been completely vanquished, difficult to detect even with peripheral vision. There was only the prospect of looking up into the heavens and wanting to drive straight up to eternity immediately. It was all mesmerizing and therefore distracting.

"Oh, my God, here comes Peter Cottontail!" Jeremy suddenly exclaimed, swerving the car slightly to avoid a rabbit scampering across to the safety of the opposite shoulder.

"I'm so glad you missed him," Maura Beth said, smiling gratefully. "If it's a sin to kill a mockingbird, I'm sure I'd feel even worse about being a party to flattening a bunny rabbit."

Jeremy waited for the slight rush of adrenaline his wildlife encounter had produced to subside. "No hint of roadkill here. I'm quick at the wheel. I've even been known to brake for falling leaves."

Maura Beth sighed quite audibly. "Oh, brother!"

"A little too poetic?"

She just smiled and raised her eyebrows, enjoying the ride.

He pressed on. "I'd really like to know what you're thinking right now, though."

Once again, she sat there, looking mysterious and utterly irresistible. "We'll get to the details later on. For now, I'll just tell you that I was thinking happily about page twenty-five."

Recipes for Loyal, Hungry Readers

No trip to Cherico, Mississippi, and the inner workings of The Cherry Cola Book Club would be complete without a few convenient recipes so that readers can duplicate the delicious dishes of some of their favorite characters. For sampling at your leisure, therefore, we present the following pages as lagniappe in hopes that you will enjoy many a satisfying meal with all good wishes in the years to come. Just turn the pages, pick out something you like, and get cooking!

Becca Broccoli's Easy Peasy Chicken Spaghetti

Ingredients you will need:

1 whole chicken
1 package of thin spaghetti
1 stick of butter
1 chopped onion
½ cup chopped green pepper
1 cup chopped celery
1 large can of mushroom soup
1 can of diced pimentos
2 cups grated cheddar cheese
Salt and pepper to taste

Cook chicken in salted water until tender. Remove chicken and dice the meat. Use chicken broth to cook spaghetti until tender. Sauté butter, onion, green pepper, and celery until onions are translucent. Add veggies to pasta; then add large can of mushroom soup, chicken, and pimentos; pour into casserole dish and sprinkle cheese over top. Bake at 350 degrees Fahrenheit until golden bubbly.

—Courtesy Mrs. Rose Williams Turner, Natchez, Mississippi

Connie McShay's Frozen Fruit Salad

Ingredients you will need:

8 ounces cream cheese
½ cup sugar
1 cup mayo
1 cup white raisins
½ cup chopped nuts (walnuts or pecans)
1 can fruit cocktail (drained)
Poppy seed dressing

Mix cream cheese and sugar; add mayo, raisins, nuts, and fruit cocktail; pour cocktail into twelve lined muffin tins and freeze; package in large Ziploc bag. (For additional flavor, add two tablespoons of poppy seed dressing upon serving.)

—Courtesy Alice Feltus, Lucy Feltus, and
Helen Byrnes Jenkins, Natchez, Mississippi

Periwinkle Lattimore's Baked Sherry Custard

Ingredients you will need:

2 tablespoons sugar
1⅓ cups whole milk
Dash of salt
3½ teaspoons sherry
1½ teaspoons vanilla
3 egg whites
1 additional tablespoon of sugar

Combine the two tablespoons of sugar, milk, and salt in a pan; cook on simmer to low heat until sugar dissolves—approximately five minutes; remove and then add sherry and vanilla together.

In a separate bowl, combine the egg whites with the additional tablespoon of sugar; whip or beat into soft-peak stage; and add the milk mixture slowly. Use sieve to strain the entire mixture into a two-cup baking dish; place dish in a baking pan with water bath (usually halfway up the sides) and bake at 325 degrees Fahrenheit for about an hour. If toothpick comes out clean when inserted in middle of mixture, custard is done. Serve warm or cold.

—Courtesy Helen Louise Jenkins Kuehnle,
Natchez, Mississippi

Becca Broccoli's Cherry Cola/Lime Punch

Ingredients you will need:

1 liter any chilled cola beverage (do not use diet variety)
1 liter any chilled ginger ale beverage (do not use diet variety)
1 jar maraschino cherries
3 limes

Pour cola and ginger ale into large punch bowl and stir. Add jar of stemless maraschino cherries and one half the liquid. Cut limes in half and squeeze juice into mixture. Stir everything together and serve.

—Courtesy Lauren R. Good, Memphis, Tennessee

Periwinkle Lattimore's Tomato Aspic with Cream Cheese

Ingredients you will need for tomato aspic liquid:

2 cups tomato juice (or V8 juice)
½ cup chopped onion
2 chopped celery ribs
1 envelope unflavored gelatin
¼ cup cold water
2 tablespoons lemon juice
Dash of hot pepper sauce
Dash of Worcestershire sauce

Boil tomato juice, onion, and celery for about twenty minutes, or until veggies are tender; drain tomato juice and set aside. Soften gelatin in 1/4 cup cold water and add to tomato juice; then add lemon juice, pepper sauce, and Worcestershire sauce.

Ingredients you will need for cream cheese filling:

8 ounces cream cheese
2 tablespoons mayo
1 teaspoon grated onion
Salt and pepper to taste
Paprika (optional)

Make small balls of filling ingredients; put at the bottom of individual molds or at the bottom of a casserole dish and cut into squares. Pour tomato aspic liquid over the cheese balls; after everything has congealed, serve chilled. For additional flavor, top with dollop of mayo and sprinkle paprika over that for color.

—Courtesy Mrs. Rose Williams Turner, Natchez, Mississippi

Maura Beth Mayhew's Chocolate, Cherry Cola Sheet Cake

Ingredients you will need for the batter:

2 cups flour
Dash of salt
2 cups sugar
1 cup any cola beverage
⅓ cup oil
1 stick butter
3 tablespoons dry cocoa
½ cup buttermilk
1 teaspoon baking soda
2 teaspoons vanilla
3 tablespoons maraschino cherry liquid
1 jar of finely chopped maraschino cherries
2 eggs

Mix flour, salt, and sugar in bowl. In separate pan, bring to a boil the cola drink, oil, butter, and cocoa. Add hot liquid to the bowl and beat heavily; then add buttermilk, baking soda, vanilla, cherry liquid, cherries, and eggs and continue beating. When well mixed, pour into sheet cake pan sprayed with non-stick spray and bake for twenty-five minutes at 350 degrees Fahrenheit.

Ingredients you will need for the icing:

1 stick butter
3 tablespoons cocoa
6 tablespoons whole milk
3 tablespoons maraschino cherry liquid

1 pound confectioners' sugar
2 teaspoons vanilla
1 cup finely chopped pecans

Heat the butter, cocoa, and milk until the butter has liquefied; add the remaining ingredients and beat well. Pour icing onto cake while it is hot or still warm for ease of spreading; cut when cake has cooled.

—Courtesy Marion A. Good, Oxford, Mississippi

Mr. Parker Place's Lemon/Lime Icebox Pie

Ingredients you will need for the crust:

1 7.05-oz box of Carr's Ginger Lemon Creme Tea Cookies
2 tablespoons of butter or margarine

Empty box of Carr's Ginger Lemon Creme Tea Cookies into food processor and pulse until crumb consistency is reached; or, empty box of cookies into Ziploc bag and pound/roll with rolling pin until crumb consistency is reached.

Pour crumb mixture into a 9-inch aluminum-foil pie pan; melt better and then drizzle into crumb mixture; mold mixture into crust, adhering to pie pan; set aside.

Ingredients you will need for the filling:

1 can fat-free condensed milk
3 eggs
4 limes or 4 lemons

Note: Using limes will give the pie a tarter taste; using lemons will give it a sweeter taste.

Pour can of condensed milk into large mixing bowl. Crack three medium eggs and separate yolks from whites (if you wish to save whites for omelets, etc., do so; otherwise, discard). Put yolks into condensed milk and stir thoroughly until blended.

Juice four limes or four lemons (do not use reconstituted lemon or lime juice); add juice into condensed milk–egg mixture in small portions and mix in thoroughly each time until all juice has been added and blended.

Pour mixture into pie pan and bake at 350 degrees Fahrenheit for about twenty-five minutes; overbaking will make the texture of the filling mealy. Cool before cutting and serving. Serve at room temperature or chilled. Serves up to six.

—Mr. Parker Place (Joe Sam Bedloe, Cherico, Mississippi)

And finally: Stout Fella's Instructions for "Islanding" Ice Cream

Ingredients you will need:

1 tablespoon (fresh and hot from being cleaned in the dishwasher, if possible; if not, blow on metal until warm)
1 gallon of previously untouched, unopened ice cream, any flavor

Take ice cream out of freezer, put it on counter, and yell at it to hurry up and soften just a tad bit. Open the hatch or the top and begin testing the edges; start scraping on all four sides; keep going deeper until you have reached the bottom and created an "island," or your wife comes in and screams at you to "Stop, you'll spoil your appetite for dinner!" whichever comes first; repeat, if she goes away, and rinse (the spoon).

—Courtesy Justin Rawlings "Stout Fella" Brachle, Cherico, Mississippi

A READING GROUP GUIDE

THE CHERRY COLA BOOK CLUB

Ashton Lee

ABOUT THIS GUIDE

The suggested questions are included to enhance your group's reading of Ashton Lee's *The Cherry Cola Book Club.*

DISCUSSION QUESTIONS

1. Discuss the female character who fascinates you the most, and give the pros and cons of her personality.
2. Discuss the male character who fascinates you the most, and give the pros and cons of his personality.
3. Assign someone to argue for The Cherico Library's existence against someone else who supports the City Council's point of view for its dissolution. Let the group decide who won the argument.
4. Does Cherico reflect some of the economic and cultural realities of your hometown?
5. Which of the couples most resembles your relationship with your spouse or significant other: Becca and Stout Fella; Miss Voncille and Locke Linwood; Douglas and Connie?
6. The character of Pamela Linwood, though deceased, plays an important role in the plot. How do each of you view that role?
7. What has your local library meant to you?
8. Over the long haul, do you think Maura Beth Mayhew is fighting a losing battle?
9. Do you think taxpayers in general have a realistic view of what it takes to keep a library up and running?
10. Do you think library services should fall into the same category for funding as firefighting, police protection, streets, water and utilities?

11. Did you ever make the sort of wish/bucket list that Maura Beth Mayhew made on page twenty-five of her journal (Three Things to Accomplish Before I'm Thirty)?
12. Pretend you are a female member of The Cherry Cola Book Club. Do you fall into the Scarlett or the Melanie category as a modern woman?
13. Pretend you are a member (either gender) of The Cherry Cola Book Club. What role do you think *To Kill a Mockingbird* played in the passage of the 1964 Civil Rights Act, if any?
14. There will be a sequel to *The Cherry Cola Book Club*. What do you hope will happen in that book?
15. What is your favorite sequence in *The Cherry Cola Book Club*?